UnderCurrents

Who Will Satisfy Their Thist?

Consortium Book 3

RICHARD VERRY

ALSO BY RICHARD VERRY

UnderCurrents

Who Will Satisfy Their Thirst?

Consortium Book 3

Richard Verry

Published by Richard Verry
Rochester NY

RichardVerry.com

UnderCurrents

Who Will Satisfy Their Thirst?

Consortium Book 3

RICHARD VERRY

Prologue

Across the centuries lives an inscrutable evil in the shadows. This darkness pervades everywhere and with anyone, maybe even with those you know and love. This centuries-old organization calls themselves, the Consortium.

They are organized and well funded. They deploy and operate agents all across the globe. Most operatives are unaware of their real purpose. They have no idea what the ulterior motives of this organization are. These agents honestly believe they are helping others. They only know the organization they work for pays well for their services.

They couldn't be more wrong.

The Consortium operates with a singular purpose. They gather up the best talent to suit their insidious and nefarious needs, hunting them as prey for the slaughter. They are always on the lookout for suitable stock to replace their dwindling reserves.

They watch and study the lives around them. No one knows they exist, not the public, not the authorities, no one. They live outside the box, beyond the reach of the authorities around the civilized world. Everyone is paid off, and those that aren't, are closely watched and reported.

Only a privileged few know the real purpose of its existence. Security is paramount. Hidden among the multiple layers within the Consortium are secrets abound. Each hand of the organization knows nothing of the others. Kept isolated from each other are Agents, Researchers, Assassins, Hunters, and Transporters. They operate in complete ignorance of one another. The elite membership of the Consortium prefers it that way.

The Chairman of the Consortium is elected for life to oversee the running of the organization. His role is a simple one. He is charged to satisfy the needs, wants, and desires of the membership. Everyone answers to the Chairman. As long as the Chairman provides suitable stock at auction, the membership is happy to delegate the details.

Always on the hunt, the Consortium enthusiastically acquires new victims to satisfy their bloodthirst. If you are young, beautiful, vulnerable, and alone in the world, you are a candidate for abduction. Who will be their next victim to satisfy their thirst?

Chapter One

Lost in her thoughts, a young hippie-ish woman stared out the window. Getting out of bed a short time ago, she threw on a pair of cotton panties and low-cut jeans before checking out the weather outside her apartment.

The morning overcast skies would soon give way to a bright, sun-filled blue sky sure to enhance her good mood. Her apartment in the NW district of Portland, Oregon, wasn't much, but it had a great view of the city. The Willamette River split the city into two on its way to join with its larger cousin, the Columbia River.

The smell of coffee brewing filled her with pleasure, enhancing the scene before her. The aromatic scent reminded her that breakfast still needed to satisfy her growling stomach. Sighing, Katie turned and began pulling out a variety of vegetables. Setting them by the sink, she washed them. In no time at all, she began dropping them in her blender. Rather than buy vegetable juices from the nearby market, Katie liked to make her preferred blend chosen with care from the local organic market two blocks over.

Taking her breakfast concoction back over to her window looking out over the river, she reflected on how much her life had changed over the past year. She moved here when the last of her family passed away. Uncertain as what to do, an acquaintance kept telling her she should check out Oregon, specifically the Portland area. He kept reminding her she would fit right in with the scene. It was a progressive city with lots of fascinating history over the past century. She would love it.

Hedging for many months and doing research on the city at the library, she decided he may be right. With nothing holding her back, she made the leap of faith and packed what little she cared about and moved. Within a month of getting settled and finding her way around, she fell in love with the city.

She explored Washington Park on the west side of the city, discovering treasures hidden just yards off several trailheads. The forest within the metropolis was old, sporting massive pines and sequoias. Watered by the rainfall that fell nearly every day for half the year, enticed its abundant flora to thrive. Checking out the Oregon Zoo, the Portland Japanese Garden and the International Rose Garden, Katie quickly fell in love with the city. The city resting on the western slopes of the Rocky Mountains became her permanent home.

If it weren't for that incidence in the park where the police showed up and took a report, everything would have been perfect. As far as she knew, they never found the guy who accosted her. She avoided the assault by fighting back, using her police whistle to draw attention. It also helped that her attacker hadn't realized that she had some skills. Kicking him in the nuts helped fend him off until a pair of hikers came by. No longer alone, the coward took off. By the time the cops showed up, they had lost him in the deep underbrush. Still, she had to give a statement and promised to file charges if they ever caught the guy. Otherwise, her time in the City of Roses was uneventful. She liked it that way.

Today, Katie headed down to Powell's City of Books to spend a relaxing day in quiet contemplation. While she had several acquaintances, her friends were of the more inanimate variety. To her, the characters contained within the pages came to life, and she loved following their adventures. The store was huge, with several floors stacked one upon the other. The bookstore occupied a full city block. It had a quaint feel to it. The smell of the old wood of the building and real paper books gave it an air of distinction from the standard fair of bookstores.

It was a busy place, with hundreds of people from all across the world filing through the doors every day. There, she could find anything, from the latest releases to rare autobiographical first editions. Not that she could afford to buy any, just being in proximity with works of art contented her. With money tight, she liked that she could spend the day reading whatever caught her eye on a comfy sofa with no one chasing her out.

Today, she took a book on the early days of the city. Hours later, she learned about how the city dealt with Prohibition. By moving the speakeasies underground, the metropolitan area maintained a healthy and legal prostitution business until the mid-twentieth century when the prudes finally got their way. Recently, recreational pot had become legal again, freeing the multitudes to buy and smoke in the open instead of keeping their passion on the down-low. What fascinated her the most was the city's underground life. She resolved to find out more and expand her explorations. All in due time, she figured, she had plenty of it.

Shortly after mid-day, she re-filed the book on the shelf and left to get a bite to eat. Walking the streets, she stopped at an interesting little bistro and ordered a half sandwich. About an hour later, she walked around the city blocks just looking. She didn't have to report to her job for a few hours. To pay the rent, she worked as a bartender at a popular hangout close to her apartment. Beyond that, she didn't have much need for money. She was happy with just the way things were.

Moseying back towards her apartment, she rested before tackling her long night ahead. Tonight, she would work a 6 to 2 a.m. shift. While the job paid the bills, what she liked were the people coming in to blow off stress, hook up, or get drunk. Each had their good and bad aspects, but overall, they were all a good bunch of people. Working with each of them allowed her to feel more comfortable in social settings, something she lacked before coming to Portland.

After lying down, Katie got up, showered, and put on a pair of short shorts, a halter top tied between her tits and a pair of comfortable shoes. It would be a long night, and she didn't want to come home with aching feet. At five minutes before six, she walked through the door.

"Hey Ed!" she called out to the bartender on duty, dropping her purse in her cubby behind the bar.

"Hello, Katie. Thanks for being on time. I got a thing tonight, and the missus will kill me if I don't get out of here on time."

"No worries, Ed. I'll take over from here. Get your ass in gear. I wouldn't want you to have to deal with your lovely bride on such a nice day as this."

"Thanks, Katie. I appreciate it," he said, balling up his bar towel and tossing it in the dirty towel trays set aside for just that purpose. "The guy on the end is looking for a fresh one, and there are two open tabs, one for that guy and then the table over there in the corner."

"Thanks, Ed. Go on, get out of here. I got it covered."

"You're the best, Katie. Have a good evening."

"Thanks," she said as she walked over to the patron at the end of the bar.

"Another one?" she asked.

"Yeah, sure."

"What are you drinking?"

"Bourbon on the rocks."

"Coming right up!"

***

As the night progressed, the bar got busy, and Katie had to hustle to keep up with the demand for drinks. Being midweek, besides the bar owner, she was the only one on duty. The owner helped when things got tight, but overall Katie handled the customers without incidence.

Several of the patrons hit on her. Only two interested her; a svelte blonde and later a taller man with a square jaw. The man went a long way to entice her by showing off his build. Still, his attempts to impress her failed. However, the blonde interested her. High-heels called attention to the blonde's long legs, leading up to a fit, athletic physique. She had long, straight hair that framed her face before spilling across her shoulders and down her back. She wore a black skirt and jacket over a white button-down blouse open to her cleavage. Peaking out was the edge of the shirt revealed a decidedly feminine lacy bra. What interested her was not her build but the way she carried on a conversation. Most bar patrons seemed to want to talk about themselves. These two didn't, seemingly more interested in Katie as a person and not a servant or object of desire.

As the night progressed, the bulk of the crowd thinned out, by either deciding to move on or hooking up with someone. With an hour to go, a few of the regulars hung on, nursing their drinks. Both of the two people Katie was interested in had left a while ago.

That is until about twenty minutes before two. The blonde was back, taking an empty stool at the quiet end of the bar.

"Hey, you're back. What can I get you?" Katie asked.

"Oh, this late, I think I'll have a club soda with a twist. I don't need any spirits to dampen my mood."

"Oh, sure," Katie said, turning to grab a glass tumbler and filling it with ice. A moment later, she placed the effervescent drink with a twist of lime in front of the woman.

"Thanks. So, I'm Shelby."

"Katie."

Thus started a few minutes of small talk, the two women getting to know one another. Feeling positive about their conversation, Katie leaned over the bar, resting on her elbows in front of Shelby.

"So, Katie, would you like to go somewhere after you close up?"

"Shelby, we close in about ten minutes and then I have some clean-up to do. I'm usually out of here by three."

"I can wait if you don't mind."

"Hmmm… okay. Let me get everyone out of here. I'll start cleaning up right now."

"Fair enough," Shelby said, crossing her long legs at the knee. "Can I help?"

"As much as I'd love the help, the boss would frown on it. It won't take long, and I can hurry it up."

"All right, I'll just sit here and watch you work."

Chuckling, Katie said, "Sure. You'd like that I'll bet. Do you want a refill on that club soda?"

With a sly smile, Shelby took a sip of her club soda, her eyes gazing over the top of the glass. "No, thanks. I'm good."

"Okay fellas, finish your drinks. It's closing time." Katie yelled out to the few patrons left.

"Aww...." came the chorus from the half dozen customers left nursing their drinks. "Hey, can I have one more?" asked one drunk.

Letting him down easy, Katie answered. "No, sorry, last call was a half hour ago."

"Oh, come on," he begged.

"You know that I got a life too, and I need to go to bed," Katie replied, smiling sweetly.

"Ya need a bit of company?" he persisted.

"That's very sweet of you but thank you, no," Katie answered, turning on her heels quickly and began stacking empty chairs on tables. After shooing everyone out, Katie locked the front door and turned to Shelby.

"Does that happen every night?" Shelby asked.

"Pretty much," Katie acknowledged. "It's no big deal. I can handle them."

"I'll just bet you can," Shelby remarked, getting up off her stool, making her way over to Katie.

Slipping an arm around her waist, Shelby leaned in and pulled Katie into a kiss. Relaxing under the warm caress, Katie could feel her fatigue slip away. Melting, she returned the kiss with a passion. Her cheeks flushed, her neck feeling very warm. Katie took her time before breaking it off.

Smiling at her companion, Katie said. "Not too bad! I'll finish up quickly, lock up and we can go."

Shelby smiled and released her. "You're pretty good yourself. Can I ask a personal question?"

"Sure."

"Are you solely into girls or do you go both ways?"

A little embarrassed, Katie finished wiping down the bar while answering. "It depends on the person whom I spend the night with. Pleasure is pleasure, no matter where it comes from."

"I couldn't agree more," Shelby added.

"I'll be ready in five minutes, and then we can go."

With the click of the door lock a few minutes later, Shelby and Katie walked into the night and got into Shelby's car. Getting to know one another, they chatted like old friends. Shelby pulled the automobile away from the curb and drove off.

Chapter Two

"Mr. Chairman, I'd like to say the addition of the new amphitheater arena worked out brilliantly. I'm not sure we can, but I foresee many opportunities to top the snake presentation. It has the potential for many forms of entertainment."

"Thank you." the Chairman replied. "You all had a hand in its creation. I'm happy that we could surprise the general membership with our inaugural event."

"Surprised them? I'd say we did more than that. They are still talking about it."

"The gist I heard was the snake swallowing a girl alive will remain the highlight of their lives. You know they want to see that again," another board member remarked.

"Yes, I'm sure they do. There is an unlimited supply of meal packs to toss to Henrietta, but they have to be the right ones to deliver the desired effect."

"By the right ones, I take it you mean that they react appropriately, deathly afraid, and panicking."

"Exactly right. I chose the girl specifically for her physical dimensions and her deathly fear of snakes."

"I'd say she had a right to be afraid of them," someone chimed in, eliciting laughter from all seven board members spread out around the room.

The executive board dealt with setting the policies of the Consortium. The Chairman oversaw the implementation of those policies, supported by various positions such as Vice-Chairman, Treasurer, and Secretary. However, the Chairman took on the responsibility of building the arena and the pen for the snake as a pet project.

"Well, as you know, putting it together took the better part of three years," the Chairman continued. "We built the holding pen for the python first, so we had somewhere to put it after its capture. Then we moved on to the construction of the arena. I envision making it into a multi-purpose deathmatch arena, capable of hosting several types of contests. Stumbling on Henrietta, jump-started the project. I agree, it all turned out splendid. Well, maybe except for the girl we put in the arena with Henrietta.

Unmoved their joviality was at the expense of the girl's life, the atmosphere in the room lightened into a cheery, spirited mood.

The Chairman continued, "Yes, yes, all. It was a fantastic performance, and we all made money on the deal and watched what hopefully will not be a once in a lifetime event. I don't believe we should think about repeating the scene at the next auction. I have some other ideas for next time. However, I'd like to elicit suggestions from the rest of you to consider for upcoming events. This last one took years in the planning. It was exhausting to put together, but the outcome was worth the effort. I'd like one of you to propose the next extravaganza and oversee its implementation. Whatever it takes, as long as this board backs it, we'll make sure the resources are available to pull it together. What do you think?"

"I think it's a great idea. However, if your stunt took years to pull together, we should also work on short-term goals, such as what we will do for the next auction."

"I agree. As for the mega-show, would one of you like to take it on to gather ideas and coordinate them with this board? As for the short-term, does anyone have any suggestions?" The Chairman asked.

Fueled by the recent euphoria, the board members started offering several ideas. Often talking over each other, their jovial mood built with each additional suggestion. The Chairman let them have their fun. Being a member of the management team was often a thankless job. The banter was good for all of them. He enjoyed it too, especially now that the stress of putting together the snake show was over.

After a long time, the Chairman asked "Mr. Secretary, I presume you are jotting down these ideas. I think you all agree many are good ones."

"Yes, Sir, I am. However, I admit it's a struggle to keep up with all of them."

"Well, do your best. There's plenty of time to try them all. However, the next auction is in a month. Normally, we would let the member next on the entertainment list provide the post-auction festivities. Do we continue with that practice or temporarily suspend it, so we can fully use the capabilities of the amphitheater?"

"Mr. Chairman?"

"Yes, Raven."

"Sir, as delightful as that spectacle was, and you all know my enjoyment of the consumption of human meals…." Interrupted by the loud laughter that broke out, the Chairman's sister continued. "… yes, sorry about that. The pun was just too irresistible to ignore."

"Brilliant, I'd say." the secretary interjected.

"I think we should integrate the two. I suggest that this board plan on one mega-event each year and let the membership continue as before. We can adjust the schedule as needed. Auction dates are often fluid based upon the availability and demand for new prey."

"I think that is a great idea, Raven," one of the other board members chimed in. "With us managing the mega-event, we'll make a killing."

Laughter broke out all around. "Sorry, I couldn't resist the pun either," nodding in Raven's direction.

"The suggestion also supports the member responsibilities to the Consortium. Our charter requires them to select and implement rotating entertainments. This suggestion reinforces the requirement to supply stock for post-auction entertainment. If this board were to interrupt those expectations, we would end up being wholly responsible for putting on all of the entertainments going forward. That is something I do not wish to do. I fully support the suggestion. Thank you, Raven."

"Oh, yes, I see what you mean. The membership would end up with all play and no work to maintain their cherished lifestyle. I like it," the secretary added. "I can also see where this could go. As the event coordinator, you would end up on the hook, please excuse the pun once again, for everything."

Hearty laughter once again filled the room.

"Thank you. I appreciate your following my logic, not that I am a logical person, I let my brother handle that. I enjoy letting my emotions take over. Being responsible for all future entertainments would be just too much." Raven added.

"Don't worry, Sis. Speaking for the entire board, we won't let that happen."

"Thank you, Mr. Chairman."

"This is what we'll do. The membership will continue to provide the entertainment, though they have the amphitheater available for use. Raven, as the event coordinator, I'll leave it to you to let the next member on the list know that they are to come up with preparing for and implementing the spectacle. You'll also let them know that in no way, are they to feel they must come up with something surpassing Henrietta's scene?"

"Sir, you know that they will feel that way, regardless of our assertions to the contrary."

"That's expected. Just remind the membership that we don't expect mega-spectacles from them. We will do everything we can to reassure the entire membership not to expect too much. They will be on the hook themselves before too long."

"Yes, Sir. Thank you. I appreciate the support. Should I put on the schedule when the next mega-event will be?"

"Leave that off for now. We have to figure out what that event might be and plan for it."

"Sir?" the secretary interjected. "I don't think we should wait too long. I recommend that we put it on the schedule within the next six months."

"Everyone, how do you all feel about our esteemed secretary's suggestion?"

One by one, they all affirmed the wisdom in his suggestion.

"Right then, you have confirmed my opinion on the matter. This board is now on the hook to put on a spectacle less than six months from now. I'm open to any practical suggestions of what we can do. We can always put the idea on the storyboard for a future date. Now, does anyone have any ideas?"

For the next half an hour, the members of the executive board discussed various options before settling upon a course of action. When the conversation died down, the Chairman continued.

"To summarize. We have a tentative plan for the next major event. Mr. Secretary has graciously accepted the responsibility to lead the effort, and the rest of us will support him to make it come off with a flourish. Raven, you'll communicate to the next scheduled member to prepare the entertainment at the next auction. Is that reasonable among all of you?"

After getting a round of approval, the Chairman continued with a new topic, hoping to capitalize on the good all-around mood of the board.

"I'd like to bring up the new member application. As you know, my property Avril has completed successfully everything this board required to warrant a full membership into our community."

"I still can't believe you are supporting this, Mr. Chairman. If she were my property, she'd be dead right now. There would be no discussion or need to deal with the whole mess."

Looking sternly over at the rude interruption, the Chairman continued. "My motivations are my own, and I will share with you what I feel is appropriate. Need I remind you that the Investigation Ministry vetted and endorsed the application. She met every demand made by this board. As the ruling body of our organization, it is our responsibility to review every qualified applicant and decide whether to allow the application to proceed to the general membership for a vote."

"Apologies Sir, but I don't understand why this is important to you. Perhaps if you shared more of why you think this is a good thing, I could support the application. As it stands now, I cannot."

"If I understand you, knowing how important this application is to me, you need further proof of my loyalty to the Consortium and our lifestyle. That you no longer trust me or my judgment, do I understand you correctly?"

"Mr. Chairman, it's not that I don't trust you or your loyalty to the Consortium, or even to this lifestyle. I've seen your commitment firsthand, and I have never doubted you or your ability to lead us."

"But?"

"Yes, there is a but. It's just that this application, by prey no less, is unprecedented. We don't do it that way. Can we trust her to fulfill her commitment to our community? That's what I struggle with."

"Yet, you witnessed her commitment when she tortured and killed that woman. She decapitated her, bathing in the woman's blood as she sawed through her neck, before lifting the woman's head from her body. You also witnessed the finesse she exhibited as she tormented the prey, eliciting screams, and ignoring her futile pleas for her life. You saw that in real time, and you still doubt her commitment?"

"Yes, Sir. I do."

"Well, I know what your vote will be."

"Excuse me, Sir, before you move on, let me add this. I witnessed her taking down that prey, binding her to the post, whipping her to an inch within her life, before decapitating her right in front of my eyes. I trust you and your loyalty to our lifestyle. That was never in doubt. Perhaps I should have rephrased my original objection by stating, I don't understand what her motivations are, aside from self-preservation that is."

The Chairman interjected, "I hope you're not implying that I disregarded the possibility of self-preservation as a motive."

"Oh, no, I didn't intend to suggest that at all."

The Chairman ignored the insincere correction and continued. "I know that self-preservation is one of the driving motivations for her application. It's just not the only one. If it were, I would agree with you and deny her application, never having gone this far. I'd have killed her, relished her delightfully agonizing screams along the way. As it is, there is something else within her, that I believe is of more importance. Deep inside her, she is one of us. She desires much of what we do. Only, it's been her societal training that has squashed the very idea from consideration. She's only now learning what she is capable of and I believe it will bring great things for us."

"Oh, come on now, can you honestly say you believe that?"

"Yes, I can, and I do."

"Let me ask you a question," Raven interjected. "Are you in love with her?"

"I will answer you this way. I have reflected upon the possibility that I may. I honestly don't know. I've loved no one before. Virtually all the membership has a spouse or partner who may or may not know about their Consortium lifestyle. They may love them or act as a public face to the world. I have no one that fills that role. I am alone in that respect. What I can tell you is that I need something in my life. What that may be, I'm not sure. Avril does something for me, on a personal level that no other, man, woman or prey has ever done. I want to allow her the opportunity to fulfill her place in the universe, and if that should compliment my needs, all the better."

"Brother, I don't know if you are in love with her. Maybe you are, or maybe you're not. I don't know. Like you, I don't have a basic understanding of what love is. Sure, I love this lifestyle. I love the thought of roasting my prey alive and then feeding upon their flesh. But that is not the same as loving another person. Even the depictions in novels and movies imply what that may be, but only those who have loved get the joke. You and I don't. I wasn't challenging you with my question. I just wanted to know if you believed that."

"Thank you, Sis. I get your meaning. As for the rest of you," addressing the entire board this time, "I think she is worthy, earning her place among us as an equal. I ask that you vote as I do and accept her application."

"Excuse me, before we put that motion up for a vote, I have another motion that will affect whether we need to vote on the current motion."

Sighing softly to himself before responding, the Chairman asked. "What is it?"

"I motion that we put to the vote on whether we as a group should require the termination of this prey once and for all."

"You mean he kills her right now?" Another committee member asked.

"Yes, that is just what I mean. If the motion carries, there will not be a need to vote on the application."

"Well, this is unprecedented," a member argued.

"So is contemplating accepting prey into our fold with full membership rights."

"Yes, I see your point." The Chairman remarked. "All right, I agree. Is there a second?"

"Second" shouted several other committee members.

"Fair enough." The Chairman began. "Mr. Secretary, please record the votes. There is a motion before us requiring the Chairman to terminate his prey immediately upon his return to his estate. I call the vote."

One by one, the committee secretary recorded the votes among the nine executive committee members.

"Mr. Chairman, the vote is as follows. Three votes for, four votes against and two abstentions, the motion is defeated. The prey lives to see another day."

"Thank you all. I recognize that this application is unusual and difficult to fathom. I felt it right that I abstain from the vote. Thank you, Raven, for doing the same. The others might think our relationship taints your vote."

Raven nodded but said nothing.

"This vote aside, I also recognize that many of you have reservations. I understand that, and until recently, I also shared those reservations. The applicant has shown behavior and attitude that this is genuine. We should consider this application in the same light as any other membership application put forth before us. The motion now is to whether we submit it to the general membership to approve or not. Is there a second?"

"Second," Raven announced.

"Please vote on it as you see fit without regard to my position. I assure you, I will not hold 'Nay' votes against anyone. Mr. Secretary, please call the vote."

The committee secretary recorded the votes and announced.

"With two dissenting votes, the motion carries. The board approves to move the membership application to the general membership for final disposition. I will tender the application at our next general membership meeting. In review, a simple majority passed the measure at the executive board level. According to our charter, it will take a two-thirds majority to accept the application among the general membership. The only question I have is, do we inform the membership that the applicant was once our prey?"

The Chairman immediately answered. "As much as I know it will taint the vote, we have no choice but to inform them of where the application arises. Yes, include that piece of information. It is better to be upfront with them that the applicant was once our prey than hide it and sow discord after they approve the application."

"Thank you, Sir. I quite agree," the secretary remarked, noting agreement among those around the room.

The boisterous owner of one of the dissenting votes added, "I still don't like it, but I will support the decision of the board."

Chapter Three

To an outsider, the air felt oppressive and burdensome, as if she was outside with a storm hanging overhead. Avril was in her room, sitting at her desk, angry. It wasn't so much that she hadn't seen Sir in over a week. After all this time, she had long since dealt with his extended absences.

It had more to do with the disappointment in herself. Avril's dark mood reflected her anger at doing the unthinkable to satisfy her membership application. Never in her wildest dreams had she ever envisioned taking the life of another person. Yet, she had and of her own volition. Not just once, but she had killed many innocents by her own hands. The sickening feeling stayed with her all this time.

When he was away, she had a hard time sleeping. The visions of their faces as they died revisited night after night burned the back of her eyes and blackened her soul. Would God ever forgive her? She wasn't so sure. She hoped God would know that she had good intentions in taking down the Consortium. Still, Avril worried that the ends would never justify the means. Night after night, she'd wake up in a cold sweat, her throat sore from groaning guttural sounds in her despair.

She used to welcome his absence as it meant relief from the agony inflicted upon her body. She struggled to maintain her composure, feeling the dark mood embedded in the walls of the house. Now, she welcomed his presence. Lying next to him in bed allowed her to sleep somewhat normally. Her bad dreams quickly explained away as nightmares resulting from his continued mistreatment upon her body.

It wasn't so far from the truth.

Staring down at the drawing paper in front of her, she watched her hands put dark, hard, angry strokes on the innocent paper. The abuse of her pencils and charcoal reflected her mood. However, it was healing in a way. Putting down the imagery plaguing her thoughts on the virginal paper seemed to help. She tried to transfer a portion of her sin on the medium as her penance. It wasn't enough. It would never be enough.

This time, she illustrated the murder of poor Misty, slicing into her neck with a long, sharp knife and decapitating her. This composition depicted the moment she held the instrument of death in one hand, while Misty's head laid at the feet of her body still tied to the post. It was not a pretty scene, but it depicted her dark state of mind.

"Oh, God. What have I done?" she murmured to herself.

She knew she couldn't vocalize her questions out loud, knowing that Sir had the entire house under constant surveillance. If he suspected what her ulterior motive was, he'd kill her in a heartbeat, but not before extracting her final, awful and painful screams from her. No, she knew she had to keep her true feelings bottled up, even if it killed her.

Flipping to the next page in the drawing pad, she started a new depiction. She hadn't so much as scratched her first few strokes with the charcoal when she heard him behind her.

"Let me see." Sir said.

How long had he been standing there was unknown? Avril turned around and saw him leaning against the doorjamb of her quarters.

"Oh, Sir. You're home. I didn't realize you came home." Avril said, quickly getting up from her chair and taking her familial kneeling pose in the center of the room. Legs spread-wide, her gaze tilted down, staring at the floor, her hands palm up on her thighs and resting on the back of her heels, she waited.

"Sir, I should have been in pose to greet you," she added apologetically.

Silently, Sir walked around her and picked up the drawing pad. Flipping the pages back, one after the other, he studied each rendering, taking in the nuances of each stroke, giving him an insight into her moods.

Finally, he said. "I'm glad to see you return to your drawing. You've been away from it for way too long. As I have told you in the past, these are good, and I will proudly hang them within the estate."

Quiet for a few more minutes, he studied her and her sketches. Avril, knowing the score, maintained her pose, kneeling on the floor facing the door. Checking for a response, she waited for permission to speak.

"I see you are working through your issues about what you did. Is it helping? I give you leave to answer." Sir said.

"Thank you, Sir. I appreciate your comments on my drawings."

"But is your drawing helping you get over your regrets?"

"I don't know Sir. I wish I did, but I don't know." Avril responded, unmoving in her perfect pose.

Sir, in the meantime, sat down on the chair reserved for him in the room and said. "Why do you think that is?"

"Sir, again, I don't know."

"Could it have anything to do with something you couldn't conceive of doing before you came here?"

After thinking about it for a moment, Avril answered. "Sir, yes, that is part of it. I still can't conceive of me doing such a thing to another person or any living thing."

"Yet, you did, without being ordered to do so."

"Yes, Sir, I did."

"Why?"

"Um, Sir, I don't understand. Why what?"

"Avril, you're bothered by your actions. I want you to say the words. What did you do? Use real words."

Taken aback, Avril broke her pose for a moment. Her back wavering from side to side, she almost dropped her head down to her knees before she recovered.

"Um... what I did? Well, Sir, I committed a mortal sin and blackened my soul."

"Avril, don't dance around with your responses. Besides, there is no such thing as a mortal sin, and I very much doubt you blackened your soul. Colored it maybe but not darkening it. Still, tell me what you did to get you into such a depressive state."

"Sir... I... I did the unthinkable for which I can't seem to shake."

"You did what exactly?"

After a long period of silence, Avril struggling with saying the words, she said. "Sir, must I?"

"Yes, you must. Tell me what you did?"

"I... um... I... I, oh please Sir, don't make me."

This time, Sir remained silent, the reticence blaring inside her head. Losing track of the minutes, Avril stammered though no sound exited her lips.

"Come now, Avril, it's not that hard. Just tell me what you did. I was there, remember? Don't get embarrassed. Just say the words."

"Ah, Sir... I, um, I killed those women."

With the words expressed, she opened up, almost yelling at him in her grief.

"I murdered those women. I took their lives. I killed them, cutting off the head of one, throttling another as I literally fucked her to death, and those were just my first. Now there are others. Since then… well, let's just say I see their faces in my sleep every night."

She went on like this repeating the words several times as tears streamed down her cheeks as her body shook in despair. Sir sat mute, letting her get it all out. After several long retching minutes, Avril finally slowed her rant, before losing control of her body and slipping down to the floor, curling up in a fetal position, still crying profusely.

In time, her sobbing subsided and her tears dried up. Sir squatted down in front of her and stroked her shoulder and upper arm. To comfort her, he then began stroking the back of her head, occasionally combing his fingers through her hair. In time, Avril could feel her body relax, the tension of the moment flowing from her to him, and out into the universe.

"There there," she heard him breathe. "Everything will be fine. Killing an innocent is hard and not without emotion. In time, you will feel better. I promise. Besides, with your belief in God, those that you killed will not suffer any longer but enjoy peace forever in the rapture of his hand."

Coughing lightly, Avril added. "Um, that's true, I guess. I had never considered that."

"Of course, it's true, at least in your belief of God and the afterlife."

"What about you, Sir?"

"Me, you mean my religious beliefs?"

"Yes, Sir."

"Avril, my dear. I have no religious beliefs. I don't believe in God or life after death. I believe it all ends when we die."

"It must be lonely then, knowing that when you die, it's over for good."

"I suppose. However, I'll give you this. I believe that our souls will one day inhabit the body and be born again. An endless cycle of living and dying, repeating over and over until the end of time itself."

"And then what?" Avril asked.

"You mean at the end of time?" Avril nodded. "Well, I don't quite know. Maybe that will be the end of my soul."

"Sir, in my beliefs, you would live beyond that, forever, loved and cherished in the hand of God."

"Emotions I've never felt before, my dear. So really, what would I be missing."

"Yes, Sir. I see what you mean. Sir, you can punish me if you wish, but I feel sorry for you."

"Punish you? For speaking your mind truthfully? I told you, I will never punish you for that."

Nodding, Avril started to sit up. Sir stopped her, and instead, slipped his arms underneath her and carried her to her bed. Lowering her down gently, he slipped his shoes off and laid down next to her, cradling her head on his shoulder and wrapping a comforting arm around her.

Together they laid there for a long time, the shadows from the gleaming sun sliding across the floor. Eventually, Avril fell asleep, resting comfortably. When she opened her eyes, she discovered him still there, surprising her to no end.

Puckering her lips, she kissed him lightly on his chest. A minute later, he opened his eyes, and resumed his stroking, continuing to calm her.

"Feeling better?" he asked.

Nodding, she answered. "Yes, Sir."

"Good, I'm hungry and not for food."

Smirking, Avril quite expected this and was well prepared to give it to him. Shifting, she leaned over him, undid his belt and pulled his shorts and trousers down. Free of its encumbrance, Avril slipped between his legs and took his cock into her mouth, enticing him into a firm erection. Studying his eyes, she knew he was enjoying her attention.

Avril watched him enjoy the sight and feel of his cock slipping past her lips and slide towards the back of her throat. It had taken her a while to learn the technique without gagging. She pushed her head onto him, feeling his fullness filling her neck and throat.

He moaned his pleasure and then did the expected. Gripping her shoulders, he pulled Avril towards him. A moment later, he slipped between the lips at the top of her legs and slid inside her. Comforted by the fullness of his cock, she rocked back and forth, sensing him match her movements with his thrusts.

Enjoying the moment, Avril fell upon him as he took control and drove faster and deeper inside her. Bouncing her up and down, sometimes lifting her knees off the bed as she straddled him, she fell upon him, his cock spearing her in building euphoric pleasure. By the time he expelled his seed inside her, Avril had lost count of the number of times she had climaxed. She may have experienced one long, multi-faceted orgasm. She would never know for sure. All she knew was the pleasure she felt as he took care of her.

When he finally finished with her, ejaculating multiple times, she fell upon him, both struggling to catch their breath. After their breathing slowed and returned to normal, they hugged each other and slept once again.

***

"Welcome back, Avril," she heard when she returned to consciousness.

Smiling, she pressed her body firmer into his. "Did you have a good trip?" she asked.

"Yes, I did."

"Did you talk about me, Sir?"

"Oh, you want it to be all about you?"

Catching herself, she added carefully. "Only, Sir if it would please you to say so."

"Well, in that case, I can honestly say, of course."

Shocked, Avril tilted her head up to look at him in disbelief. "Sir?"

"Really. What do you think? That you're always on my mind."

"Yes, Sir. I do."

Feeling him smile, Avril relaxed and dropped her gaze once again, seeing the full expanse of his body stretched out before her. Her eye in contact with his chest, she saw him as if she were looking out upon a landscape. Following a line from his sternum, her eyes traveled a path down the rippling of his abdomen, dipping briefly into his belly button, and over the slight mound that followed. Her gaze slowing, she stopped momentarily to gaze upon his flaccid cock, still slick with her juices. Getting her fill of his awe-inspiring manhood, she continued her journey down his legs right down to his toes. Comforted by the sensation of one of his arms wrapped around her as his free hand stroked her breasts, she waited for him to tell her what she already knew.

"Oh, you fox. You know you were the subject of conversation at all levels of the Consortium."

"And Sir?"

"And nothing. On my last trip, I officially submitted your membership application to the executive committee. On this trip, it was all about arguing the merits of accepting you. Mostly, I stayed out of the discussion, answering questions as they directed towards me. Everyone knows I support the application, so there was no need for me to comment."

"So, Sir. I presume that the conversation was spirited and contentious?"

"Oh, you could say that."

"And?" she led.

"And nothing. The membership is still contesting the application. How it turns out, I don't know. What I can tell you is if they turn you down, it's over. They will not accept a new application from you. If it passes, then it goes before the entire membership for a vote. In that case, you will need to garner a two-thirds majority. Again, if you don't, it's over, and you will never become a member."

"That would be too bad, Sir."

"For you, for sure."

"Sir, what then?"

"Then, well, that's simple. You remain my property to do with as I please."

"To kill me? I thought our agreement would remain in effect. I remain your property, and you maintain my life, even as your pleasure and torment me."

"Oh, you think?"

Slapping him playfully, she responded. "Really, Sir? You wouldn't go back on your word."

"The way I see it," he teased, "the agreement becomes null and void. Therefore, I could kill you immediately and be done with you."

Catching her off guard, he waited a while before continuing, letting her stew in her raw emotions.

"The agreement is still in effect. The agreement was contingent upon submitting your application, not having it accepted. You'll do your part, and I'll do my part."

"Whew, you had me going there for a minute, Sir."

"I did, didn't I?" Sir smiled playfully, the teasing moment passing.

Resting her head back again, she asked. "So, Sir. What do you think?"

"You mean, your chances at being accepted?"

Avril nodded her affirmation.

"It will be dicey. I usually have a handle on what will happen with applications. In your case, I don't know. The committee members are not sharing their opinions on how they will vote. I only know of the objections, of which there are many. I can't say that some don't have merit. They do, and I agree with them. Whether the weight of my support will be enough to turn the vote your way is unknown. All we can do is wait and see."

"Thank you, Sir, for your honesty and faith in me."

"You're welcome, my dear. Now, I'm hungry for real. Let's go shower and then eat."

"Yes, Sir!" Avril strongly affirmed, jumping up and skipping to the bathroom and turning on the shower. A minute later, they were washing each other, and sharing one more private and intimate moment before exiting the cleansing water.

After drying each other off, Sir got dressed again, leaving aside his tie and jacket, and Avril donned her heels. When both were ready to exit her room, she tipped on her toes and kissed him. Together, arm in arm, they walked out into the hallway and headed for the dining room.

Chapter Four

Listening carefully at the door, she waited until she was sure something occupied her sister. Heather knew her sister well. They were best buds, even though Rachel would call her a brat. Still, wasn't the job of the younger sister to tease the older one, and see how much she could get away with?

Cracking the door to Rachel's bedroom, the music on the other side streaming out into the hallway, Heather squinted through the crack in the door and peered into the room.

"Ah, she's sitting on the bed with her back to the door." Heather discovered.

Carefully pushing the door open so it wouldn't squeal on her, she slipped into her sister's room and carefully closed the door behind her.

"So far, so good," she thought.

Crawling, she made her way to the side of the bed and slithered under it to wait for the perfect opportunity. This was the hard part for Heather, the waiting. Inside her head, she gleefully replayed the scene in her mind of how she would scare her sister. As a young eleven years old, the anticipation was killing her, and she wanted to get the fun started.

The minutes dragged on. Rachel continued to sit on the far side of the bed, the music playing throughout the room, unaware of the intruder waiting in wait. She was singing along to one of the latest pop songs on the radio. It wasn't one of Heather's favorites. Despite that, she liked it because Rachel liked it.

Rachel shifted, and the bed creaked. Slithering further under the bed, Heather waited.

Singing loudly now along with the music, Rachel began walking around the room, a skip in her step, absorbed in the music and the magazine in her hand. Heather smiled to herself. The time was approaching. She knew her sister was unaware of her presence, and she almost giggled out loud before covering her mouth with her hand.

Peeking out, she saw her sister standing in front of her dresser, looking down at something. A moment later, she tossed the magazine on the bed and opened her jewelry box.

A sudden fear crossed Heather's mind. "Would she notice the missing bracelet that even now, encircled Heather's wrist?" Biting her lip, she remained as quiet as a mouse.

A moment later, the jewelry box's cover slapped closed, her apparent 'theft' undiscovered. Breathing a quick sigh of relief, Heather resumed her vigil in preparation to bounce on her unsuspecting sister and scare her.

Watching feet walk around the room, Heather prepared. The moment was soon upon her. Eventually, a pair of feet with ten brightly painted toes approached the side of the bed where Heather was hiding.

"Oh, yes. Any second now." Heather breathed in building anticipation. The plan was, she would grab her sister's ankle just before she was about to climb into bed. And there it was, just inches away.

Opening her hand to grasp the villainous ankle, she was just about to spring out and grab it when suddenly, the bed skirt right next to her face disappeared, replaced by Rachel's face.

"Boo," Rachel yelled.

Unprepared, Heather jumped but with the bed frame inches from her face, she smacked her forehead instead. Her plan thwarted, she yelled in a combination of pain and disappointment.

"What are you doing under there, Heather? Get out of my room before I wallop your backside."

"You wouldn't dare. Mamma would wallop you."

"Don't count on it, brat. Mom wouldn't like knowing you were about to do the same to me."

"Oh, she wouldn't mind. Besides, I know how to get what I want from Mom when I need to."

"Yeah, right?" Rachel said incredulously, watching her little sister slide out from under the bed. "What are you doing under there?"

"Oh, nuttin," she said. "Hey, how d'you know I was hiding under there, anyway?"

"Don't you know? Like Mom, I have eyes in the back of my head. I knew the instant you crawled through the door."

"Really?"

"Yup! The very instant the door opened. I watched you sneak in, close the door behind you, and slither under my bed like the snake you are."

"Why did you wait so long then, leaving me hiding under there for hours?"

"Oh, come on now. It wasn't hours. Minutes, yes but hours, no way."

"Well, it felt like forever."

"Serves you right. Besides, what is that around your wrist?" Rachel asked as Heather quickly hid her hand behind her back.

"What?"

"My bracelet, that you're wearing right this very minute."

Defiantly, the eleven-year-old Heather stuck her hand out in front of her and said. "Oh, this stupid-looking thing? You want it back? I'll give it to you when I'm good and ready."

"Oh yeah? Well, keep it for now. Just don't lose it."

"Really? I can wear it?" Heather exclaimed, the excitement in her tone self-evident.

"Sure, just don't lose it. I'll let you wear it for the rest of the week, and then you can return it. If you don't give me an argument about it, maybe I'll let you wear something else."

"Honest? I can wear it?"

"Yes, but only if you return it as I asked."

"Oh, Rachel, you're the best big sister a girl could ever have." Heather squealed as she jumped on to the bed and patted the mattress beside her.

Taking the cue, Rachel sat down next to her, and wrapped an arm around her younger sister's shoulders, tucking her close to her.

"Heather, I can't stay mad at you. Not at my age. Besides, you're my only sister, and even though you're a brat, I love you anyway."

"That's not so. I'm not a brat."

"Yes, you are, and you'll always be my bratty sister, even after we're all grown up."

"Will we live together? I mean when we're all grown up?"

"Maybe for a while, as long as you're good, and only until I get married."

"Can I live with you even then?"

"No silly, you'll probably have a guy fawning all over you."

"Speaking of guys, what was it like to kiss Sam Hutchinson?"

"What? How did you know I… oh, wait a minute? Have you been reading my diary?"

Heather sheepishly dropped her head, just a touch mind you, but enough that Rachel, four years older, could tell. Pushing her aside, Rachel opened her bedside table drawer. Sure enough, the diary had moved.

"Heather, you know it's not polite to read other people's diaries. It's personal."

"Well, how was it?" Heather asked, ignoring the scolding.

"None of your business."

"Ah, come on, spill it. Was it wet?"

"Wet? Where do you learn such things? No, it wasn't wet. It was nice. That's all I will say."

"Awe, come on. There must have been more."

"No, you little scamp. That's all I will tell you."

Just then, there was a knock on the door just before it opened.

"Girls, it's time for bed. It's a school day tomorrow, and you're both up past your bedtime. You especially, Heather."

"Oh, mamma. Do I have to? We're having such a good time."

"Yes, you do, Heather. There will be time for more tomorrow and the day after."

"Oh, all right," she said dejectedly and hopped off the bed. Before leaving, though, she turned to Rachel and said. "And we're not done. You will tell me."

"In your dreams, brat."

Smiling, Heather skipped down the hall to her bedroom.

"Did you brush your teeth?" Mom reminded the young girl.

"Oh, yeah," Heather answered before moving off towards the bathroom.

"And do it right, you hear!"

"Yes, mamma," the back of her head remarked as it disappeared into the bathroom.

"Don't stay up too late. You have school tomorrow too!"

"I won't, mom, I promise."

"I know you won't," she said, reaching for the door. Before stepping through, she stopped and turned to her firstborn and asked.

"How was kissing Sam Hutchinson? Did you like it?"

"Mom! Really? That's private."

"Sweetheart, I get it. Just be careful, all right. Do you still keep condoms in your purse?"

"Yes, Mom, I still have it. I will not use it for years, you know."

"I know dear. Whether or not you need it, I want you to keep it handy at all times. Trust me. I know these things. You never know when you will need it until you want it. Your father and I want nothing to happen to you, and this is just one small way we can keep you safe. Please promise me."

"I promise Mom. I'll always have one handy. I'm still not going to need it."

"Yes, dear, even better. And remember, I'll give you new ones every three months. They wear out even when sitting in your purse."

"Yes, Mom, I remember. It'll be alright. I promise."

"Thank you, dear. I will feel so much better if you do, and so will your father."

"Daddy?"

"Oh, yes, your father too. Why do you think I married him and had two terrific girls with him? We think alike."

"Will you tell me again the story about how you two met and fell in love? I love hearing that story."

"Sure, but not tonight. School night, remember?"

"Yes, Mom." Rachel said, as she reached over and turned off the music. "Do you mind if I read a little while before turning off the light?"

"All right, but don't stay up too late. I don't want to have to drag you by the ankle out of bed tomorrow."

"No, I wouldn't want that either. Good night Mom, and thanks."

"Thanks for what?"

"For being you, that's all."

Smiling, Rachel's mom turned and just as the door closed, she whispered, "Love you. Sweet dreams."

"Love you too, Mom."

As the door closed, Rachel heard her mother snap at her sister. "What are you still doing up? Get to bed little one before I thrash you."

The sound of feet running followed and then the sound of her mother following Heather in to tuck her in bed.

Before she dived into the book she was reading, Rachel smiled as she heard the two of them say goodnight along with the customary 'I love you.'

The phone rang, bringing Heather out of her reverie. She had been looking out the window and got lost in her daydream.

"Hello?"

"Hello Heather, how are you doing tonight?"

"As always Daddy, not so good. I won't be until we find Rachel and bring her home."

"Yes, I understand. I don't sleep too well myself these days. Neither does your mother."

"Momma? Is she all right? Did something happen to her?"

"Nothing like that, Heather. She's fine. Like all of us, we're missing Rachel, and need her back home and knowing she's safe and sound."

"So, any word on the search?"

"Heather, I'm sorry, but nothing concrete. The FBI and the Justice Department have several crack investigators working on it, but so far, they have reported little of use."

"Daddy, I can't help get the feeling that she never returned to Chicago from the conference."

"You know dear. I can't either. Everything seems like she did, but there is something that I can't quite put my finger on. Her stuff was all there, as if she walked into the apartment, took some stuff out, and went to bed. After that, she just disappeared."

"Daddy, she didn't sleep in that bed that night. Honestly, I don't think she ever came home."

"Heather, I think you may be right, but why do you think so?"

"I couldn't smell her on the sheets. I've slept with her enough to know how she smells and how the sheets smell afterward. I can't think of a reason, that's all."

"Well, I'm assured that teams in both cities are combing every nook and cranny to figure out what happened. However, I agree. I don't believe Rachel ever boarded the plane to Chicago. I think a doppelganger took her place."

"Someone pretended to be her on that flight? That's what you're saying, isn't it?"

"Yes, dear. It's possible. Remember, like you. I have my doubts she returned home to Chicago. I've asked Justice to look seriously into that possibility."

"Daddy, I have my reasons for thinking she didn't make it home. What are yours?"

"Well, to be honest, it's a gut feeling. As you said, her apartment looked normal and all, but if that was Rachel on the plane, she took great care to prevent the hundreds of security cameras at the three airports to get a good look at her. Even going through security, where cameras would surely get a good image of her, there was something about the image that didn't seem right."

"Can I see some of those photos?"

"Sure, I don't see why not? I'll send them to you today."

"Do you have any other suspicions? Can I help with anything?"

"Beyond my gut feeling, I don't. I'm letting the investigators do their job. They are very good at this kind of thing. However, you could help. I hadn't realized you could tell she didn't sleep in her bed by smell alone. I'll let the investigators know and have them talk to you again. I'll also ask them to let you help, but I don't know how they'll feel about a civilian becoming an active member of the team."

"Thank you, Daddy. You know I don't intend to sit by and wait. I might fly out and visit the hotel where she stayed at and stop by the conference center. I might stumble on something useful."

"I don't suppose my telling you that might be a bad idea will deter you."

"No, Daddy."

"No, I didn't think so. Just be careful. Promise me that. We don't know what we're up against."

"I will, Daddy. If I think of anything or find out something, I will let you know."

"No doubt, honey. I know. Just be careful."

"I will. I love you, Daddy."

"Love you too. I mean it. Be careful. I don't want to lose you too."

"You won't. Bye."

With that, Heather rang off, more determined than ever to find her missing sister with every beat of her heart. Picking up her smartphone, she opened a browser and started checking out airline flights out of the city.

***

Senator Ladensen hung up the phone, a new look of worry appeared upon his face.

Pressing the call button on his desk phone, his secretary Ben Clark stepped into his office. "Yes, Sir."

"Close the door," the Senator asked.

With the door closed, Ben asked, "Yes, Sir. You need something?"

"Yes, Ben. Get me the agent in charge of my daughter's disappearance at Justice for me."

"Yes, Sir. Right away."

"And Ben, keep this private. I don't want too many people to know I'm reaching out to Justice."

"Sir, everyone knows they're helping with the search for your missing daughter."

"Still, keep this between the two of us."

"Yes, Sir. Right away."

After the door closed, the Senator closed his eyes and leaned back in his chair. With two fingers rubbing his eyes, he murmured, "Damn, my daughter will be the death of me yet."

Chapter Five

Sitting at her kitchen table, Shelby pondered what she would write. She was of two minds about Katie. On the one hand, she liked the girl. They hit it off nicely from the first day when she had picked her up at the bar. Taking her home, they fell into bed and pleasured each other until dawn.

Shelby discovered something about herself on that first night. She was multiorgasmic. Never had a lover kept her climax running for such a long time with barely a break. She had lost all sense of time. All she knew was that almost from the moment they stripped each other's clothes off and fell on the bed, her body climbed to new heights that never seemed to stop. Frankly, the time on the clock surprised her. At least two hours had passed in what seemed like minutes as her mind fell in upon itself, among the waves of pleasure emanating from her core and radiating outward.

"What was it about this girl?" she wondered. "I could get into her."

The trouble was, Katie was an assignment. Her employers expected her to write up an accurate, factual report, along with her opinions and subjective analysis. They wanted her to sleep with the girl if the opportunity arose, and it did. It turned out that not only was she fun in bed, but she was also fun in everyday life.

"Am I falling in love with her?" Shelby asked herself.

"How can I do this?" she added, referring to her analysis report for the Consortium.

The problem was, Shelby knew that they expected a professional and honest report. Deceiving them would surely mean the loss of her job or her life. Even worse, they'd designate her as prey, seize and sell her into lifelong bondage.

She had little idea of what became of those taken by the Consortium. Frankly, she didn't want to know. All she knew was that whenever she submitted a positive review of an assignment, that person disappeared forever. They paid her handsomely for her honest, professional analysis and didn't ask questions.

She was of two minds about Katie. If she wrote an accurate analysis, then she knew Katie would disappear forever. She didn't want to give up on what may be the love of her life. Shelby liked Katie, maybe even loved her. She didn't want to contribute to whatever would become of her.

Scratching her head, she got up from her table and made herself a cup of tea. Her mind struggled with indecision. She knew one thing for sure. She did not want Katie to suffer the fate a positive assessment would do to her.

"Oh, why did I ever get involved with them?"

The answer was easy. It was the money. Until now, Shelby never had a problem with handling an assignment. If she was honest with herself, these targets didn't interest her. She befriended them, got to know them, slept with them, and had a good time. However, none of them ever enticed her to fall in love with them.

Until Katie, that is.

"Katie, Katie, Katie. What am I ever going to do with you?"

Shelby struggled with her decision for a long time. The trouble was, she had already delayed filing her report. They were waiting, and they were insistent. They wanted her assessment, and they wanted it today. There would be no more delays, no more deferrals. It was now or suffer the consequences.

"Damn, why did I have to fall for her?"

"Do I have a choice?" she asked herself for the hundredth time. "No," was always the answer.

Resigned, she sat down and began writing her report, favorable for the Consortium but not for herself or Katie. Writing it depressed her, but she knew she had no choice.

Shelby added an addendum to the report, documenting her feelings for Katie, wishing it would make a difference, but knowing inside, it didn't. The Consortium was not a compassionate bunch. They were ruthless. What she didn't want to know was how vicious.

With a sigh of despair, she folded up the papers and stuffed them into an envelope. Picking up the phone, she dialed a number long ago committed to memory. After a single ring, she heard a tone before the line disconnected.

Hanging up, she sat down, staring at her cold and uninviting tea. Tonight, she'd be taking a walk, making the drop, and exchanging the favorable report for cash to her handler.

Cash in hand and stuffed in the pockets of her overcoat, Shelby strolled back to her flat. She was feeling terrible. Katie, who might have been the love of her life, would soon disappear, forever. With head down, staring at her feet, she barely heard her phone ring. It's constant ringing finally got through to her. Taking the phone out of her pocket, she looked at the caller ID.

"Shit," she muttered. Her thumb hovered a moment over the decline button before taking the call.

Putting on a good face, "Hey Katie. How nice to hear from you? This is a surprise."

"Hi, I'm bored. The bar is nearly empty, and I've got nothing to do except think about you."

"Well, I'm flattered, my dear. I'm sorry about being bored. Anything I can do?"

"I thought you would never ask. Can you come by, if you're not doing anything?"

"Oh, I don't know Katie. I...."

"Please Shelby. I'd like to see you."

"I'm exhausted, my love," Shelby begged.

"Well, I can take care of that."

"Oh, no doubt. I'm sure you can."

"Then you'll come?"

"Well..." Shelby hesitated.

"Please? I need to see you, and right now, I could use a friend. I have this terrible feeling. A feeling that something awful is about to happen."

"About what?"

"Come by, and I'll tell you. Hey, I'll give you a hint. 'It's about us, and it's something not good. I'll tell you the rest when you get here."

"I don't know Katie. I'm exhausted."

"Well, if that is what you want to do."

"Katie, I don't believe I'd be good company for you."

"Shelby, please. I always feel better when I'm with you. Remember three months ago, when we first met."

"Sure, I do. That was a wonderful night. You had me going. I'll never forget it–ever."

"Then you know how much I can do for you. We can both help each other tonight."

"You're right, of course, Katie. All right, I'll be there shortly. What time do you get off?"

"Closing."

"What else is new. All right, I'll get there beforehand. Pour me a drink. I need one right now."

"You got it, babe. I'll have it ready for you the moment you step through the door."

"See you soon," Shelby said as she hung up.

"Shit!" Shelby thought. "I don't need this right now. I'm betraying her, and now she's bored and wants to see me."

Chapter Six

Leaning back, Sir rubbed his belly. "That was delicious. You chose well when preparing for the meal upon my return."

"Thank you, Sir," Avril replied with a sly smile on her face.

"Just what I needed after a long trip and even a longer session with you in bed. If I am not mistaken, Avril, you're becoming a nymphomaniac. You need sex almost as much as I do."

"Sir, you know I always liked sex. Being with you has opened up so many more avenues to experience. I dare say, you made me realize there's much more to explore."

"And explore you do. I love watching you move from mere to desire to a primal need for satisfaction as you indulge in your lust and desire. When you're on the verge of tipping over in your approaching climax, you disappear inside yourself."

"Sir, I don't mean to, it just happens."

"Don't worry about it. I like it. I enjoy watching you fall into the abyss and lose yourself. It's fun to watch."

"Sir, when I do, which I admit I like ever so much, I can't seem to feel the world around me. I don't care about time, where I am, or whom I'm with. I know you're there. But it's up here in my head. I know that. The rest of me, well, I don't care, except that all I want is to go on experiencing the joy of what I am feeling."

"Avril, it's entertaining to watch you do that. Do you have any sense of how long you are in that state?"

"No, Sir, I don't. I don't think I've ever thought about it."

"You go right on not thinking about it. What I can tell you is that your orgasmic state goes on until I let it stop. Often enough, I keep you tilted for over a half-hour without letting you come down."

"A half-hour? Is that even possible, Sir?"

"Oh, yes. Over the years, you've learned to give in and let go. That's the key. Sure, you waver in intensity, similar to gentle waves in the ocean. You bob up and down but never drop so far that you exit your climatic state. Rather, I keep you there. Your orgasms are mine, whether I withhold them or share them with you, they are mine. Just as I own you, I own your orgasms."

"Sir, if I may, I know you've told me that before, but I am only now just starting to realize what you mean by that. You're saying that in my giving of myself to you, submitting to you, turning ownership of my body and mind to you, you take possession of all that is within me. That includes my climaxes and pains."

"Yes, my Avril. That is exactly what I mean. Even as I make you scream in torment, those are my screams, extracted as I see fit. The same goes for your pleasures. Your orgasms belong to me. I own them, and I will share them with you as I see fit."

"Yes, Sir. I understand though I need to reflect upon the idea more, though I now see what you mean. Apologies if I have been dense until now."

"Are you saying you're sorry?"

"Ah… no Sir. That would violate the rules."

"Quite right, my dear. Quite right. So what did you mean?"

"Sir, only that I was in error and I need to adjust my thinking," Avril blurted.

Smiling under his breath, Sir picked up his coffee cup and drank. With the wheels turning behind his eyes, Avril waited to see how he would respond. He stayed silent for quite some time, allowing her nervousness to climb. After all this time, she knew she had to remain silent. Silence was the best option at the moment.

After many minutes, where Avril fidgeted under the table, he finally spoke.

"Time to play. Take care of your bodily needs and meet me in the playroom in fifteen minutes. I'm ready to explore more of you."

"Yes, Sir. I'll be ready."

Right on time, Avril was in the playroom. She knelt in the center of the room, in a posture that showed her respect for her Master and Owner. Her ass planted firmly on the back of her heels, Avril spread wide her knees, granting him a full view and access to what lay between her legs. She rested her palms on the tops of her thighs, palms up and fingers flat and extended. With a deferential attitude, Avril sat upright, threw her back straight, shoulders back, and chest out, providing a sweet, delicate curve of her body. In this pose, he called 'Nadu,' unlike the usual poses, she held her head down, staring at the floor in front of her.

There she waited for him. She waited for her Sir to collect her. She did not know what he had in mind for the night. Whatever it was, considering how much fun in bed she had earlier in the day, she sensed she would feel just the opposite.

It had been a while since she knelt for him. Not that she minded, she used to enjoy kneeling for him. At first, when she was first taken and brought here, he had her kneel under duress. To survive, she learned to kneel, prepared for his needs, and eventually found the exercise fulfilling. Now it was different.

She found solace in kneeling for him, assuming he was around. Still, she had fallen out of the habit. It had been at least a month since she last knelt. Her joints were getting sore. As much as she enjoyed exercising, kneeling absolutely still was a workout she had not practiced in a long time. Now she didn't see the value in kneeling.

"Where is he?" she thought to herself.

She was getting anxious. Half of her wanted no part of what was about to come. The other half was excited to get started. His need to extract her screams was painful, but it was an intimacy she never thought she could experience. It shocked her to find out she wanted and needed this kind of play. It gave her a sense of closeness to her Master she would never have expected. Years ago, she wished she had a man who could control her in bed. It was a wishful thought, and one she never thought would happen. Now she had one, and it amazed her how good their relationship turned out.

At the start of every session, she felt nervous with trepidation. As the course of the playtime went on, she lost the sense of pain and felt pleasure. As the scene progressed, pleasure turned into excitement, and eventually, she climaxed.

"Where is he?" she asked herself a second time.

"How long has he kept me waiting?" Avril considered. "I don't know. Without watches or clocks, she didn't know. Had it been fifteen minutes, thirty, an hour?"

What she knew was that she had to wait, no matter how long. Further, no matter how much it hurt to stay in pose, she had to maintain it. Sir was likely watching her. How, she never found out, but sure as hell, she knew he was.

So, she continued to wait, holding her 'Nadu' pose, her knees aching and her thighs and calves burning. Even after what felt like hours, he hadn't made an appearance.

"So, where the fuck was he?"

She continued to wait.

***

Her legs numb, her body crying in pain, she paused and waited. She started to fidget. To deal with the stiffness in her neck, she rolled her head from shoulder to shoulder. It felt good to ease her stiffness. She knew she was taking a chance. Odds were, he would know, but she couldn't help it.

Her ankles were feeling it now, joining her knees in moaning. Fortunately, the ache in her thighs and calves had settled down.

Long ago, she had stopped asking where the fuck he was. He would come in his own sweet time. What she knew was, when he came, she had better be in position and ready for him. However, she would soon be a pool of mush, unsuitable for extracting her screams.

Her mind going blank, she lost focus and wavered. Catching herself, she stopped herself from falling over. She had to break posture and steady herself by putting a hand to the floor.

Of all the time, he opened the door and walked in on her, out of position and a hand on the floor.

"Sir!" she tried to call out. "I'm–"

"Don't give me that. You know what I expect. You've fallen out of practice. I know you've not knelt for me for some time. You've been lax. How do you expect me to support your application for membership if you don't do the simplest of tasks required? All I ask is that you kneel for me every day. Yet, you don't put in the effort. How can I trust you?"

"Sir, I am sorry. I will do better."

"So, even now, you break the rules." Sir jumped on her words, chastising her for apologizing, a violation of the rules.

"Sir? Oh, I see."

"What should I do with you?"

"Sir, whatever you feel is appropriate. I will accept your decision. You're right. I have failed you, and I submit myself to your discipline."

"That's better. Now, get up."

"Yes, Sir," Avril said as she put her hands on the floor to assist her body in standing.

"No hands. Just get up."

"Yes, Sir. I'll try it."

"No trying. Do it."

"Yes, Sir."

Pulling her hands back, she tried to unfold her body and stand. Part way up, her legs failed her, and she fell over, landing on her side.

"I'm waiting." Sir spoke sternly to her.

"Yes, Sir."

Moving slower this time, she righted herself, and carefully stood up. It took a while, but eventually, she made it.

"Inspect," he commanded.

"Yes Sir," she responded, assuming the pose he demanded of her. Standing straight up, she locked her hands behind her head and spread her legs wide, her feet beyond shoulder width apart. Staring straight ahead, she said.

"Sir, if it is all right, I have a question."

"You want to know how long I kept you waiting."

"Sir, yes, Sir."

"It's none of your business. You know I require you to kneel whenever I demand it and stay there until released, no matter how long it takes."

"Yes, Sir, I do."

"Then you also know that I could require you to kneel for hours or days on end, without moving."

"I do Sir."

"Then you also know that you failed me."

"Yes, Sir."

"Don't move. Is that understood?"

"It is Sir."

Walking around her, Sir dragged his fingers across her body, feeling its tension and her apprehension. Her back to him, he snickered to himself.

"How dare you disobey me," he said instead.

Avril kept quiet, zipping her lip. She knew that no matter what, there was nothing she could say to appease him.

Patting her ass, she felt him walk away. A minute later, she heard clanking metal and something dragging across the floor. She wondered what he was doing, but ultimately, she didn't care. Eventually, she'd find out. One thing she knew, it would not be good.

"Come here," she heard.

Turning, she started walking to him and then stopped. Fixated, not on Sir, but what he was standing beside she stared. Dread started consuming her.

It was a steel cage. Only, it wasn't just a cage. Whoever built it, designed it with steel, shaped into the form of a person. And it was a small, tiny in fact. What's more, it had a door, and it was open, presumably waiting for her.

"Get in," he commanded in no uncertain terms.

Gulping, she nodded and approached the cage. Grasping the sides with her hands, she paused. Knowing what Sir wanted from her, she did not want to climb in for fear of the coming discipline.

"I'm waiting."

Resigned, she turned and backed her way into the cage. Pressing her body against the back, she waited for him to lock her inside.

"Don't keep me waiting again."

"Yes Sir," she said as he closed and padlocked the door, crushing her between the steel bars. It completely enveloped her, from the crown of her head to the balls of her feet. It held her tightly, squeezing her from all sides. She could not move barely more than an inch. It was a tight fit, and she could scarcely breathe.

Resigned, she waited for what was to come next. She didn't have long to wait. First, he reached out grabbing each of her nipples. She moaned in delight. There was one thing about Sir, her nipples loved his attention, standing upright and firm for him. Sometimes she wondered who demanded more attention, herself or her nipples. They were almost separate entities, different people.

Nodding, he looked into her eyes, drilling deep. She stared back, hoping to reveal the dark desire of his soul. The deep black of his eyes only told her he had something genuinely sadistic on his mind. No one had to tell her she was about to experience an unusual and particularly cruel punishment. She dreaded what came next.

Releasing her nipples, he pulled out of his pocket a light-weight chain and locked them to her nipple rings. As he released them, she realized nervously that the connecting chain rested outside of the bars. Any movement she may make would pull on the interlinks, stretching her nipples. It allowed him the opportunity to play with the chain, pulling on it and swinging it back and forth, just to see her tits perform by his command.

After a parting yank on the chain, she watched him walk off behind her. A minute later, she heard the clanking of a winch above her head. In no time at all, she sensed the cage rise off the floor and her with it. Freely swinging, the cage spun freely from side to side.

The sound stopped, and her upward travel halted with it. Sir reached over and grabbed a pair of large clamps on the end of a long wire stretching out her view. He attached the black one to the back of the cage just below her shoulder blades. He clamped the red one to the floor of the cage.

Gulping, Avril knew what was coming. It would not be fun.

"Avril, I know you know what these are."

"Yes, Sir, I do."

"For failing me not just once or twice but consistently over the past weeks, you will suffer their effects until I feel you have suffered enough and repent your sins against me."

She nodded.

"You should know, I attached the leads of the clamps to a generator controlled by a timer. At regular intervals, the generator will deliver a powerful electrical shock to the cage and through your body. You will feel it all over; everywhere the steel touches your body. The nipple chain resting against the steel will intensify the effect. As you writhe in anguish, you will shake and squirm, bouncing the chain against the bars. Electroshocks will stab deep into your nipples, sending its energy through your breasts and deep into your chest. As much as I love your tits, I would hate to see them burn away and fall off. Understood?"

Nodding, she said in a soft, nervous voice. "Yes, Sir. I will do my best."

"I'm sure you will." Sir said as he turned on the timer.

It immediately went off, and Avril screamed. Feeling the agony of the current coursing across her body told her one thing. It was not a pain that would elicit an orgasm. On the contrary, the electricity attacked every cell, simultaneously tormenting their connecting neurons everywhere. When it was over, she felt drained and worn out, sweat covering her entire body.

"That was only two minutes. They'll be more at irregular intervals. You'll never know when they are coming, nor will you be able to predict the next one. I'll leave you now to your misery. Have fun!"

"Yes, Sir, I will," she said under her breath.

"I'm sure you will," he said, walking out the door.

As he turned out the lights, the timer went off, and Avril screamed. Electrified crackling sizzles lit up the room as his punishment fried her body. Avril was certain she would soon die.

Chapter Seven

Walking into his office, the need for a cup of coffee strong, Sir walked to the beverage bar and turned on the coffee machine. As the device warmed up, he stepped over to the window and looked out. It was late morning, and he felt rested. Birds flitted about, scratching what they could find out of the ground. The sun was bright and barely a cloud in the sky. Odd for this time of year, it was a peaceful scene, set apart from the rest of the world.

And that's how he liked it. His estate stood in the middle of nowhere, insulated by miles of thick, dense forest. He owned miles of land all around him to keep interlopers at bay. Occasionally, some developer would reach out to him and propose a lucrative project. They were all the same, profitable to the developer but not to him. The real value was to keep everyone away so he could enjoy his life by indulging in his passions. No, they would never get him to sell off any of his precious lands.

All seemed right with his world, even though Avril's behavior of late still bothered him. With a ding, his coffee machine alerted him that his coffee was ready. Preparing it just as he liked it, Sir took his first sip.

"Ah…" he uttered his deep sigh of satisfaction. Turning, he relaxed on his sofa and picked up the first of his newspapers from around the world. Increasingly dissatisfied with them, they always seemed to be a day or two behind in current events. He preferred getting his news on his tablet, which was more up-to-date. Still, there was always an odd tidbit or two in the paper that he'd miss from the online version. He quickly went through them, tossing them all aside in short order. Distracted, today's daily briefing from around the world held little interest to him.

Picking up his tablet, he accessed an app that granted him access to the video monitors in the playroom. The room was blacker than sin, but the infrared cameras provided a good view of the subject of their attention.

Avril was visibly exhausted, her body sagging in the metal form-fitting cage she occupied. Her eyes closed even as her mouth clenched. Looking at the counter on the monitor, she suffered in there for about sixteen hours now. It was hard to tell if she was alive or dead.

He'd be disappointed if she died during her ordeal. He still wanted her. Still, she needed punishment. She failed him. Anyone else and it would be different. He'd punish them without a second thought, unconcerned whether they lived or died. Often enough, he savored their final screaming moments. Avril was another case. He had plans for her, and her death would cause years of lost progress in achieving his goal.

He needed a mate. He needed someone to share his passions, enjoy his lifestyle, and to carry on his legacy. He needed someone to carry his child. The trouble was, as much as he enjoyed his obsession, he was a romantic at heart. His baby mama needed to be someone he cherished. At the moment, Avril had all the makings of being that mate.

Watching her on the tablet, in some small way, he felt sorry for her. He wished she had kept up with her kneeling for him, whether or not he was there. He desired more from her than just obedience. He wanted her to feel close to him, honoring their relationship while performing this simple act without prompting or encouragement. That she had fallen out of practice was a setback and would likely delay her admission into the Consortium, not to mention his good favor.

Just then, as he gazed at her, she went all stiff. Her jaw clamped even tighter, and her eyes clenched tightly closed. He could tell she was screaming inside her skull, even as the jolting electricity coursed through her body squelching the screams.

Looking at the anguish on her face, he smiled. Getting up, he walked to a paneled wall and simultaneously touched it in three places. Immediately, a portion of the wall revealed a door which opened outward, and Sir walked through.

As the door closed behind him, an array of dozens of video monitors lit up, showcasing his inventory of captured prey in their cells and rooms. Ignoring the others, he dialed up the primary large screen monitor to focus on his Avril, surviving the latest electrocution ordeal as it ended.

She was shaking her head in a rage. Later, he'd review the recordings of the overnight ordeal, but the real-time feed interested him. He also configured several other monitors to show him the scene from various angles as she dangled in her electrified steel cage.

"Well my dear, how are you doing this morning?" he casually asked himself before sitting down in a thickly padded, leather lounge chair and putting his feet up on the desk. His coffee forgotten, he leaned back to enjoy the movie.

Reviewing the setup in his mind, he knew that he set the timer to activate roughly every ten minutes at random intervals. That meant approximately ten shocks per hour.

"Hmmm," he muttered, doing the math "she's suffered about a hundred sixty electroshocks since the start. Impressive girl, I have to admit." The numbers might horrify an observer, but Sir only pursed his mouth and smiled.

"I'll give her a few more hours until tonight, and then we'll see." He would only halt the near-execution if she became unresponsive, or she satisfied his resolve in accepting her punishment.

Without actively thinking about it, he knew that each session started at random, lasting anywhere from thirty seconds to two minutes. The intensity of the current also varied to a mere annoyance to near-fatal levels. The machine carefully timed and executed each session to be as painful as possible without killing the victim. Experiments done on other prey over the years had given him an excellent idea on how much current to deliver without fatal results. That he had killed a few during the experiments was inconsequential. It gave him sufficient data to perfect his technique.

The timer on Avril's next shock was counting down and getting close. Picking up the remote, he turned up the volume. He wanted to hear everything.

The countdown reaching zero, he watched her exhausted body stiffened once again. Looking at the meters, he noted that this was one of the more intensive shocks, reaching near maximum intensity and duration.

"Perfect," he reasoned to himself, observing small electrical sparks of light bounce all over her body, as she involuntarily moved, trying in vain to avoid touching the electrified steel of her cage. He heard moaning which filled him with an almost insurmountable pleasure. He knew she'd feel more as the electroshocks ravaged her body.

As she twitched, the cage spun around, giving him excellent views of her suffering. As the current session wound down, Avril opened her mouth wide, still unable to scream out loud. Inside her head, Sir knew it was another story. Leaning forward in his chair, he eagerly awaited the end of the current so that her lungs could pass air over her vocal cords, eliciting a satisfying vocalized scream.

It ended, and she did. Catching her breath, Avril muttered, 'mother fucking bastard' as her body sagged once again.

Satisfaction filled him, and he leaned back. He was having a good day. He thoroughly enjoyed it when they cursed him out and called him various expletives.

Looking at his coffee, now cold, he got a fresh cup. Returning to his observation seat, he sat down and slowly drank the hot coffee.

As he studied her anguished face, his secure phone rang. Looking at the caller ID, he frowned. Seeing who it was from, he knew that this was not a welcoming call, but one that he had to answer.

"What is it?" he snarled, annoyed at the interruption, much preferring to watch his precious possession suffer.

"Sir, sorry to bother you. We have a situation."

"Yes?"

"It's one of our senior agents, a team leader."

"What about him?"

"Actually, Sir, it's a woman."

"Fair enough continue."

"Yes, Sir. We assigned her to investigate a candidate out of Portland, Oregon, on the west coast of the United States. From the early reports, it looked as if the target was a suitable candidate, one that might interest you for yourself."

"But…?"

"Yes, Sir, there is a but. After months of investigation, we were expecting good news, and I had already tagged her to submit to you for final selection. Yesterday, I received her final report on the candidate, and it is disturbing."

"How so?"

"The agent has completely reversed her findings. She's now reporting information that makes the candidate unsuitable. In the report…."

"Get to the point."

"Ah, yes, Sir. The point is, I suspect something else is in play here. As a result, I assigned a new team. However, instead of investigating the candidate, I've assigned them to investigate our agent. I did not inform them that their target is one of us. I want them to assess as if the agent was candidate prey."

"Let me get this straight, so I understand. You're saying that our agent is behaving erratically, and we may not trust her. Then, to validate your suspicions, you've assigned an independent team to investigate the agent. All good. So, what's the problem?"

"Sir, when you put it like that, there is no problem. I felt I should make you aware of the situation."

"Rightly so, you thought correctly. Is there anything else of immediate importance?"

"No, Sir. That is all."

"Thank you. I appreciate the call. Now I'm very busy."

"Yes, Sir, and thank you, Sir," the assistant said as he rang off and disconnected.

Sir thought about the situation for some time staring at his cold coffee. It's not that this hadn't happened before on his watch, but it concerned him that his assistant thought it so important that he felt it worth disturbing him at home.

He briefly glanced at the monitors where Avril stood caged and breathing heavy before calling up the latest reports on the prey out of Portland, Oregon. Glancing through the reports, he quickly found the candidate referred to and started reading in depth.

His assistant was right. There was a significant disparity between the early reports and the later ones. In reading the reports of the others on the agent's team, he found nothing of significance that would prevent this candidate from being picked up. The girl interested him and was potentially a welcome addition to his stable. Further, he knew the agent and her work. Until now, she was a valuable asset to the organization.

"What changed Shelby?" he rhetorically asked himself.

Looking into the database, he found and flagged her investigation, which would alert him whenever someone updated it.

Just then, movement on the big screen monitor caught his attention. Avril's timer had just started shocking her, and she bounced stiffly against the electrified bars of her cage. A gleam in his eyes, he watched sparks of light flashed as the nipple chain bounced against the bars, completing a circuit and electrocuting her tits.

As the timer ended its shocking session, Sir smiled as he heard her exclaim between recovering breaths. "Fuck!"

"Sir, please stop this? I can't take any more of this," she begged, trailing off at the end.

Sagging her body as much as the cage allowed, tears flowed again, and she mumbled, "I'm sorry."

Leaning back in his chair, he sat back to watch the entertainment. Checking the time, he gave Avril a couple more hours. Maybe then he would release her.

Chapter Eight

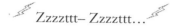 Zzzzttt– Zzzzttt...

Sounds of sizzling flesh crackled and burned under the torment of electrical energy. Bright sparks of light flashed briefly illuminating the dark room. Alone in the dark, isolated and blind, Avril writhed in agony and despair as the heartless electrical storm ravaged her body. Little by little and with extreme efficiency, the electrocution was killing her ever so slowly.

Mauled by the unceasing barrage, Avril lost all sense of time or space. She lived inside a universe of agonizing lightening. The electricity elicited a stinging misery she had never felt before. She couldn't sense her surroundings, but she was very well aware of the bars squeezing her body. Her nipple chain bounced and sparked against the metal bars, sending strong shocks deep into her breasts, penetrating her chest dozens of times per interval.

The on-again, off-again energy exhausted her. At the height of each electrical onslaught, her body stiffened as her fingers and toes curled. During the ever so brief reprievals, her body relaxed from the agony of the electrocution. Resting, she sagged against the metal bars of the cage, ensuring solid contact at the next formidable assault.

She cycled through periods of sheer agony to welcome relief. If it were possible, she'd fall to the floor and lie in blissful slumber. As it was, the cage was so form-fitted to her body that it was impossible to move. What movement it allowed, only seemed to enhance her misery as new contact points allowed electricity to flow into her body. Her arms locked in position, the inflexible steel kept her tightly contained and immobilized.

Every muscle in her body strained to contract upon themselves as they tensed up, further exhausting her. She didn't care about that. All she cared about was the terrible agonizing current tormenting her body. Any movement promised a new excruciating adventure in electroshock punishment. No matter how she moved, how she shifted, she could not avoid the sizzling, stinging sensations all over her body.

She saw flashes of blinding light dancing while sounds of popping and sizzling sounds filled her world. Starving for air, trying as hard as she could, Avril couldn't breathe. The paralyzing electrical assault prevented her lungs from working. Finally, the ordeal stopped, and she felt exhaustion took over. Her starving lungs took in their first deep breath.

"Mother fucker, how much longer you bastard?" she venomously uttered.

Early in her ordeal, she tried to figure out whether the electricity flowed from her feet and out her chest or was it the other way around. Now, she didn't fucking care. She just wanted it to stop. Whether it was a release from the cage or life, she didn't care. She wanted it to stop. Now wouldn't be soon enough.

She knew one thing. The fucker would soon electrocute her again.

"Bastard," she sneered.

In her exhaustion, she wanted desperately to sleep. The cycles of electroshocks and relief prevented it.

Taking the time to rest as best as she could, she considered the electrical burns that she knew covered her body. There was nothing she could do about them. If she survived this ordeal, she knew that Sir would treat her injuries, just as he had done on other occasions. Still, enough was enough.

"What more do you want of me?" she yelled out into the dark void.

Even as she mumbled the words, she knew the answer. He wanted her to suffer. The thing was, how much more could he do to her that would surpass this agony? Some time ago, she thought she had suffered the worst of his torments. Over time, he continued to surprise her, coming up with harder and more painful ways to kill her without causing her death.

"When is the next one coming?" she casually asked herself, not wanting to know the answer. It would come soon enough.

But in the dark, unable to see even the bars trapping her, she felt outside herself. She was so, so tired. She felt as if she could sleep a week.

Shutting down, she stopped thinking. She only existed and dreaded the next shocking session.

Had it been just seconds, minutes, or hours since the last electrifying escapade, she did not know. It was at that moment that she sensed a change in the surrounding air. Somewhere in the distance, she sensed a dim, out-of-focus light coming from somewhere. Slowly processing the new sensation, Sir startled her when he spoke just inches away from her nose.

"Where did he come from?" she asked herself.

"Hello, Avril. Having fun?" he teased.

"Fuck no, you fucking bastard," was all she could say.

"No? Too bad. I can let you continue until you do. Would you like that?"

Finally, understanding what he was talking about, she shook her head 'No.'

"I didn't think so. Before I do, what do you have to say for yourself?"

Again, it took time to figure out what he was asking. Her mind was working slowly from the fatigue and the painful ordeals.

Eventually, Avril answered, "I'm sorry."

"Wrong answer." he snapped. "Your apology violates the rules." Try again.

Trying to concentrate on the correct response, she failed. She had forgotten why Sir put her in the cage and electrocuted her.

"You don't remember, do you?" he finally said several minutes later when she could not come up with an answer.

Slow to respond to the shifting question, Avril answered slowly, "No—Sir."

"Why were you punished?" he demanded.

Avril slowly processed the question without coming up with the reason. He would punish her for any old reason. It didn't have to be for an infraction. She shook her head 'No.'

Impatiently sighing, Sir reminded her, "I punished you for not respecting our relationship. To do that, you're to kneel daily, reflect and honor our ties to each other. I know you haven't kneeled in over a month."

Avril tried to assimilate the new information, but like the question, she was slow to process his statement. Eventually, she focused on the keyword, kneel. Slowly, she nodded her head 'Yes.'

"Good," he said. "Now what do you have to say for yourself?"

"I... will try to kneel... as required."

"No! Not try, do!" he snapped, interrupting her.

Nodding, she took her time to rephrase, "I will kneel."

"When?"

"Every day," she whimpered.

"For how long?"

Not knowing the answer he expected, she thought about it for a moment and then said, "For as long as you… require it."

"Good. For now, an hour a day will suffice. Now, are you ready to get out, or should I resume your punishment?"

Avril didn't have to think about this one. She knew the answer to the question, but it was not the answer she wanted to give him. Still, she wanted out, and the best way was to appease him.

"Whatever pleases you, Sir."

"Fine, then let's continue, shall we?"

And with that, he reached over and flipped a switch, resuming the torrents of highly charged electrical current coursing throughout her body. Avril knew only one thing.

She despised him and hated him. She hated him as she never hated him before. Her mind and thoughts consumed her with a loathing that pushed all other thoughts from her.

Then, replaced with an all-encompassing stinging pain, her body tensed as her jaw clamped shut. Involuntarily, she smacked her head on the back of the bars and felt her fingers and toes shoot bolts of lightning from their tips. Throughout, somehow, she knew she was no longer breathing. Her chest throbbed even as her nipples burned. The restraints on her body prevented her from doing anything except dance to the lightning striking her. Her muscles strained; exhaustion overwhelmed her.

The tingling, burning sensation went on forever, and then suddenly, it was over. Again, she sagged as electricity vacated her body. She took a few autonomous breaths even as her forehead slipped forward and banged into the flat steel bars in front of her face.

Unable to contain herself, she whispered, "Bastard."

In the all-encompassing blackness of the room, she didn't see him smile at the insult.

After a few more cycles of agony and relief, he removed the wires to the cage and opened the door. Avril fell out. If it weren't for him catching her, she would have landed on the floor in a heap. In seconds, she was unconscious, uncaring what became of her.

She woke up with a throbbing head, and in a dense fog. Coming to her senses, Avril found herself curled up in a fetal position. She laid there for some time, trying to resolve the pain resonating throughout her body. Even though she slept, every muscle in her body ached. Avril rolled over onto her back and covered her eyes with an arm.

Lying there, still languishing over her ordeal, she tried to make sense of her situation. Her thoughts came slowly to her, and it took time to measure each fleeting word speckling her brain.

"Ow!" was the only word that escaped her mouth.

Eventually, she removed her arm and opened her eyes. Looking through the fog, she sensed she was not back in her room. But where was she? She was lying on a small cot with something barely like to a mattress pad. It took effort, but she soon found herself locked inside a small cell with steel bars for a door. Groaning, she dropped her head back down and closed her eyes.

She attempted to clear her mind and go back to sleep. She almost succeeded when her bladder made itself known. She tried to fend the message off, but eventually, it forced the issue.

Groaning, she opened her eyes and threw her legs over the edge of the cot. In that simple action, she felt a stout resistance. Looking down her legs, she discovered a chain locked around her foot and ankle, shackling her to a heavy-duty eye bolt embedded in the cement floor.

"What now?" she lamented.

Groaning through her massive headache, she noticed a bucket at the foot of the bed.

"Really?" she complained.

Humiliated, she squatted over the bucket and emptied her bladder. Looking around for something to wipe herself, she didn't see so much as a corner of a bedsheet. With nothing to clean herself, she stood up and rubbed herself against the mattress pad. She might regret the action later, but it was better than nothing.

Sitting down on the edge of the cot, she considered her next move. Exhausted and in need of sleep, she knew Sir wanted something from her. He would not allow her to leave this horrid cell until she did as he wanted.

"What?" she wondered to herself, her head still in a fog of pain and fatigue. "What do you want?"

"Think Avril—think." She willed herself.

Fatigue overwhelming her, she curled up on the cot and drifted off to sleep.

***

Returning to her senses, she felt more rested this time. Still, she kept her eyes closed, hoping that she could fall off once more. She knew she was tired, and she ached all over. In her nakedness and without a sheet to cover her, she was cold. Goosebumps covering her body, she tried to curl up tighter to warm herself. She failed.

After a time, she groaned again, and sat up, putting her heels on the floor. Resting her head in the palm of her hands, she sat there for a time, trying not to think. After a while, she recognized the futility of the desire and looked up at the world around her.

Much to her chagrin, she remained chained to the floor in her tiny cell. Standing up, she looked at the nearby bucket. A foul odor arose from it.

"Crap!"

Then she walked over, squatted over it again, and spilled her water into it. Afterward, she felt better and cleaned herself as she had done the first time. Shaking her head, she knew he would make her eventually clean it up. He might even punish her for using the mattress for something other than for sleeping. No matter, she needed to maintain a lady-like appearance.

"Appearance? Oh, shit, I must look like a fright!" she realized. Touching her hair, she could feel the knots in the strands and tried to comb it with her fingers.

"What does he want from me?" she wondered, dreading how she looked.

"How did I survive that on-again, off-again, electrocution?"

"How many times did he shock me?"

"How long did it go on?"

These and several other questions flooded her head without getting an answer.

"Why did he punish me?" she asked herself again and again. "Why?"

She could not remember. She couldn't remember anything that transpired after dinner and going with him to the dungeon. All she could remember was that he locked her in a cage and electrocuted her repeatedly for hours on end.

"Electrocuting me? That's right. He electrocuted me several times over," she realized. "He locked me in a cage and shocked me with electricity repeatedly." Avril began scanning for injuries. Sure enough, burns covered her from chest to feet. What's worse, is that her nipple screamed in pain, though she could not remember why.

"But why? Surely, he said why? Why can't I remember?"

Struggling, she tried to remember, knowing that he would not release her from this cell until she resolved the issue to his satisfaction.

Standing up again, still shaky, she paced around, dragging her chain around with her.

For the life of her, she could not remember, her brain still scrambled. Deciding to rest again, she curled up on the cot and finally fell back asleep.

***

A long-time later, she woke up. She did not know how long she slept. The light still burned above her head. Just as when she first came into Sir's service, he used the ever-burning light to prevent her from telling time to any extent. She could have been asleep for an hour or a day. She did not know.

"Well, I have one idea. I need to go to the bathroom." Avril mused as she opened her eyes to look in the foul bucket at the foot of her cot. It smelled nasty, the rank odor permeating the entire room.

Getting up from the mattress, she used the humiliating bucket by adding more of her water to the putrid stench inside. Afterward, she resumed her seat on the thin mattress, contemplating what Sir wanted from her.

Then it came to her. She realized why Sir punished her so severely.

Feeling more rested than the last time, she found an empty spot on the floor and knelt. Taking a restful pose, she clasped her hands behind the small of her back and spread her knees wide apart. She concentrated on maintaining a perfect pose. That was what he wanted from her—to kneel.

Thinking about kneeling, she wondered why he wanted her to kneel.

In all this time, they had never talked about it. Sure, it was one of the formidable rules in the damn rule book but still why? Since day number one, Sir always has a reason for what he does, what he decides, what he demands of his prey, and what he wants of me.

Considering the question, "Was it to do homage to Sir as her Master and owner? Possibly but that didn't seem right to her. Was it a means to control her? But what did he gain from it? There must be something else at work here, but what?"

For sure, he wanted her to obey him and kneel. So that was what she would do. For how long?

The simple answer was, for as long as it took. Or, was it for as long as he liked? Both responses were likely correct. Therefore, she would kneel until he released her or until she fell over, however long it would take. She emptied her mind and forced herself into a meditation trance, allowing her to maintain the pose for a very long time.

"Avril?"

Deep in a trance, she barely heard her name.

"Avril, attend me."

The command shot through her trance, and she opened her eyes with a start.

"Yes, Sir."

"Stand up."

Nodding, she put her hands on the floor to steady herself as she stood.

"No hands, just stand up," he rebuked.

"Yes, Sir," Avril replied, removing her hands from the floor. Leaning back on her heels, she centered herself and extended a pair of wobbly legs. It took effort, but eventually, Avril stood up. Standing upright, legs shoulder-width apart and her arms crossed behind her back, she waited.

"Now, what do you say for yourself?" Sir asked.

"Sir, thank you for my well-deserved punishment. I will kneel daily for you as required."

"My dear, you don't know how close you came to feeling my

ultimate wrath."

"Yes, Sir."

As she stood there, he walked around inspecting her. Afterward, he told her he would treat her wounds, reassuring her they would heal without long-term marks.

"Thank you, Sir."

"Put your foot up on the edge of the bed."

As she did so, he interrupted. "No, the chained foot."

"Oh, sorr... ah, yes, Sir."

With that, he unlocked her chain, and she fell prostrate onto the floor. Not just fall over, but she toppled over, her limbs splaying out in all directions, and her face ate the ground. She reminded Sir of a dead body. Utter exhaustion kept her from moving into a more comfortable position.

Before leaving, Sir told her, "You may return to your room to get cleaned up." Pointing to the foul bucket in which she relieved herself, he said, "First, take that and empty it. Then rinse it out and return it to this room. I'll meet you in my private dining room in an hour and a half. I expect you cleaned up, hair washed and smelling sweet. Don't be late."

"Yes, Sir. Thank you, Sir. I won't be late." Avril uttered, the sounds of her voice bouncing off the floor.

Chapter Nine

"Come on, get out of bed lazybones," Shelby said, slapping Katie on the ass. "I'll take you to breakfast."

Groaning, Katie slowly opened her eyes. "What time is it?"

Shelby threw her legs out of bed and stood up, giving herself a long, satisfying stretch.

"Nearly nine. Come on. Get your ass up. I'm hungry."

"Another hour, please. I closed last night." Katie mumbled, closing her eyes once again. "Besides, sleeping with you, it's a wonder either of us gets any rest. Not that I didn't like…."

Katie trailed off, her pillow catching the rest of the comment.

"Ow!" she screamed, when Shelby slapped her again on the ass, only much harder this time. "Okay, okay. I'm getting up."

Instead, Katie pulled the covers over her head, trying to shut out the morning light and hiding from her new lover. Only Shelby wouldn't have any of it. Walking around to the side of the bed, Shelby gently pulled back the covers, uncovering Katie down to her waist.

Giving her breasts a loving caress and her warm lips touching her exposed ear, Shelby whispered. "All right. First, we'll breakfast on each other and then get some breakfast for our bellies. What do you say?"

Reaching up, Katie wrapped her arms around the back of Shelby's neck and pulled her into the bed alongside her. "Deal, but you're buying."

Wrapping each other in a tangle of arms and legs, they first devoured each other's mouths, reigniting the passion from the night before. Before long, Shelby spun around and dived into Katie's delicate patch between her thighs. Katie barely sucked in a satisfying breath before she reached for Shelby and kissed her on her mound.

Before long, each woman licked, sucked and kissed each other into a frenzy, until Katie felt her head crushed between Shelby's powerful thighs as her partner orgasmed. Feeling the heat and desire of her friend's entrance into ecstasy, Katie joined her. Neither cared what happened next so long as they resumed the frenzy of the night before and satisfying them back into reality.

After one last toe-curling orgasm, Shelby rolled off her lover, landing on her back. Covered in sweat, she stared at the ceiling while her panting subsided. The top sheet and blankets were missing, despite Shelby's feeble attempt to pull them over her. She found them on the floor at the foot of the bed. Too weak to reach for them, Shelby collapsed on the bed.

Gasping, she said, "Katie, you're a wild one. How you can go on and on in one long orgasm the entire time is beyond me. How can you have so much sexual energy stored inside you for one so young?"

"Shelby, you're not so bad yourself. How many did you have? I lost count."

"You were counting? I wasn't. I don't care if I have one or a hundred. They're all good. That's what I love about us. We can bring each other off so easily. It's a delight to be with you."

"Thanks. I feel the same towards you."

"Katie, I think I love you."

"Think?" Katie teased.

"All right, bitch. I love you. There, I said it. What are you going to do about it?"

"Nothing whore, except love you back. I love you too. The question is, now what?"

The question brought Shelby back to reality. Her unfocused eyes suddenly distanced her from her lover. She had a job to do, and it did not allow her to fall in love with the target. They paid her well to investigate potential candidates for the Consortium. Getting personally involved was not in the job description. She knew very well they had an unwritten rule denying her a private life with candidate prey.

"What is it?" Katie asked, feeling the sudden change in the disposition of her lover.

"Nothing, a work thing just flew into my mind. It's not important. I'm starved, let's go to breakfast."

"I'd rather have you for breakfast."

"Didn't you just have your fill?"

"Well," Katie faded off as if fondly remembering their time together. "I could go for seconds."

Laughing, Shelby patted her belly as she stood up. "Come on now. I'm hungry. I don't think I could last another round without some food in me."

"Oh, all right." Katie pouted in a sad but happy sort of way.

It was a trait that Shelby loved about the girl. No doubt about it, she was an animated lover. Too bad, she was a perfect fit for the Consortium. She hoped her last couple of reports downgrading her candidacy would work. Still, without the lead forwarded on to the organization, she might never have met the girl. If they took her, she would lament her lost love. Maybe it was time to get out of the business.

"Let me use the bathroom first if you don't mind. I'm about to burst." Katie told her as she ran ahead of Shelby to the bathroom.

"Need any help?" Shelby teased.

"You helped enough." Katie teased right back. "Just give me a sec."

Smiling at the jovial banter between them, Shelby stripped the bedding, and put them in the launderer and started the wash cycle. Grabbing a fresh set of sheets and pillowcases, she made up the bed.

Proud of her work, she walked over to the window and looked out. The sun was streaming in, making the room bright and cheery. Scanning up and down the block, she saw that lots of people filled the Portland streets, some walking with a destination in mind, and others just hanging out.

"What a life," she thought to herself, wishing that she was among them.

"Ready?" she heard from the bathroom as Katie bounced out, freshened up and looking gorgeous.

"I will be when I get in there," she said, closing the door behind her.

"Hey, I will never get used to the idea that you need the door closed just to pee. You know I've seen it all already, don't you?" Katie chastised.

"Never you mind," Shelby answered. "I like it this way. Maybe next year."

"So, you think we'll be together that long?"

"Could be love. You never know." came the answer through the door.

"Hey, thanks for making up the bed. I suppose the sheets are in the laundry?"

"Yep, now let me be so I can finish up. I'm hungry."

"Yes, Ma'am."

Katie grabbed a pair of shorts and a tank-top. Standing by the window, she looked out as she pulled her top over her perky tits and pulled on her jean shorts.

"Hey, Shelby," she yelled across the room and through the door. "We got ourselves a pervert."

"What?" Shelby howled as she jumped into the bedroom. "Where?"

"There," Katie pointed at the window across the street. He's gone now, but I know he was there."

"Really? How rude?"

"Yea, rude. Come on, let's eat."

"Can I get dressed first?" Shelby complained.

"Why? He must have seen it all. Come on, hurry up! You got me up early, and now I'm waiting for you. What's with that?"

Shelby stared out the window in the direction. Katie pointed but saw nothing. Still, it worried her. She had given her team the night off so no one should have been watching them. Now, the prey had glimpsed their surveillance. She'd have to check it out.

Putting on underwear, a bra, slacks, and a top, Shelby fluffed her hair and told Katie. "Let's go. I'm starved."

"I thought you'd never ask," Katie replied, taking Shelby by the hand out of the apartment door.

A short time later, as the two of them sat at a window table, giving their food order, Shelby scanned the street outside. There was nothing there that implied someone was watching them, that she could detect. Still, that meant nothing. If they were as skilled as she was in surveillance, they could sit at the next table over, and not know someone was watching her.

Still, Katie's observation back at the apartment warranted looking into the question. "Were they watching her or Katie?" Shelby asked herself. With the Consortium, one never knew.

Shelby knew that she was running a risk to stop the Consortium from looking at Katie as prey for capture. She didn't know what ultimately happened to those that the Consortium seized. Frankly, she didn't want to know. What she knew was that it likely wasn't safe for her lover. Further, she didn't want to become prey herself. Her training taught her that if they wanted to, she would be perfect prey for their agendas. She wanted nothing to do with that.

"Shelby?"

"Huh?" Shelby said, startled by the interruption of her thoughts. "Are you all right?"

"Yes, of course. Is it my turn to order?"

"Yes, that's what I've been trying to tell you. What do you want? The waiter is waiting."

"Oh, sorry."

"That's all right, Ma'am. Anytime you're ready." The waiter remarked.

After giving the man her order, Shelby turned to look out at the street beyond the window.

"Hey, is everything all right? I mean, we had such a good time last night and then again, this morning. I'm still tingling with excitement. You seem off. What is it?"

"I don't know Katie. Maybe it was that peeping tom you caught."

"Him? Phew, he's not worth the time of day. If he wants to watch two women go at it, cock in hand and jerking off, I don't care. He means nothing to me."

"Oh, Katie. You are such an innocent. However, you may be right. I'm sorry. Will you forgive me?"

Taking Shelby's hand, Katie said, "there's nothing to forgive. Let's enjoy the day. Just remember, I have to be at work in a few hours."

"Already?"

"Yes, dear. That's what happens when you sleep in."

"Uh, I don't remember sleeping much, do you?"

"Of course not, silly, unless you slept through it as I devoured your delicious petals and licked you clean."

"Sleep through that? You've got to be kidding. Of course, I didn't sleep through that. I enjoyed myself."

"Me too! I can't wait to do it again."

"You're insatiable. How about another round after breakfast?"

"Thanks, and sure, why not? We make a good pair, don't you think?"

"Yes, I do Katie. We've got a good thing here, and I would like to keep it going."

"As do I," she started. "Here comes the food," observing the waiter returning carrying two plates of food.

"Great! I'm starved."

"You keep saying that. Did I wear you out that much?"

"Yes, I think you did." The two of them laughing at the thought of going back again for another round.

Just then, Shelby glimpsed someone loitering just down the street. The woman looked like she belonged there, but to Shelby's trained eye, there was something off about her. Her posture spoke volumes. The orientation of her body and position on the street showed that she could see everything about the restaurant, including the occupants. She was certain. Whether the target was Katie or herself, they were under observation.

A chill ran down her back.

Chapter Ten

"Come in, Avril. Have a seat."

"Thank you, Sir," apathetically taking a seat.

Her blasé attitude spoke volumes even though she remained silent. As usual, he sat at the head of the table, while she sat to his left. She placed her hands together and laid them on her lap.

As usual, she wore heels and nothing else. In preparing for dinner, she spent the bulk of the time washing and conditioning her hair. After her ordeal, it had been a knotted, stinking mess, not to mention the rest of her body. Plus, she hurt everywhere right down to the roots of her hair. The constant near-fatal electrocutions wore her down, and numbness and pain persisted long after they stopped.

Since she had little to wear, she paid attention to dolling up her long hair. It was one of the few luxuries she could indulge in and feel somewhat normal. Today, she had it up, held in place with a set of hair combs encrusted with dozens of sparkling crystals — a pair of complementing earrings dangled from her lobes.

The only other accommodation, she found a fresh new pair of heels in her room. She gladly exchanged them for the foul-smelling, damp heels she wore during her ordeal. They went down the shoot to the laundry facilities the moment she stepped into her ensuite. "Good riddance," she muttered to herself as they disappeared into the darkness.

"Avril?"

"Huh, oh, sorry," she replied automatically, even though it was against the rules. Right now, she didn't care.

"Avril, I asked, would you like a cocktail."

"No, thank you, Sir. I'll just have water with lemon, please."

Snapping his fingers, their attendant went to the beverage bar and poured the water and a good pour of Macallan, one of her master's favorite single malt scotches, over ice. Depositing them in front of Sir first and then Avril, the bought and paid for servant resumed her place in the room's corner. Like Avril, she was also wearing heels plus the skimpiest of aprons around her waist. It did nothing to cover her nakedness. Just above the apron, she sported a serving tray, though she was not supporting it with her hands. Instead, a belt around her waist held it in place while a beaded chain threaded through her nipple rings and around her neck held up the front. All combined, it supported the tray and kept it from tipping over. As Avril looked on, she half-heartedly recognized that if there were anything on the tray, her nipples would stretch well beyond their average length.

Seeing the nipple rings with the chain through them only reminded Avril of her nipple rings. After her electrifying ordeal, she couldn't feel her nipples anymore. They didn't hurt. They didn't ache. Instead, there was nothing. Even when she touched them, she felt nothing.

She was beyond caring.

"Avril?" she finally heard him speaking to her.

"Uh, oh, yes, Sir."

"Avril, that's the second time I had to get your attention. What's bothering you?"

She shook her head.

"Are you bothered by your punishment?" Sir asked. "That was a week ago. Are you still angry with me?"

She just looked down at her lap, not responding at all. She was numb all over and beyond caring about much. In fact, at this moment, she hated being in his presence.

"Avril, I'm speaking to you. I require you to answer."

She nodded in acknowledgment but again said nothing.

"With that nod, are you bothered by the punishment or only acknowledging my order to answer me?"

"I... don't know."

"Don't know what?"

"I..." she trailed off, mumbling under her breath.

"Avril, you're not making any sense. Speak up," he commanded in a stern voice.

She looked up at him—her blasé apathy plain in her posture. Out of the corner of her eye, she noticed the attendant looking worried, compassion in her eyes. Avril knew she wouldn't move for the world. To do so, would incur his wrath with a severe punishment to follow. The girl remained still, too afraid to move, too scared for Avril.

"I don't know."

"Again, don't know what?"

Avril looked at Sir, not knowing what he wanted.

"Aren't you missing something in your reply?"

Tilting her head ever so slightly, she eventually replied, "I don't know, Sir," in a surly tone.

"Careful Avril. I won't have that tone at this table."

She remained silent and immobile.

"Avril," he spoke sharply at her.

"Yes, Sir," she answered absentmindedly, her eyes downcast.

"Avril, are you bothered by your punishment?" he asked once again.

"I suppose so."

"I suppose so, Sir," he reminded her.

Acquiescing, "I suppose so, Sir," she repeated.

"All right, we'll take this up after you've eaten."

Not caring, she nodded, noting that he didn't seem to care an iota about the ordeal she recently suffered. He seemed more bothered by her attitude than not using his title.

She was about to ask about that when he turned to the attendant and said. "You may serve."

"Yes, Sir," the attendant replied. As the girl prepared the dishes, he added. "Make sure she gets extra protein."

"Yes, Sir," the girl answered.

A moment later, a plate appeared in front of Avril. Barely looking down, she half-heartedly noted the plate piled with scrambled eggs, several slices of bacon, and a small portion of home-fried potatoes.

"Breakfast Sir, in the evening?"

"Yes, I know of your fondness of breakfast. I thought you would like it."

"Thank you," she nodded.

"Sir." he reminded her.

"Thank you, Sir."

"Give her juice," he instructed the servant.

In no time, a tall glass of orange juice and freshwater replaced the empty water glass. "Thank you," Avril whispered warmly to the attendant. She knew he would notice the difference in her warm tone with the server and the cold shoulder she continued to give him, but she didn't care. It surprised her at how cordial she was after all that she had been through of late.

"Please eat," he asked. "You need the food to hasten your recovery."

"So you could torment me further?" Avril replied surly.

"If need be, and I so wish it." Sir said calmly.

"Of course, you will," Avril confirmed testily, returning to her withdrawn, disturbed attitude.

Picking up her fork, she looked at the food, done to perfection, just as she liked it. Indifferent, she wasn't interested in eating. Her mind was still blank. It was an inability to process thoughts, something she had never before experienced in her life. She couldn't think, and it bothered her.

She had been thinking about it since he released her from her shackles and told her to clean herself up. Her prolonged and erratic thought processes felt like she lived in a dark, dense fog. For the first time in her life, she didn't trust herself or her body. Perhaps for the first time since her captivity, she felt a fit of anger to a degree she never felt before. She was furious, a seething outrage that left her feeling hollow and alone. A part of her wondered why she hadn't until now.

Twiddling her fork on her plate, she had yet to lift any of the food to her mouth. In a moment of sporadic clarity, Avril quelled the rising tide of emotions of raw, angry, distraught feelings. They threatened to spill over, turning her into a raving, savage beast.

Lifting a small portion of her eggs on her fork, Avril put it in her mouth and swallowed.

"Good, eat up."

"Yes, Sir."

Answering him as he expected, she played with her food more, dancing it around the plate but not eating it. With her free hand, she absently brushed past one of her nipples. Her hand detected the contact, but her nipple did not. Contempt overwhelmed her.

"Sir, why?" she asked though not expecting an answer.

"Why what? Why do I want you to eat?"

"Now you're dense. No, why you nearly electrocute me to death?"

"Avril, you know the answer. You did not follow the rules, specifically rule number one-forty-four and one-forty-nine."

"And for that, you nearly killed me in the most painful way possible?" she retorted.

"Most painful way? No, I could have done much worse, keeping you alive for weeks or months, watching you suffer in even more painful ways."

"I'm sure," the venomous tone coming through loud and clear.

"Avril, you're on thin ice. I suggest you tone down your rhetoric."

"If I don't, you'll hurt me more, punishing me even further." She spit back at her owner and master.

In the corner of her eye, she saw the attendant cringe, trying to make herself small and disappear into the wall. Noticing Avril's minor distraction, he motioned to the shaking girl.

"Go."

"Yes Sir," she said, her heels clicking rapidly on the floor as she left quickly towards the kitchen and freedom.

Once gone, Sir turned towards Avril. "You had best control yourself, young lady. I've had just about enough of your crap. You brought it upon yourself. I did not force you to skip sessions. You did that all on your own. I don't have to justify myself to you. You have no standing or rights in this matter. I own you and your body. You are mine to do with as I please. Sometimes, you know the rules better than I do. You did not kneel despite knowing what I expected. I see it as a conscious act of defiance, and I punished you, fairly I might add."

"Fairly?" Avril rebuked, raising her voice at the same time. "Fairly? I doubt it. You subjected me to uncalled for and excessive punishment. The discipline was cruel and unusual. Only an insane person would ever extract such suffering and anguish on a living human person."

"In your opinion," Sir threw right back at Avril. "Uncalled for and excessive, absolutely not, you earned every second of that punishment. And cruel and unusual? Who said I wasn't cruel? You know perfectly well, I am. Therefore, it should not be unusual. You know that I can and will be cruel with you as I see fit."

"Well, you should just then go about it and kill me already."

"I could and maybe I should. However, I made a promise I wouldn't."

"Oh, like that means anything. You also promised not to punish me." Avril retorted, the argument building.

"To be clear, I did not promise that. I only said that I would not punish you without cause or reason. I also said that in my need, I would hurt you, sometimes severely. I will do my best not to cause you permanent harm."

"Oh? Then what about my body, or rather, my nipples? I can't feel a fucking thing with them. They can't sense anything, not the touch of a washcloth, a crushing pinch, or anything else. It makes me sad to see how much they have suffered. I thought the pain of piercing, followed by welding the rings together was bad enough. Now they feel nothing."

"You earned the punishment, and now you will have to deal with the consequences. You had better hope that feeling returns to them, as I intend to play with them, hurt them too, many times in the coming years."

Raising her voice, Avril spoke out. "God, you're incredible. Can you hear yourself? You're actually saying you intend to hurt me more! Kill me already! I give you my permission. In fact, I may just do it myself. I realize the women you've bought, tortured, and killed already are better off than I am. I stuck here, suffering your cruelty again and again, for years. At least they didn't survive all that long, and now they are at peace. Me, I will never be at peace."

"Maybe they are Avril. Why you ever proposed the agreement and then negotiated a modification to join the Consortium is beyond me. I still have trouble convincing the membership when I don't understand it myself."

"That makes two of us."

"Avril, you should know that at the executive committee level, they voted a motion on to kill you outright rather than grant your application to proceed to the general membership for acceptance. You prevailed but just barely. You beat the motion by one vote."

"Or lost the motion by one vote, depending upon how you look at it. I wish I lost. I would be better off and at peace."

"I doubt it."

"Doubt it? Why the fuck do you care whether I would be at peace?"

"Avril, within your religion, you've committed a mortal sin, many in fact. Without absolution, God will condemn you for eternity to suffer for your sins."

"God will forgive me, seeing the circumstances."

"Do you honestly believe that? I don't know. Since I don't believe in the fires of hell and all, I am at peace with my preferences. Can you say the same for yourself?"

"Fuck you, you know I can't. Fuck you, fuck you, fuck you." Avril screamed at him as she started to get out of her chair.

"SIT DOWN," he commanded as loudly and forcefully as he could muster.

The sudden strength in his tone stopped her in her tracks, and she settled back down in her chair. Avril was seething, her face flushed with anger, her eyes burning holes in her plate. If she had laser emitting eyes like Superman, she would have drilled a hole clear through her plate, the table and into the floor.

"Damn you to hell," she muttered.

"If I believed in hell, you're probably right. Now, it's time to resume using my title."

"You've got to be kidding! I think, after what you have done to me, I have earned the right to know your real name. What is your name anyway? I demand you tell me." Her voice was growing angry again.

"I am Sir to you. That is my name and my title. You will use it in every response directed to me."

"Ha! Why should I? If I don't, I suppose you'll punish me again, maybe even more severely than I just suffered. I don't think so."

"Don't test me, girl. There are far more and better ways to punish you, so you'll regret your behavior. Besides, in this tirade of yours, you've broken so many rules, I've lost count."

"Oh, woe is me. Why should I care? Eventually, you'll do it to me, anyway. Why should I behave? And another thing, in the first years of my captivity, you made me the center of entertainment among your compatriots, teaching me to enjoy sex and all. I grew to enjoy servicing your friends, getting fucked by several of them, all at the same time, being insatiable to feel their attention as they ravished my body. It's been months, if not a year since you included me in that play. I miss it. When are you going to lie me down on a bench and let them have their way with me?"

"Is that what is bothering you? Are you such a narcissist that you need the attention of the others servicing you rather than just me? Is that it?"

"I'm not a narcissist. You taught me to love being fucked simultaneously by multiple partners, male and female alike. Now you've withdrawn that simple pleasure and replaced it with silly pain and torment. Why shouldn't that be upsetting?"

"I can promise you this young lady. In this mood, I wouldn't let you near them. They would smell the anger on you. Instead of fucking you, they would torture and kill you."

"Hmmm, that's a thought." Avril challenged.

"Maybe you're on to something there. I sensed your growing anger for some time now, and this may have been one reason I held you back from enjoying the pleasures of poly-sexual encounters. I have to think about it."

"You do that." Avril snapped back. "And you're right. I am angry. You stole my life and took me off the streets to do with as you pleased. Undoubtedly, when you tire of me, you will toss me aside like trash. Even if you don't kill me, you could sell me to another one of your buddies, and they'll kill me. You can even wash your hands clean, knowing that you lived up to your promise."

"You're right. I may do that. In the meantime, EAT." He commanded.

"Fuck you," she said sullenly, her anger dissipating by the second. After a time, tears fell from her eyes, which ran down her cheeks, landing on her lap.

Sir let her mellow for some time, remaining quiet. As she processed her feelings, he took their plates, refilling hers with fresh food and set it down before her. After a time, her eyes bloodshot and damp, she looked up at him.

"You know Avril? I've been waiting for you to blow up at me. What in Gaia's name took you so long? You've bottled this anger up for years now. You shouldn't do that, keep it bottled up like that. Sure, I've seen you determined, depressed, upset, and sullen. I've never really seen the anger like you displayed today. I hope that by letting it out makes you feel better."

All Avril could do was nod, exhausted by the argument.

"Don't worry. I won't hold this tirade against you. Now we can again move forward with your training."

"Fuck you, Sir," she said with half a smile.

Chapter Eleven

Staring at a bill summary on his desk, Senator Ladensen read the same page of the abstract a dozen times without understanding the words written thereon. Rubbing his eyes, trying to concentrate, he started again. Halfway down the page, he gave up and closed the document. His mind was elsewhere.

He turned his chair to face the window though he didn't look out it. Staring blankly ahead, he didn't want to see the office and the responsibilities that went with it. He was of two minds, and both mattered and yet, only one was important.

He couldn't stop thinking about his missing eldest daughter, Rachel. She had been missing for months now, and no one seemed to have any answers for him. As a ranking member of the Senate Committee on the Judiciary, he had pulled out all the stops. Rachel was missing, and no one could tell him why or where she was.

The strange thing about her disappearance was it didn't seem to involve foul play. It was as if she stepped out one door and through another into an alternate reality of sorts. Literally, to the Senator, she stepped off the face of the Earth without warning, leaving no message, or indication of where she was going.

Was she running from something? Was she hiding from the family? Did he or his job as a U.S. Senator put her into jeopardy? Is she in hiding and that's why she ran off? Questions like these plagued his thoughts since the moment he found out she was missing.

"Rachel, where are you?" he softly muttered as he processed a problem for which he had no solution.

Solving problems and getting answers was what he was good at doing. Throughout his life, he saw problems as challenges in search of a solution. Most times, he found the solution, or at least, a way around the problem. His problem-solving talent gave him an edge in politics, making him a powerful adversary that few went against him. When he got involved, his opponents almost always lost. He liked it that way. It also made him someone to befriend and keep close. Either way, there were few in his life he could depend upon and trust.

For the first time in his life, he felt powerless and incapable of solving the question of his missing daughter, his baby girl, his firstborn. His emotions were in the investigation's way, and he knew it.

He resolved to let the experts investigate her disappearance objectively. The talent he tapped to find her were the best of the best. He relied on those in charge of the investigation and in-turn, the operatives under their control. Well, at least he depended on them only so far. He was a politician. Which meant he kissed babies as he took their bottle. He trusted no one, knowing full well that every politician had their own hidden agenda.

Right now, though, none of that mattered. The Senator and father wanted his little girl back. He would go to the ends of the earth to bring her home, or find out what happened to her.

Spinning around, he tapped a button on his phone, signaling his assistant, Ben.

"Yes, Sir?" came the sound of his voice through the speaker.

"Have the lead investigator on my daughter's case see me today. If they are out of town, have them call me directly on my private line. I don't care how late."

"Yes, Sir. Right away."

A few minutes later, Ben stepped into his office. Talking to the back of his boss staring out of the window, his hands in his pockets, he began.

"Senator, the lead investigator will be here within the hour."

"Thank you, Ben. I appreciate it. I am also grateful for the extra handling of the senatorial work. I've not been up to my game, and I know it. Thank you."

"No problem, Sir. I understand."

"Well, thank you anyway."

***

Just under an hour later, the senator heard a knock on his office door. At the moment and stretched out on his sofa, he tried calming himself. Slowly standing up, he had just gotten to his feet when he heard a knock on the door.

"Come," he responded.

The door opened, and Ben entered, the lead investigator in tow.

"You can stay, Ben. Close the door," the Senator led off. Turning his attention to the investigator, he commanded. "What's going on with my daughter?"

"Yes, Sir. We've made progress in tracking her movements, and we are fairly confident that she made it back to Chicago."

"Why do you say that?" the senator queried.

"Well, we established a timeline of her trip, which we feel is accurate. She arrived on the Sunday afternoon before the start of the conference. She checked into her hotel. The check-in surveillance and signatures prove it. A few hours later, she came out and had dinner in the hotel restaurant. We presume she napped between check-in and dinner. It was a long trip for her and...."

"Yes, get on with it." the senator remarked, his annoying urgency evident in his tone.

"We've interviewed the wait staff at the restaurant and checked her hotel bill against the meal she ordered. The restaurant staff remembered her and confirmed her identity using the photos we showed them. After dinner, she spent about forty-five minutes in the hotel gym and then returned to her room. There was no activity in or around her room for the rest of the night."

"Confirmed via hotel security video I presume."

"Yes, Sir."

"Go on."

"The following morning, she registered at the conference and attended it every day that week. We interviewed the presenters and several of the attendees. They were of little help. Several people admitted to remembering her, and one, in particular, tried several times to pick her up."

"Horny bastard, I presume."

"That was our assessment, Sir. She rejected his advances several times, but he kept at it all week long. We interviewed some attendees who remarked about his interest and felt she handled him gracefully. However, by the end of the week, she got visibly annoyed with him and let him know in so many words."

"That's my girl."

Smiling, the investigator continued. "On Tuesday evening, after the conference adjourned for the day, she went to a bar and allowed a gentleman to buy her drinks and dinner. According to the bar staff, she left with him, and hotel security recorded them entering her room together. He left two hours later. She slept in, getting up for breakfast in the morning."

"I presume you tracked down this guy."

"We're working on that. He paid cash for the dinner and drinks, so there is no paper trail to follow. We'll keep on it."

"And the rest of the week?"

"As best as we can tell, it was much of the same thing. Up early in the morning, a trip to the hotel gym, breakfast and attending the conference. During lunch, your daughter hung out with a few female attendees, presumably to avoid the wolf. After the day's activities were over, she ate dinner in the hotel restaurant and back to her room. Tuesday night was the only departure from the routine."

"What about after the conference was over?"

"Yes, Sir. The last day, the night before her flight home. We tracked her returning to the hotel and eating in the hotel restaurant. She appeared exhausted, rubbing her eyes and walking lethargically. After dinner, she entered the hotel elevator and got on. She did not get off on her floor. Instead, she returned to the lobby, stepping into the hotel lounge for a drink. She finished her drink and went back to her room."

"Wait," the Senator interrupted. "You're saying she just had dinner after a tiring day. Then afterward, she headed to her room, only to change her mind and go to the bar for a drink?"

"Yes, Sir."

"That seems unlikely. She just had dinner, alone I might add. If she wanted a drink, she would have had it then. Why leave and go back? If she were as tired as you say, she wouldn't sit at a bar for a drink, especially if she wasn't interested in picking up a guy."

"I don't know, Sir."

"What did she have at dinner? Did you review the receipt?"

"Sir, I don't have that information at hand. I'm sure the team checked and would have reported anything out of the norm. I must get back to you."

"You do that. I know my daughter. She wouldn't do that. Look into that."

"Yes, Sir."

"Please continue."

"At four in the morning, hotel security footage has her leaving her room and grabbing a shuttle to the airport. Her scheduled flight departed at six forty-five a.m. Airport security cameras show her checking her bag at the counter, scanned through TSA security and getting onto the plane."

"I presumed you verified her identity with the TSA?"

Revealing a subtle annoyance over the question, the investigator answered in the affirmative. The irritation was so minimal that only a person trained and used to noting body language, such as the investigator would even notice. The Senator perceived it, yet said nothing.

The investigator went on. "The flight she was on had one layover in Houston before continuing onto Chicago. Airport security in Houston shows a woman answering her description, walking to the gate where she sat until boarding. She boarded and never left the plane until it arrived in Chicago. Flight attendants on both flights remember her. They all reported that she kept to herself, resting for much of the flights, declining the offered in-flight snacks. She took a cup of coffee on the first leg and water for the rest."

"Did she use the restrooms?"

"Yes she did, both in Houston and again in Chicago. We don't know about on the plane. There was nothing peculiar about either of the visits. There are no cameras in the restrooms, but security footage shows a woman answering her description entering and leaving in both cities. The woman was dressed the same as Rachel when she left the hotel that morning. There was no indication of foul play."

"That doesn't mean there wasn't."

"No Sir, I mean yes, you are correct. However, it is our estimation in watching the footage before and afterward that no other woman answering to her description entered or exited the restrooms within an hour plus or minus when your daughter used them."

"Go on."

"After arrival in Chicago, security footage tracks her collecting her checked bag and taking a taxi home. The fair for the trip was fifty dollars. We identified the cab company and the driver. The driver remembers her as she gave him a nice tip. He remembers her going to the building but did not stay long enough to watch her go in. We think he was lying at that point, as GPS shows him outside her building for several minutes but not long enough to execute a snatch and grab. We think he admired her walking into her building, checking her out. Another minute to check in with dispatch, and he was off to pick up another fare. In our opinion, the cab ride was without incidence."

"So, Rachel attended the conference, picked up a guy one night for dinner and sex, spent the rest of the week by herself, having a few drinks and returned to Chicago when it was all over."

"Yes, Sir. That's about it. We searched her place. We found no evidence of foul play or anything to show that anyone abducted her."

"She just dumped her suitcase in her apartment, emptied a few things, laid down on the bed and disappeared."

"I can't explain it further but yes Sir. That's about the size of it. We are still investigating, but the trail is getting tenuous. If it weren't for Heather's inability to reach her throughout the next day, we'd have thought she stayed in all day. There's no trace of her after the cab ride from the airport."

"Yet, it appears she got home, went to bed and sometime shortly after that, left the apartment never to return."

"Yes Sir, that's about the size of it."

"Did she go out for a jog? She does that sometimes."

"Heather told us about that. We looked into it, but we can't find any evidence that she did. City cameras did not pick her up at any of her favorite routes. There are also no cameras in or around her apartment building. We even checked the footage of two ATM's within two blocks of her but noted nothing of interest."

"My little girl disappeared, and no one seems to know anything?"

"It would appear so Sir. We are still following up on a few leads…" he started to add.

"But don't get my hopes up, is that what you're saying?" the Senator interjected.

"No Sir, that's not what I mean. We are treating this seriously, and we'll keep looking."

"You do that. Find my little girl."

"We will. We are pulling out all the stops on this one."

"You had better. I don't want to find out that Rachel's disappearance is in any way related to me or my position. No matter who they are, they will not compromise me."

"As to that, Sir, has anyone contacted you?"

"No, that's the thing. When I first found out Rachel was missing, I prepared myself to get a ransom call or at the least, something along the lines of blackmail. Instead, nothing. It's like the only one who cares is her family."

"Let me reassure you, Senator. We care, and we'll keep on looking."

"Is there anything else?"

"We've looked into the money trail, her credit cards and banking records, her cell phone usage, to name a few. She's not used any of them since her return to Chicago. GPS on her phone shows it briefly connecting near her apartment on the day of her return, but nothing since. We presume her battery died and needed charging. She has not used it since then, and we did not recover it. We don't know where it is. We're still looking."

"That's not like her, letting her phone battery die."

"Sir, Heather said the same thing to us. We know she used it in Houston. She searched for items and articles related to her conference and job."

"You pulled the carrier records then?"

"Yes, Senator, including the Wifi logs at the airports. Unfortunately, the Wifi logs reveal little. She used her carried data connection at all times. Those logs were more useful, which is how we could figure out what the phone was doing until it shut off."

"Yes, we taught her not to trust local Wifi, and use the data plan at all times. So that is not unusual."

"A wise choice Senator. Local Wifi is too easy to spoof. We recommend that to all of our staff and those that we protect and serve."

"Yet, in this case, it didn't seem to help, did it?"

"No, Sir. What I can assure you is that we take Rachel's disappearance seriously. There is still a lot more we are doing. It's just that there is nothing more we can report right now."

"So, there is something else you are working on that you don't wish to tell me? Do I have that right?"

"Yes, and no. We are still working on her disappearance, and no, there is nothing we don't wish to tell you. I've told you everything we have so far."

"What's next, then?"

"We are looking at two things. The hours after your daughter returned to Chicago…"

"If she returned at all."

"Ah, yes, Sir. That's the other front. We are digging deeper into her trip, looking to see if a double took her place at the conference. Until she registered, no one there would know what she looked like. If a doppelganger took her place, no one would have been the wiser."

"Seems excessive to me and a lot of planning to pull that off."

"We agree. Still, it's an avenue we are pursuing."

"Keep me informed."

"We will Senator."

With a brief wave of his hand, Ben showed the investigator out.

A minute later, Ben returned to his boss's office.

"Is there anything I can get for you?"

"My daughter."

Stumbling, the Senator's aide didn't know what to say.

"Keep on it. I will not let this go."

"Neither would I, Sir. I get it."

"Can you get Heather on the phone for me?"

"Certainly, right away," Ben promised and then left the Senator to suffer in private.

A minute later, the Senator's phone buzzed. After pleasantries, Senator Ladensen filled in his remaining daughter with the progress of the investigation.

"Daddy, I don't get it. If what you're saying is true, then Rachel made it back home. I don't believe it. It just doesn't pass the smell test."

"Heather, I think you're right. Something tells me that Rach did not make it back to Chicago. They are pursuing that angle, but I don't think they'll find anything. It's almost as if there is a conspiracy in play to stop me from finding out what happened to your sister."

"Daddy, I think you may be right. I think something is going on that we are missing. What should we do?"

"Heather, we will investigate for ourselves. Trust no one. Do it all without outside involvement. I don't want to say much more on the phone. I'll be home in a couple of days, and we can work out a plan of action."

"Come quickly, Daddy. I don't like sitting around on my hands. I miss her, and I want Rachel back."

"You and me both, kid. Take care of your mother, and I'll see you soon."

"She's a wreck, in case you didn't know. She tries to hide it, but she's suffering."

"I know kitten. I know. I'll see you soon."

"Thanks, Daddy, thanks for believing in me."

"Always kiddo, always. Give my love to your mother."

"I will. Bye."

"Bye."

Sitting back in his chair, the Senator contemplated his next move. He wasn't sure what he would do next but damn it all; he would take the bull by the horns and sort this out.

Never in his political life had he not trusted his staff and the agencies of the Federal Government to do their jobs. Now he had his doubts. He knew he had to figure it out and make sure that Heather and his wife knew he had a plan, even if he didn't. He was the captain of this ship, and under no circumstances could he elude that he did not know what to do. He was trusting no one. With all the years they had worked together, trusting his aide Ben was out of the question. Trust no one but blood. Everyone else was suspect.

"What? Am I behind the iron curtain?" he asked himself without saying a word. Not believing that his office or phone wasn't bugged, he made his first decision. "Time for burner phones and leave them on vibrate."

After reflection, he would purchase two burner phones, from different stores, only not in Washington. In Chicago, he knew where he could go and not have anyone ask questions.

Reaching over to his phone, he buzzed his aide. "Ben, book me on a flight to Chicago the day after tomorrow."

"Yes, Sir. Right away. Shall I cancel your appointments?"

"Please and for several days after that. I'm going home to be with my family. If anyone asks, I'm going home for personal reasons."

"Yes, Sir."

Chapter Twelve

Sitting at the table, having breakfast alone, Sir contemplated what to do with Avril. She was understandably angry and disturbed by the surroundings of her punishment. He couldn't grasp what was her issue. In the first six months after coming here, she struggled to follow his rules, but she did well. Over the next two years, she excelled in following them. She pleased him with her attitude. The last several months were another story. It was almost as if she didn't care to obey them. Was she becoming too comfortable in her position within the household?

In his mind, not kneeling was a severe breach of protocol and required a punitive adjustment. Besides, it satisfied him to torment her so much. He had gotten out of the habit of taking his time with her in the dungeon, and it was high time he got back to it.

"Besides, didn't she agree that she would submit to his painful torment?" Sir remarked to himself.

His plate not quite empty, he pushed back from the table and signaled his attendant to take his plate away. The petite brunette wearing only his shock collar and heels moved in from the kitchen and swiftly removed the plate.

"Would you care to have your coffee warmed up?" the cute little thing asked.

"Yes, thank you." Sir said absentmindedly, lost in thought.

Returning with the coffeepot, she leaned in and poured the coffee into a fresh cup she brought along. Smiling, he wantonly gazed at her pendulating breasts swinging about as the hot coffee splashed into the cup.

"After I finish breakfast," he told her, "go back to your room and get cleaned up. I'll come for you shortly."

"Yes, Sir. I'll be ready." Her hesitant reply evident of the apprehension she felt in the coming hours ahead.

Dismissing the girl, not caring about her apprehension, he went back to his thoughts of what to do with his Avril. He didn't understand her or why he felt that he should care at all. He never did before and believed he would never honestly care for any of his prey, except for what they offered him.

He couldn't fathom what was troubling Avril. He thought more about her than what she could do for him. He was at a loss. Why had she behaved with such disrespect and then get angry with him for punishing her? It was her transgression.

Perplexed, he got up and walked to his office to catch up before heading down to the cells and collect his plaything for the morning. Maybe diving into his Consortium work would make him forget his dilemma and get back to normal.

Opening his mail, he began to read and delete multiple messages. Most were simple notifications and did not require his response. The work on the modifications to the 'Bowl' for the up-and-coming auction were proceeding well. He smiled in anticipation of the next event the arena would hold.

He was planning an archery tournament, whereby the membership would buy into competing for bragging rights on their kills. It will be a fun event and a fantastic opportunity to replenish the coffers. Membership dues aside, the proceeds from the auction and the entertainment that followed was very lucrative. Keeping the membership entertained and coming back time and time again was a challenge. As he mixed things up, they responded, and attendance was up. Even if many didn't purchase their offerings, they enjoyed themselves and spent money during the entertainment phase of the proceedings. He was quite pleased with the numbers.

He was about to scan the auction inventory when a communication bubble request appeared on his screen. It was from his aide and executive assistant. He knew better than to bother him when he was at home. Contacting him at home meant it was important.

Opening the bubble, he opened the secure private video conference window. Greeting his aide, he said. "This must be important. What is it?"

"Sorry to bother you at home, Mr. Chairman. A report just came in that warrants your attention."

"Go on."

"I just received a report from the team on Senator Ladensen's investigation on the disappearance of his daughter. If you recall, she is the girl we harvested the heart to prolong the life of one of our members."

"Yes, I recall the details of that. What has changed?"

"Yes, Sir. Well, shortly after her disappearance, the girl's sister began searching for the woman. When she got nowhere, she reached out to her father, Senator Ladensen, for help. By that time, we had a team following the sister and then dispatched a second team to keep tabs on the father. Senator Ladensen is a ranking member of the Senate Judiciary Committee and has power."

"Which we've been able to redirect attention away from us, I presume."

"Successfully, Sir, yes. Our operative reports that the Senator was just filled in on the status of that investigation but did not appear satisfied with the report. Our monitoring devices in his offices and surrounding private spaces didn't reveal much. Then he suddenly canceled future appointments and booked a flight back home. We are still following him. It was through that surveillance we observed some particularly disturbing behaviors."

"What kind? We have people assigned to the case to misdirect the course of the investigation as it occurs. They are reporting back the 'progress' of the investigation as they follow the trail we leave for them. So what's the problem?"

"Yes, Sir, that's all quite true. At issue that upon arriving back in his hometown of Chicago, he didn't go straight home. Instead, he stopped off at two different outlets and bought four burner-phones, all without the knowledge of his federal handlers or security. We do not know the numbers of the burners, nor can we listen in on his calls. We suspect he is not trusting his investigation teams and is striking out on his own."

"So what? Don't we have him under surveillance? We can get the numbers of the burners, isn't that correct? Who did he give the burners too, anyway?"

"Yes, Sir. We're working on that from multiple angles. The team reports that they believe he gave one to his daughter and maybe one to his wife, though they think the latter is improbable. The wife is not thinking about the security of the situation, whereas he trusts the daughter. They believe the two of them are starting a private investigation."

"What makes you think so?"

"They just both booked a flight to the city where we snatched the missing daughter."

"That is significant."

"Yes, Sir. Also, the Senator withdrew a significant amount of cash from his accounts, allowing him to do things without leaving a trail."

"Yet, he booked airline flights."

"Yes, Sir. That may be a blind or something else. Airline flights require traceable identification and payment. We're looking into it."

"What do you think?"

"Sir, I believe this is something to concern ourselves over. It was risky taking the daughter, and if we had more time during discovery, we would have passed on her. As it is, the relationship of her family only came to light after her capture. We've been playing catch up ever since."

"Well, keep on the Senator. Find out what he is doing and what he finds out. Do not alert him to our presence. Everything we do, we must do covertly. Tell me, do we still have the body of the daughter?"

"No, Sir. If you recall, with the harvesting of her organs, there was too much evidence left in the corpse that might lead them back to us. We disposed of it in the usual manner. There is no way they can find the body or link it to us."

"So, we utterly destroyed it, and there's no trace left?"

"Yes, Sir, that's what I'm saying."

"Well, that's something anyway. Without a body, they will be hard-pressed to track down what happened to the girl."

"Sir, there is something else."

"Yes?"

"The lead hunter on the team that snatched the Senator's daughter is also the same agent we are investigating in Portland, Oregon."

"The one whose reports on the prey investigation has suddenly changed in tone and recommendation?"

"Yes, Sir. That's the one."

"Hmmm...."

"Sir, our agent may know we are investigating her."

"That makes sense. The agent is one of ours and highly trained to be on the lookout for such things."

"Sir, it is our contention, that the agent may have fallen in love with her target and is actively looking at her options to safeguard her."

"Fallen for the prey? Not that hasn't happened before, but the connection between the two issues is too important to ignore."

"I agree."

"Terminate the agent immediately. Make it look like an accident if you can, but the priority is that she cannot survive to talk in any capacity."

His aide was about to respond when the Chairman interrupted. "Better yet, if possible, pick her up and send her to the auction house as prey. I have something special in mind for this one. We need to send a message to our agents that if you fuck with us, this is the price you pay. However, if you can't snatch her, just end her, better dead than talking."

"I expected that would be your decision. I'll send out the contract confirmation today."

"What about the prey? Is she aware of what our agent was doing?"

"As best as we can tell, she is not aware of the agent's activities or motivations."

"Is the prey still a viable candidate for collection?"

"Sir, the other team we assigned believes so but hasn't had the time to do an independent investigation. Based upon their initial report and of the earlier reports of the first team, she would be a viable candidate. From the reports I've seen, I would have included her in my summary to you for final disposition."

"Send me the report on her right away. I'll decide today whether to seize the target. Our operator has outlived its usefulness. We can not let the agent leak any information to the Senator."

"I'll see to it right away."

"Is there anything else?"

"No, Sir."

"Then I won't hold you up," the Chairman said, disconnecting the line.

Leaning back, he closed his eyes, trying to predict the ramifications of these latest events. Not that the situation worried him. He had dealt with similar circumstances before, successfully squashing anything that might lead back to the Consortium and him. So far, his decisions and the actions taken led to a favorable outcome.

What worried him was Avril. What was he going to do with her? Focusing his attention, he felt both fronts would resolve themselves in time. The question of the Senator would come naturally to a satisfactory conclusion. It was Avril that bothered him. The path to deal with her to his satisfaction was cloudy.

For the first time in his life, he did not know what he would do with this kind of problem.

Unable to focus on work or the Consortium, he got up, closing the door to his home office behind him. Walking down to the lower levels, he looked up the cell location of the breakfast servant. Excitement growing in his pants, he stepped up to her door and walked in.

Smiling, seeing her kneeling in the center of the cell awaiting him, he offered only one word. "Nice!"

He walked up to her. Standing in front, he slapped her hard across the cheek. Reeling backward under the blow, she had barely enough time before he grabbed her and threw her on the bed in her cell.

Moments later, he was inside her, ravishing her. That she was weeping didn't phase him in the least. She was his property, and he could do with her whatever he wished. He'd fuck her long and hard before taking her to the dungeon for some real fun.

An hour later, with the girl strung up from the rafters, he pulled out a three-meter leather whip and tested its action. Ignoring her cries for mercy and relishing her screams, he began lacing her body with bright red welts. The whipping did little to settle his tortured mind. The problem of Avril consumed him. When he finally dropped the whip onto the floor and walked out of the room, the strung-up prey hung limply from the shackles. She would never move or feel pain again.

She was, in fact, very dead.

Chapter Thirteen

Sitting at her desk in her room, Avril scratched a drawing pencil against the sketch pad. Her mind remained mired in a dark place. She wasn't paying much attention to the images appearing on the paper. Her last meal with Sir days ago didn't turn out well, at least from her perspective. She was still fuming about her near-death experience by his cruel hands. Even knowing his tendency to kill on a whim, only to experience the awful screams and pleads for life, she never thought he would be so fucking cruel and vicious with her.

In so many ways, she wished he had killed her in that fucking electrocution cage.

Surviving that day was nothing to brag about to anyone. Her body still tingled from the memory of the agonizing electricity. Most concerning was the thousand little lightning strikes going off in her fingertips and toes.

Avril was in a lot of distress. Even after several days, Avril did not know if she could ever forgive Sir. Maybe in time, she would forgive him, only not now.

So instead of confronting him further, she sat at her desk drawing, charcoal dust all over her fingers and smudges on her face and body. The etchings on her scratchpad were chaotic, dark, and full of rage. Though she was the artist, she did not see the renderings in her mind. Only her emotions took over and placed the images on the paper, page after page of her sketchpad. She drew, wearing down the charcoal sticks in her hand, one after another. She was in pain, not only physically but mentally and emotionally.

What bothered her now was the desire to die. This was something she struggled with every day. Her faith prevented her from taking her own life, and yet she felt God In his infinite wisdom would forgive her. Was it to be? She did not know. Had she reached her limits—possibly? Time will tell. Determined to figure this out, Avril meant to survive, escape, and take the Consortium down. The how was yet unresolved.

Her body aching, she extended her arms behind her head, stretching her back. It was at this moment that she heard a subtle cough coming from the doorway. Turning, she saw Sir standing there watching her.

Quickly getting up, she said, "Sorry, Sir, I did not know you were there." Avril apologized, quickly moving to the center of the room and knelt in the pose she knew would please him the most. It was also in that moment, she remembered rule two-hundred and six, 'Never say you're sorry.' Biting her lip, she hoped he would let it slide.

"That's all right. I saw you were self-absorbed with your drawing. Thank you for kneeling. I appreciate that."

Breathing an internal sigh of relief, she said, "Thank you, Sir, I appreciate it."

"Avril, I just came in to see how you were doing. Are you having any aftereffects?"

"To be honest, Sir, yes, I am."

"Tell me about it. What's bothering you."

"Sir, I still feel the electrical energy surging throughout my body. It tingles everywhere, and most especially in my fingers and toes. It feels like I have ants crawling all over my body. My muscles seem to spasm on their own. It's very frustrating."

"All of those symptoms should go away in time. I expect them gone by the end of the week."

"I hope so, Sir. They are distracting and annoying.

Is it alright if I am honest with you? I know I shouldn't ask, but this is important."

"Always my Avril. I insist on it."

"Sir, I hope you are right and that it will dissipate in time. But please, I beg you, do not do that to me ever again. I would rather that you kill me outright."

"Avril, I don't want you to die just yet. I don't want you to die at all. However, you know me, my preferences, and my needs to torment. With you, I restrain myself in going too far. To be just as frank and honest with you, it's hard. So instead, I take my pleasures on others, many of whom do not survive even a single session."

"Just the same Sir, I'm worried. These ongoing symptoms are affecting me, and I can't stop wondering if what I feel will go on for the rest of my life."

"Then, Avril, you need to learn to deal with them. I will not apologize for punishing you. You knew the consequences and earned the punishment. Speaking of which, when I first stopped by, you said, you're sorry. Don't think I didn't note that once again, you broke a rule. These rules are there for a purpose. I have a reason for everything I do and a reason for every decision I make."

"Sir, I submit to your punishment. You are correct. It just came out, as I would have commonly done in my old life."

"Is that an excuse? Shall I let it go just because you said it inadvertently?"

"No, Sir. I didn't mean it as an excuse. I knew as I spoke that I broke rule number two-hundred and six. I realized it much too late to keep my mouth from saying the sentence. I had hoped you missed it, even though I knew you wouldn't."

"See that it doesn't happen again. Now, get up and lean over the chair. We'll take care of the punishment for your failure right now."

"Yes, Sir."

With that, Avril got up, turned towards her desk chair, and leaned over its back, grasping the seat with her hands. Her ass stood open, exposed, and proud to him. Gritting her teeth as she heard him undo his pants belt, she waited for the inevitable. Based on her experience, she knew what was coming and that it would be painful.

He didn't disappoint her. The first strike of Sir's belt landed across both her ass cheeks, just above the place where her legs merged with her hips. Pain shot throughout her body. Her knuckles turned white as she clenched them around the edge of the chair seat. Her lungs paralyzed; she couldn't breathe for a time. Still, she grunted out the one word she knew he expected from her.

"One,"

A moment later, another smack of the belt landed on her ass, reinforcing the previous strike and adding another red mark next to the last one.

"Two," she groaned out as the searing of her derriere continued.

He stopped at twenty. When Avril was sure he finished, she croaked out. "Thank you, Sir, for my well-deserved punishment."

"Break the rules anytime Avril. I enjoy punishing you."

"Yes, Sir… I mean, no, Sir. Oh, I don't know what I mean."

"See that you don't. Now stay there. I enjoy looking at you. The fire in your ass turns me on."

"Yes, Sir," she said as she relaxed her body over the chair.

She didn't know how long she remained in the position, but it didn't matter. It was better than being beaten. In time, she felt something new on her ravaged bottom. It was the head of his cock, searching for an opening. Instinctively, she spread her legs, her body knowing what to expect. He didn't disappoint her or her body. In one smooth motion, he entered her.

An inadvertent moan leaked out of her mouth and pleasure consumed her, compensating the painful punishment she went through. She felt him. She felt all of him, filling her up, stretching her pussy, and pressing against all of her insides as far as he could reach.

Barely able to process his entry, she felt his hands grasp either side of her hips. Holding her still, he thrust in and out, slowly at first but firmly establishing a building tempo of faster and harder plunges into her pussy.

Her knuckles white again, only this time for a very different reason, she held onto the chair with all her might and will power.

Enjoying the hard fucking, she let go of her logical, conscious self and let the emotions of her pleasure take over. It didn't take long until the surrounding room disappeared. Sensations from her core washed over her and devoured her with a welcoming fire. Suddenly, her world got small, and she didn't care in the least. She was happy and content, as one orgasm after another consumed her.

Sometime later, how long she didn't know, she returned to the here and now. Opening her eyes ever so slowly, focusing on the seat cushion below, she took in her surroundings. Still draped over the chair, almost as if she had passed out, Avril reviewed her condition. Her arms were weakly dangling over either side of the chair, and the chair back pressed up hard into her abdomen.

Stretching her senses outward, she reached for him. Disappointment set in when she realized she was completely and utterly alone. His need resolved, he left her draped over the chair and returned to who knows where. She knew he wasn't one for aftercare but still, he could have at least made sure she was all right.

"Fuck," she silently grumbled.

Thinking about standing up, she returned to her position folded over the chair. Her legs atop sky-high heels were tingling and wobbly, unable to support her weight on her heels.

"Great!" she grumbled, realizing that getting up might take a supreme effort.

She was cold and shivering. The only thing she wanted was to get to her bed and climb under the covers. She couldn't fathom why she was cold. Sir kept the residence at a constant temperature. It was warm enough so that her constant nakedness didn't suffer from the cold. But now she was. Goosebumps speckled her arms. Chilled to the bone, she felt as if she was freezing.

Resolved, she held onto the chair and tried to stand up. She had almost made it when her legs gave out, and she slipped slowly to the floor, thankful for the chair, helping to slow her descent.

Lying prostrate on the carpet, she rolled over to her side, her legs sprawled wildly. Tilting her head towards the bed, she stared at the beckoning object of her desire. Recovered for a moment, she began edging towards the bed. It took effort; her exhausted body was failing her.

It took lots of work, but she eventually made it to the bed, pulled herself up, and slid under the welcoming covers. Exhausted and warm, she positioned her pillow under her head, tucked the covers up underneath her chin, and fell instantly asleep.

***

Waking up hours later, she felt relaxed and wholly gratified. Even her ravaged butt cheeks felt better by the post-beating ordeal. She laid there for several minutes staring at the ceiling, not thinking of anything in particular. Instead, her mind was welcoming blank of anything. The minor imperfections in the ceiling captured her interest, enticing her to look for others around the room. In reality, she didn't care about what she found. All she wanted was to maintain a clear mind, free of every concern, relishing the calm peace immersed in every cell of her body.

In time, the real world invaded her thoughts, encouraging her to get up. She had little idea how long she remained unaware of her surroundings from the moment Sir enjoyed her body. She sensed it was a long time. He might await her appearance.

Deciding, she sat up, though her full bladder helped choose for her. After relieving herself and cleaning up in the on-suite, she returned to the main area of her quarters. Stretching to take the kinks out of her joints, she looked around, settling her eyes on her desk.

Suddenly worried, she noticed for the first time a note written in Sir's handwriting.

"Oh shit," she thought to herself.

Hurrying over she picked up the note.

"Avril, I'm going out, and I won't be back for several days to a week. While I am gone, I want you to reflect upon your behavior of late. Of concern to me is your lack of respect for the rules and me. Are you still determined to become a full member of the Consortium? I have my doubts. You will need to prove to me your continued interest."

"I also want you to work on your domination skills. There are several subjects in the cells for you to do your best. I won't mind if one or more are missing from my inventory when I return. Whether any are missing, is entirely up to you."

"Outside of that, I require you to kneel three times a day for a minimum of an hour each, alternating between the waiting and inspection poses. My observations of each of these poses revealed that your posture needs work. Your elbows are sliding forward way too much, and your back is not straight with a gentle curve to your spine. Work on it. I expect perfection in your poses. I will evaluate your progress upon my return. I hope to see significant improvement."

Breathing a sigh of relief, she sat down on the edge of her bed. The note was good news. She hadn't missed an appointment with him. Nothing in it demanded immediate action, though she worried about his doubts on her conviction to join the Consortium. Was he picking up on her deception? She resolved to be more careful, which meant being forced to kill again.

She'd deal with that tomorrow. She was hungry, ravenous in fact. After washing up, she strolled out of her quarters and headed for the kitchen to take care of her hunger. Arriving, she found one of the house slaves already there, ready to prepare a meal for her. She wore heels and an apron. Around her neck, she wore the standard obedience collar depicting his ownership encircling her neck. It was exactly like the one Avril herself wore.

"Mistress, what can I make for you?"

"What's available? I'm hungry after a long ordeal and too much sleep." Avril replied. "Anything. You know what I like."

"I do ma'am. I've already started on something anticipating your needs. I was holding up the final preparation until you came down for dinner. Give me five minutes, and I will serve you."

"Thank you. You've been most kind."

"You're welcome, Ma'am. The Master also left word that you may have a cocktail or two. I've staffed the beverage bar in the dining room for you. You may indulge yourself."

Avril nodded her acknowledgment and turned towards the dining room. Stepping through the door, she sought out the bar. Besides it, stood a stately woman wearing nothing more than a pair of black, closed-toe six-inch heel pumps, a shirt collar without the shirt, and a black bow tie. She had long, straight, black hair that reached the small of her back. Her hair contrasted well with her fair skin, just as the shirt collar set off the bow tie. Unseen under the shirt collar, rested the symbol of Sir's ownership and dominance over every member of his stable.

Approaching the bartender, she ordered a very dry vodka martini with a twist and sat down at the dining table already set out with a place setting.

As she sat there, she pondered the thought of whether these slaves would soon suffer by her hand, possibly dying. Putting the idea out of her mind, she closed her eyes and waited, a dread invading her thoughts.

Come what may, she knew what she had to do. She had best get on with it.

Chapter Fourteen

"What will you have?"

"Beer, I don't care which kind, just beer. Hold on, make that a craft beer, a pilsner on draft."

"Yes, Sir, coming right up," bartender Katie said to the customer sitting at the bar.

Katie had been working an entire shift and a half. Her replacement hadn't shown up. Frankly, she was dead on her feet. Still, she liked the job and the regulars more. Grabbing a chilled beer mug, she placed it under the tap and began filling it with the aromatic scent of a locally brewed craft beer. This one was one of her favorites. She was positive her new patron would like it.

Pondering him as the golden liquid filled the mug, she wondered who he was. She had never seen him around before, yet he moved like he knew his way around. As the door closed behind him, he stood there a moment, scanning the bar, before his eyes settled on her. Immediately, he stepped up to the bar, took a stool, and ordered.

Capping off the draft beer with a beautiful head of foam, she brought it over to the guy.

"Here you go? Would you like to open a tab?"

"No, that's all right. Here," he said, pushing a twenty towards her.

"Out of twenty," she replied automatically. Ringing up the sale, she deposited the bill in the cash drawer. Dropping the change in front of him, she checked on another customer at the end of the bar.

Out of the corner of her eye, she kept tabs on him. There was something about him that bothered her. Without a doubt, he wasn't one of the usual crowd. After checking the other patrons, she had a moment to herself. Grabbing the bar towel, she wiped down sections with spilled beer and drink. Turning her attention to the bar sinks, she washed, rinsed the dirty glasses, putting them back in their usual places to await another customer. It was busy work but necessary.

That done, and not seeing anyone in need of a fresh drink, she scanned over the table areas, looking for thirsty customers. Katie liked the floor attendant, who was keeping everyone satisfied. She had spunk and didn't take shit from rowdy customers. She had a way of calming them down when they got too grabby, unruly, or obnoxious. She had learned a lot watching her.

Leaning back on a cabinet, she rested a moment, taking some weight off her feet. As she watched, the customer that caught her attention, downed the rest of his beer, left a tip, and turned to leave.

Katie breathed a sigh of relief. At that moment, just before the guy reached for the door, it opened. Looking at the newcomer, she was happy to see that it was Shelby. She enjoyed her company and welcomed her arrival. Her presence meant she would have a lovely night and morning ahead of her.

Just then, as Shelby stepped through the door, she stopped and looked long and hard at the leaving patron. A strange look appeared on her face, sidestepping the guy as she walked over to the bar. The guy gave her a second look but continued through the door and out onto the street, closing the door behind him.

"Shelby, I'm glad you came by. I've missed you."

"Katie…" Shelby began.

Katie interrupted, "Do you know that guy, Shelby"?

"Uh? Oh, no, I don't." Shelby replied.

Katie knew her mate too well to understand that she was lying. Still, Katie respected her privacy.

"Oh, I thought maybe you did, the way the two of you looked at each other. No matter. I'm so glad you stopped by. I've missed you."

"Ah, Katie, that's kind of why I stopped by. I have to leave."

"Leave? You just got here. Can I stop by after my shift is over?"

"Katie, I have something to tell you."

"What?" Katie asked, detecting the severe tone in her lover's voice.

"I have to leave."

"Leave? You mean not just tonight but forever?"

"Yes, Katie. I do."

"Why? What about us?"

"It's complicated."

"Isn't it always? Have you found someone else?"

"Uh? Ah, no. It's not that. I have to go, leave town."

"Is there anything I can do to help?"

"No sweetie. There's not. Just know this. I love you, and it's because

I love you that I have to leave."

"Shelby, you're not making any sense. What is it?"

"Katie, I can't tell you, but please trust me. It's because I love you that I have to leave. I... I am trying to protect you."

"From what? Who? I don't understand."

"No, you wouldn't, my dear. You're so sweet, why would you. No, my love, you can't help. To keep you safe, I have to leave."

"I don't understand."

Please trust me. I have to do this."

"Will, I ever see you again?"

"No, you won't. That is if everything goes the way I hope. I'm sorry. I can't say anything more."

"Shelby, I will miss you."

"And I will miss you, Katie. You have saved me, and for that, I will forever be grateful."

"Kiss me before you go?"

"Sure. I can't think of anything better than a kiss from you." Shelby said, leaning in and cupping her face, kissing Katie full on the mouth, stirring her insides and her excitement.

"Watch your back, my love. Stay alert and watch your back." Shelby finished before spinning on her heels and heading for the door.

Breathless, Katie leaned back, worried about her lover who was not only walking out the door of the bar but out of her life forever. Katie stared for a long time at the closed door in disbelief and anguish.

"Katie, can I get another one?" she heard from the other end of the bar.

"Oh, sorry. Yes, right away." Pouring the insignificant draft into a fresh mug, she dropped it in front of the regular.

"Is everything all right?" she heard him ask, only to nod and walk away. She didn't want to talk about it, not now, and maybe never.

***

Shelby stood in the shadows down the street from the bar. Dread consumed her. Seeing that guy in the bar told her all that she needed to know. She knew him by reputation. She had hoped she would never see him.

He was another hunter for the Consortium. The problem was that he wasn't just a hunter. He was an elite hunter. His presence at the bar could only mean one thing. He was after her.

When she stepped out on the street outside the bar, she quickly scanned the dark streets. For her assignment, she had studied the area thoroughly. She knew every crook, every hiding place in the area. She saw nothing that worried her, and that in of itself, bothered her.

Still an hour before closing, she surveyed the surrounding buildings before taking up station within sight of the bar. Worry consumed her. Were they after her or Katie? She had hoped to dissuade the Consortium from targeting the sweet Katie. She had thought she had done that all right, but the events of the last couple of days worried her. Ever since she identified the tail when she was out with Katie the last time, she knew time with her lover was short. She had hoped to avert the snatch, but it looked like now that she would fail.

"Over my dead body," Shelby promised herself, chuckling at the idea that it just may come to that.

Satisfied that all was well for the moment, Shelby found a dark corner and slipped inside to wait. Checking her watch, she had just about an hour before Katie would close up and go home.

***

Katie was late locking up. Shelby checked her watch for the umpteenth time. "Come on, girl. Go home."

At that moment, the bar lights turned out, and the door opened. Katie stepped out, turning to face the door to lock it. She didn't notice the van driving slowly down the street, stopping just in front of the door.

"Oh, shit!" Shelby exclaimed. "It's going down now."

Running down the expansive length of the street, in her heart, she knew she would be too late. As she ran, the van side door opened, and a man jumped out.

"Run Katie," she yelled.

Katie, oblivious to what was about to happen, turned in bewilderment. As she did so, the man grabbed her from behind and shoved her towards the van.

"Katie, I'm coming!" Shelby yelled, knowing in the back of her mind, it was fruitless.

A moment later, the van door closed, swallowing up the love of her life. The van drove off and disappeared into the night.

Shelby stopped and leaned over, her hands on each of her knees. "Fuck! I'm sorry, Katie. I'm so sorry."

Straightening up, she caught her breath and began walking away, in search of her car. Turning the corner, she noticed her car wasn't alone, and she quickly ducked out of sight. Taking a quick peek, she knew in an instant they were onto her and planned on taking her out. Reversing course, she ducked between the buildings, making her way to a safe house. They didn't know about this one, at least she hoped they didn't.

When she arrived hours later, on foot and backtracking several times, she waited in the shadows to see if the streets were clear. After a time, she figured she was safe for the moment.

Entering her safe house, she cleared each room. Satisfied, she took no chances. Accessing a hidden cubby, she was happy to note that her escape case remained intact. Opening it, she inventoried its contents. In it were dozens of gold coins, several bundles of cash amounting to ten thousand dollars, a cache of handguns, a silencer, an automatic rifle all with matching ammunition, and four sets of identification, including matching passports, all forged. It would, for the time being, keep the hunters from tracking her movements.

Selecting the identifications, appropriate firearms, and ammunition, and pocketing the cash, she closed the case and left the safe house for good. In a nearby garage, she got into a new car she hoped they knew nothing about and pulled out onto the street. Finding her way to the interstate, she headed north towards the airport.

"Maybe I can get her back before they fly her out of here," she prayed. She would do whatever it takes to get her back.

Once safely away, driving just above the speed limit on cruise control, tears began falling down her cheek. As hard as she had tried to protect Katie, it wasn't enough. They had taken her anyway. No one would ever see her again.

"Oh, Katie. I am so, so sorry." Shelby lamented between her racking sobs.

She had to do the best as she could to get her back. No way in hell would the Consortium get to keep her.

***

Arriving at the airport, she carefully made her way to the private hanger she knew the Consortium used. Avoiding their surveillance cameras and security people, she parked well away from the airplane hanger.

Picking up a pair of binoculars, she scanned the area. Sure enough, she arrived just as the van Katie was in pulled into the hanger. Not seeing anything she couldn't handle, she got out, softly closed the door, and crept towards her target.

Thankfully, she was wearing dark clothes so she could stay in the shadows with relative invisibility. Creeping slowly, trying to keep out of sight, she held her breath, careful not to advertise her presence. Crouching low, she looked for a way in without going through the front door. Having been here enough, she knew what measures they would take to keep things quiet. Unfortunately, every time she had been here, she was acting as a hunter turning over her captured prey. This time, she was an unwelcome adversary, plotting to free one of their captured prey.

Circling the sides and back of the hanger, she found no obvious way into the building. Further, with the building sitting out in the open as it was, there wasn't a way to the roof to look for a concealed entrance. Taking a moment, she considered her options. Decision made, she'd have to slip in the front door and do the best as she could.

First, she'd have to take out the security guard positioned outside the hanger door. The hunter she was, she slipped silently behind the guard, and with a chokehold, she took him down. Looking at his face, she realized he was a member of her team.

"Sorry," she whispered to the teammate.

Sliding up to the door used for people, she carefully listened before testing the door latch. It was unlocked. Cracking the door open, she peeked inside. As expected, the action was at the far end of the hanger. They parked the van behind the wing of the private plane, its doors standing wide open. Knowing their procedures, she figured that she only had minutes to rescue Katie and get her out of there. She was running out of time.

Slipping inside, she quietly closed the door behind her and crept to a hiding place just inside the hanger. The sounds of activity came from the far end of the vast open space. Keeping low, she quickly moved along the walls, ducking behind whatever cover she could find, getting closer to her goal with each step.

In no time, she made her way to a point where she could see the interior of the van.

"Damn, they've already moved her," she realized.

Whether she was already on the plane or in a side room packed for transport, she didn't know. Watching the people gathered around the plane, she figured that they were waiting for something. It wasn't much, but it implied that Katie might be in a room, packed into an acrylic transport crate. She might have a chance.

How to find which room? It was probably the normal one used to strip and transfer an unconscious person into a crate. She'd have to be very careful.

Surprise was her only advantage. Determined to free her friend and lover, she went in.

Waiting until those gathered around the plane seemed distracted, she slipped to where she guessed Katie was and entered the room.

"Ah, there you are Shelby. Just in time. We've been expecting you."

Stunned, she froze in her tracks, realizing her mistake. She was in mortal danger. A quick look around told her they already sealed Katie inside the acrylic transport box. It would challenge her to free her and escape together unscathed.

The person who spoke out was unknown to her. However, she was familiar with the tone of the voice. It felt like hours as she processed this new information. Instinct took over, and she slammed the door into the person hiding behind it, knocking him to the ground.

Closing the door in front of her, she dived back into the open space of the hanger, her senses searching for other opponents attempting to take her. They were right behind her and barely a second away from grabbing her.

Spinning on her heel, she delivered a whirling kick to the closest guy, connecting the back of her heel just under his chin. He went down in a heap and didn't move. Focusing on her other attackers, she jabbed at a second man, nailing him in the solar plexus. While he went down, giving her precious seconds, instinct told her he wasn't out.

A pair of strong arms wrapped around her frame, intent on immobilizing her, while another attacker circled her flank, preparing to sucker punch her in the gut. She slammed her spiked heel on the foot of the owner of the arms binding her. The sudden freedom allowed her to focus on the fist swinging towards her midsection. She had just enough time to deflect it and return a gut strike.

As the front attacker doubled over, she focused on the one behind, about to re-secure her in his powerful arms. Bumping him backward with her butt, she turned and faced him, delivering a wide crosscut to the chin. His head snapped sideways, and he went down. Not caring that she broke his neck, she turned to the attacker in front and kicked at his groin, connecting smartly right between his legs. He doubled over, howling as he went down.

In the corner of her eye, she saw several other guards running towards her. Outnumbered, she took off, abandoning her mission to save the poor Katie. Hopefully, she could do something about that later. Unable to help at the moment, she took off, dodging while making her escape.

In the darkness of the shadows outside the hanger, she ran. A half-hour later, from the shadows, she watched with regret. The private plane exited the shelter and made its way to the runway. With a roar of its engines, it lifted off into the night sky, taking her love with it.

"I'm sorry, Katie," Shelby said with deep remorse. "I will get you back," she resolved.

Chapter Fifteen

Blue, clear skies ahead and cruising at thirty-two thousand feet, the pilots sat monitoring the instruments and answering the occasional radio chatter from ground control. Their focus should have been on flying the Gulf Stream 510 luxury jet. It was not. Instead, their thoughts were on their passenger.

In the nearby cup holder, sat a single malt scotch on ice. A clear fluid floated on top, indicative of a forgotten glass. The preoccupied owner of the drink didn't care, knowing a fresh one would appear just as soon as he was ready for it.

Most corporate jets carried business people engaged in idle conversation, working on a presentation, reviewing and responding to email, or just napping. Here, the primary passenger on board, though a businessman, never conducted business while traveling. There was too much to lose if any of his business concerns ever leaked outside the Consortium.

Instead, Sir maintained an entourage of beautiful women to occupy his time. On this flight, two of them serviced him, each woman dressed in their standard flight uniforms. That is to say, nothing except for their sky-high heels and obedience collars permanently locked around their pretty necks. They wore the heels because Sir liked them. He used the collars to control and prevent their escape. They had earned Sir's trust and relished the freedom from the painful torment in his cellars. They found freedom in being taken care of, never wanting for anything, for only the low price of occasionally servicing him sexually.

On this trip, something agitated Sir. Each was servicing him orally, trading off while the other rested and relaxed. Even though he enjoyed their attention, they detected his agitation through his body. Under normal conditions, each could satisfy his needs with little effort. Not this time, instead, he was rough on each of them. Renowned for his stamina and ability to recover quickly, each felt they were in a fellatio marathon.

Time after time, their owner and Master, jammed his cock down their throats. He demanded that they each accommodated his length and girth deep into the back of their mouths. He gave them no opportunity to enjoy the moment. On this flight, he clamped their heads against his groin and shot his load directly down their throats, where their esophageal muscles carried his ejaculate directly to their stomachs.

Indeed, something agitated him, they thought.

Still, the attendants preferred this, then spending special time in his dungeons. They knew from experience that most of his playmates never left the nether regions of his estate. They were content to deal with his occasional agitation. Besides, he took care of their sexual desires, and they were all the happier for it.

Their names were unimportant to him. As long as their names didn't rise to the top of the replacement list, they were content. Despite knowing that Sir would kill them both one day, they gave up the thought of escaping to their previous lives. Just the other day, they found out that one of their kind, tasked with dining-room duties, had not returned from the dungeons. They knew he killed her. They didn't want to know any more.

All that mattered now was to please him and ease his agitation as best as they could. In recalling that moment, the attendant currently swallowing his cock, felt him reach his climax. Almost as if he detected her thoughts about his tormenting members of his stable, he grabbed the back of her head and pulled it tight against his loins. He had a way of doing that, reading their body language or minds. No one knew for sure.

As he shot his load, her associate licked and fondled his balls, ensuring that every precious drop of his ejaculate disappeared down the other girl's throat. It was something they enjoyed doing for him. Each wasn't sure he even cared. In those final stages, he went inside himself, oblivious of the world around him, and wallowed in a kind of pleasure that neither of them understood.

She felt him grow in girth and length before he came. Struggling to breathe, she gulped a small amount of precious air, knowing from experience, she wouldn't be able to breathe for a while. Thankfully, she quickly refilled her lungs moments before she received his gift, shooting past her tongue and into the back of her mouth.

Her companion steadied her, wrapping an arm around her back to hold and comfort her. It helped her through the worst of it, preventing her from upchucking stomach slime all over him. Not that he cared if she did. She hated the foul and burning acids that would stick to the insides of her mouth and nostrils for some time to come.

Resolved, entering her kind of trance to deal with the inability to breathe, she tasted his seed time and time again, alternately contracting and expanding his cock in each firing. The sensations reminded her of those cartoons she used to watch as a kid. The gun would shrink and then suddenly grow longer as a bulb flew down the length of the barrel, ejecting the bullet. In many respects, she loved these moments, knowing that it was she that pleased him.

There was no doubt about it. She loved sucking on Sir's cock, draining his balls.

After a time, she felt him relax, releasing his death grip on the back of her head. Slowly he started sliding out of her throat, allowing her to take another breath. However, she knew that in no way, was she to withdraw completely, and move away from him. No, it was in these final moments that he liked better than the actual climax. He needed her to care for him, holding him inside her mouth, even as his cock deflated and returned to its average size and shape. She thought of it as his aftercare of sorts.

Gently holding on to him with her tongue and mouth, she caressed his cock with her tongue and cheeks. For a moment, she thought she could sense his escaping cum and quickly closed off its path to freedom. She gladly relished its flavor, adding his essence to her own.

Sometime later, he leaned back and released her, patting the seat next to him. Smiling, she leaned up and kissed him.

"Thank you, Sir."

"My pleasure," he answered and then including the two of them. "You were both delightful, and I appreciate the attention you each gave me."

Each nodded, accepting the compliment.

"You're welcome, Sir. It was our pleasure." The other attendant answered for both of them. Then looking at the glass with the melting ice, said. "I'll get you another," picking up the glass and standing up.

Sir nodded, not caring if he drank it. His attendants knew whether or not he drank it, it was their responsibility to always have a fresh drink at the ready.

"Sir, we'll be on the ground in about a half-hour."

"Thank you, Captain."

"We'll start our descent in about ten minutes. Skies remain clear, so we shouldn't have too much trouble during our descent and landing."

"Very good, Captain. Carry on."

"Yes, Sir." the pilot answered before signing off.

Looking at his companions, he cradled them in his arms. He never tired of admiring their graceful lines. He loved seeing their soft, feminine curves resting against him. After a moment of admiration, he tapped each one on the shoulders.

"You heard the Captain. Time to finish up and return to duty."

"Gladly Sir," the one attendant uttered while the other squatted over his erection and lowered herself on him.

"Don't be too quick about it. You know how much I like to finish just as we touch down."

"So you can dive in and split me wide open, Sir?"

"You understand completely."

"Gladly, Sir," said the one who wrapped her pussy around him and began rocking.

The other attendant busied herself by stroking the back of his head and kissing his neck. Sir took the face of the one fucking him, and pulled it close to his mouth, kissing her vigorously. She melted before him, kissing him back while competing with her companion to hold the back of his neck.

Before long, Sir was enjoying their little competition. Right on cue, the moment the aircraft touched down and applied reverse thrust, he speared her, shooting his seed deep into her uterus where it would never find a target.

The plane slowed and taxied to the terminal.

"Thank you, girls. Remind me to tell your owner how specular each of you was on this trip."

"Sir, forgive me, but that is unnecessary. We're sure he already knows."

"He does, doesn't he? Never forget that. All right?"

"Never a doubt, Sir, never a doubt."

Slapping each of them on the ass, he kicked them off his lap. After downing the last of his single malt scotch and allowing the girls to put his trousers back on, he kissed them both. Pinching each of their nipples amid his kiss, he smiled when they yelped at the minor discomfort to their nips.

"Stay like that until I deplane," he commanded them, meaning that they should remain nude and on display as he admired their bodies one last time before ducking through the hatch.

"On second thought, straighten up here and follow me to the car. I'm not done with either of you yet. And don't bother with your uniforms. You're perfect just as you are."

"Yes, Sir!" they both answered eagerly.

Stepping through the hatch, he noticed that they remained in place until he deplaned. As he walked down the jet stairs, he could detect the faint giddy sounds of females enjoying themselves. Presumably, in the time it took him to deplane, they were already following behind him, ready to service him once again.

"How was the flight?" Sir's executive secretary asked.

"Fine. Just right, in fact. You did well with training those two."

"Thank you, Sir. Soon, I'll have replacements ready for you."

Snorting, Sir added. "Then I can really have fun with these two."

"Indeed, Sir." his companion added, holding the door open for his boss.

By rights, the executive assistant was much more than a secretary. He was the Director of Operations for the Consortium and Chief Director of the Facility. He ran much of the behind-the-scenes operations in the search and fulfillment of stock for the membership. Though Sir in his role as Chairman and Chief Executive Officer for the Consortium had the final say and set policy, the assistant put them into action via procedures and active campaigns. He directly managed the hunters, seekers, guards, and team leaders in field operations. Tightly compartmentalized, even he did not know everything there was with the activities of the Consortium. Only the Chairman knew it all, and he was happy with that.

Climbing in, Sir took his usual spot in the limousine. Reaching for the scotch on the rocks at the ready, he took his initial sip. The two girls climbed in beside him. One immediately cupped her hand over his groin, stirring it into action.

"Hungry little bitch, aren't you?"

Smiling coyly at her Master, she said. "Yes, Sir. If you don't mind, may I have your cock?"

"Were you a good girl or a bad little girl in need of a spanking?"

"Oh, most definitely a bad girl Sir." She said with a sly knowing grin. Sir tapped the top of his thighs.

Happily, the girl draped herself over his lap, presenting both of her cheeks to him. As she situated herself on him, Sir looked over to her companion and asked her the same question.

"Sir, I've been both a good girl and a bad girl. Shall I present myself for discipline as well?"

"Seeing how this greedy little bitch has taken up my entire lap, why don't you help me spank her."

"Sir?" she answered, unaccustomed to such a request.

"Spank her."

"Ah, yes, Sir."

At which point, the two of them spanked the bad girl until her ass was a flaming red mass, forcing Sir to situate her legs under his to prevent her from squirming under the brutal spanking. Howling as she endured the spanks, her eyes flooded with tears under the onslaught.

Rubbing her hot, red ass when he finished, Sir asked. "How many was that?"

"I'm so… sorry Sir, I don't rightly know. I tried to keep count… but with the two of you spanking me, they came in such disarray that I… lost count. I deeply regret my failure." She answered, barely able to get the words out between her sobbing.

"Care to guess?"

"One hundred fifty?" she sobbed.

"That's a good guess. I'll let you off for good behavior."

"Thank—thank you, Sir," she said, getting off his lap, but not transferring to the offered seat. Instead, she knelt before him on the floor of the limo.

Sir turned to the other girl and said. "Your turn."

The girl almost made a snide remark but thought better of it. Gulping, she said, "Yes Sir," and laid across his lap.

Looking at the prostrate and sobbing girl in front of him, Sir said. "Go ahead. Give as good as you got."

It took a moment before she realized what he had asked. When she realized, she said. "Yes, Sir. Thank you, Sir," even as she swung her hand in the air to connect with the second girl's sweet-ass.

She smiled, tears replaced with a gleam in her eye, her welcome reward resulted in a delightful yelp from her companion. After a few dozen hard spanks on the tender cheeks, Sir's hand joined in and helped her. It wasn't long before the second girl's hot-ass was just as inflamed, turning a bright red and shifting from warm to hot under the assault.

Sir let the punishment go on much longer, feeling that the girl earned twice as many spankings as the first one did. It was because of her hedging remark about being both a good and a bad girl. She knew the correct answer Sir was looking for and yet, made a joke of it, earning a more severe punishment. He wondered whether she would realize that was her mistake. He doubted she would. No matter, he enjoyed himself, loving hearing the tearful screams he forced from her lungs.

After the limo arrived at the facility, the Chairman, ignoring the whimpering girls, walked across the underground garage and made for his office, his executive assistant in tow.

"How was the trip, Sir?"

"Enjoyable. The inflight entertainment helped pass the time, just as I enjoyed the ride from the airport."

"Good, I'm glad to hear you say so. I take it you found the attendants to your satisfaction?"

"Indeed!"

"I handpicked and trained them myself. I'm pleased you found the girls acceptable."

"You did a fine job training them. They work well together as a team."

Stepping into the office, the assistant closed the door and then stood before his superior. The Chairman had seen this look before in his secretary. His scowl implied something wasn't right.

"What is it?" the Chairman asked sternly.

"Sir, it appears one of our agents, the special team leader of one of our hunter groups went rogue. She is…."

"Is that the one you informed me about last month, the one whose reports have suddenly changed in tone and recommendation." The Chairman interrupted.

"Ah, yes, Sir. The team leader tried to interfere with a grab-and-go of one of her assigned targets. Based upon last month's conversation, we put a second team into place to investigate not only the prey but also on the team leader."

After a brief pause, prompted by the Chairman to continue, the assistant went on.

"Yes, Sir. As we suspected, our agent got romantically involved with the target, which turned out to be an excellent candidate for collection. The agent tried to intervene, attempting to stop the pickup. When that failed, she tried to take back the prey back at the airport. Several of our guards were critically hurt. One may not survive."

"You stopped her, though?"

"Yes, Sir. The prey is on her way here as we speak. She's scheduled to arrive tomorrow in the customary air freight shipment."

"I see, and what of the agent?"

"I regret Sir, that she escaped and is on the run from us. We have teams out there looking for her with orders to end her without prejudice in all due haste."

"I need not remind you that as a team leader, she knows our procedures and enough information to damage the organization."

"No, Sir, you don't. She's also intelligent and well trained to stay out of sight and undercover. I have three teams searching for her."

"I don't enjoy telling you how to run your operations. You know them as well or better than I. Are three teams enough?"

"I expect so, Sir. I am balancing the need to capture the agent with our need to keep things close to the chest. Too many groups, too many people charged with finding and eliminating her, increases our risk of exposure exponentially."

"I understand and will let you run with it. I need not remind you what would happen should the agent reveal too much information about the Consortium, do I?"

"No, Sir, you don't."

"Keep me informed. I want daily reports on the hunt to find this bitch. Is that understood?"

"Yes, Sir. I am to report daily or more frequently as events dictate."

"We understand each other, good! What else?"

"Sir, the next batch of inventory will arrive tomorrow, along with the previously mentioned prey. I linked the summaries of each of the individuals to your account, as previously approved for pickup. I think you'll find several interesting candidates for your stock. I've taken the liberty to flag them for your attention."

"Thank you. Anything else?"

"Yes, Sir. The guards are all in place, the cells cleaned and ready, and training will begin immediately after unpacking the shipment."

"What about entertainment? Have you decided on what that will be?"

"Sir, we've settled on the shooting gallery. The idea floated months ago. Here, we will not use firearms. Rather, to boost the competitive value of the event, we will offer bows and arrows to the membership. And to keep everything fair, we will not allow hunting equipment. Rather, they will use student grade equipment."

Interrupting, the Chairman finished the sentence. "Which will have the effect of several misses and wounded prey, before the final kill shot."

"Exactly, Sir."

"What about members who don't know how to use a bow and arrow?"

"Sir, we considered that they had better learn. However, we felt that the membership would balk at that prospect. Instead, we'll supply a limited set of student grade crossbows on a first-come, first-served basis."

"Excellent. And those that miss out on the crossbows will have to use bows. I like it."

"Yes, Sir. Just another creative way of using the Amphitheatre."

"Speaking of which, how is Henrietta doing? Has she acclimated to her new home?" The Chairman queried.

"She seems to, Sir. We regularly feed her live food. She has plenty of water and places to hang out. Her color looks good. According to the vet, from all measurable standards, she's doing well and is happy."

"It's getting time to feed her as part of the post-auction entertainment. Have any suitable candidates appeared?"

"No Sir, though I agree we need to use the snake soon. The problem is, we did such a good job the first time, we may likely disappoint our membership. As you will recall, it was the prey's deathly fear of snakes that made the whole thing work. We need that same fear the next time. Otherwise, the food may figure out a way to escape or worse, injure the snake. That wouldn't do at all."

"Right, that wouldn't do at all. Do your best to find and vet a suitable candidate. Use the same criteria as the last one. Let me ask you. Are there any candidates in the pipeline?"

"A couple, we're investigating. In fact, because of the success, we had the first time, I immediately added a deathly fear of snakes as a most desirable in the hunter's evaluation criteria for acceptance."

"Good, it sounds like you have everything in hand. I heard our member with the new heart has returned to his old ways. As I understand it, he'll wear out this heart in no time. What a shame? I liked that girl. She would have been a fine addition to my stable. Still, she was unlikely to pass muster, her family connections and all. What's the news on that front?"

"So far, we have the situation contained. The Senator opened a private investigation into her disappearance, besides the one run by the FBI. I'm not too worried about the FBI investigation. We have agents in place to redirect that line of inquiry into blind alleys and dead ends. It's the unofficial investigation I'm worried about."

"Why is that?" the Chairman asked.

"The Senator and his remaining daughter are investigating on their own, using resources outside normal channels. We have limited visibility into what they are doing."

"You've got them under observation; I take it?"

"Of course, Sir."

"My apologies. I know you wouldn't leave that alone. What are they doing?"

"Sir, the Senator has made several unscheduled trips, one or two home, but most to other regions of the country. Some trips are under the umbrella of a reelection campaign. However, he is doing things not campaign-related on these trips. His daughter is also traveling, something she doesn't normally do. To an outsider, nothing they are doing is suspicious. To us, very suspicious but nothing concrete just yet. We need more information on these side dealings."

"You'll keep probing?"

"Absolutely."

"Good. Anything else?"

"Sir, the proclivities of that member who mysteriously drowned in Hawaii last year are surfacing. It's causing quite the scandal among the horde. There is no point in paying off the victims, nor trying to shut-down the story. We are just going to ensure that his involvement with the Consortium never surfaces."

"The prick. If he hadn't died, I'd have killed him myself. I presume you wiped all financial records tying him to the Consortium?"

The two men knew well enough that the Chairman had orchestrated the member's death. The Chairman took the hit out on the pedophile. Despite knowing how the member died, they liked to talk as if they didn't.

"Yes, Sir. Those accounts are all closed and redirected to dead-ends. It took some work, as he wasn't all that careful with our privacy."

"I'm sure you have it well in hand. Anything else?"

"I'll have the first batch of captured prey cleaned up and ready for your inspection shortly after we unload them. They're still groggy from sedatives, but they'll be aware enough to know who's in charge."

"Good. One more thing, segregate the one that our agent was trying to protect. I might use her to find and terminate the agent."

"That's a good idea, Sir. I'll see to it. Would you like a personal session with her?"

"Hmmm, yes, I think I like that idea too."

"I'll see to it."

"Very good. You may go."

"Thank you, Sir." the assistant replied and left, closing the door behind him.

Chapter Sixteen

Strange sounds, blurry images, and a stank smell invaded her senses as Katie slowly returned to reality. A severe headache squeezed her skull as she laid in a pool of fetid water.

Not wanting to open her eyes, she tried to figure out her strange dreams. There were scenes she could not understand. One minute she seemed fine, and the next, they frightened her to death. She couldn't shake the image of powerful arms squeezing her from all sides. She recalled a foul smell filling her nostrils. All the dreams ended the same way, everything turning black.

A later dream, or was it a memory, seemed to imply that the blackness no longer surrounded her. Instead, she thought she was alone and yet not alone. She couldn't figure it out. People were all around her, and yet, segregated from her.

What she remembered in the final installment were her screams. Afraid in a way she had never been before, all she could remember was screaming until her throat hurt followed by slipping into darkness.

Now she was wide awake and still afraid to open her eyes. It was in that moment, a level eight headache, powerful enough to make her moan, escaped her mouth.

"And what was that stank smell?" she complained to herself. If she didn't know better, it smelled like old urine. But she would never in her wildest dreams even enter a dirty bathroom that smelled.

"What the hell?"

Lying down on her back, she thought about opening her eyes. Before she could do so, she felt herself moving, sliding back and forth before crashing into a wall. The pool of fluid followed behind, and suddenly, she was swimming in the water.

Opening her eyes wide, she discovered she couldn't focus. Everything was a blur. She slid about, crashing her head into a wall. Reaching out to steady herself, she felt smooth plastic on all sides of her. In trying to sit up, she smacked her nose on more plastic. Blood streamed out of her nostrils and into the back of her throat. Choking on her own blood, she felt like she was drowning.

Even as she was trying to control her panic, she slid again. Now it felt like she was bouncing back and forth, with dark shadows slowly coming into focus all around her. As her vision cleared, a foul-smelling liquid splashed all over her face. It burned her eyes and filled her mouth. Spitting it out, what progress she had made to see normally, suddenly reversed itself. Stinging eyes, she clamped her eyelids shut, as tears welled up.

After more jostling, she and her box fell roughly to the floor. Or was it a floor? Whatever it was, a moment later she was moving, over an occasional bump and around corners. Her eyes still stinging, her nostrils irritated, she attempted to take a peek. Through bloodshot eyes, she saw walls slide by as a massive brute of a man pushed her plastic enclosure. Looking wildly about, she saw no avenue of escape.

Banging on the roof of her box, she yelled, "Let me out of here. Do you hear me? Let me out!"

Her pleas landed on deaf ears. The man just kept pushing the cart down the hallway. As he pushed the cart, Katie saw the ceiling lights flash by, one after the other. Unconsciously, a sliver of her mind counted the lights as they floated by, not that she cared. She was too scared. Her throat getting raw from the yelling and the foul stench in the box, she clamped her mouth shut. Whatever and whoever they were, she knew she was in big trouble.

Coming to a stop, a second burly man joined the first one and moved her to the floor. The first man and the cart disappeared out of a door and around a corner. Looking around, the second man approached her with a kind of power tool. Minutes later, after running the device around the top of the box, the top flipped over with a crash.

Immediately, two pairs of hands rudely grabbed her and lifted her out of the box, as if she were a feather. Where did they come from?

"Let go of me," she yelled. "Let me go!"

Frustrated, he and another man dragged her to a room. The room reminded her of a large shower room in a school gym. Every three feet, a showerhead poked out of the wall, alongside it was a stainless-steel ring. The guards dragged her to the back of the room and pushed her under a showerhead. Alarming her further, they fitted a leather ball gag harness over her head, stuffing the red ball firmly into her mouth. With a closing touch, they snapped a metal band around her neck and tethered her to the ring.

She wasn't alone. Looking around, she noticed they chained seven other people. Over time, they dragged in dozens of other people, men, and women of every color and race, and secured them naked as she was to a wall. She lost count how many, several dozens for sure.

Turning to the woman hitched beside her, she pleaded with her eyes. "Who are they? Do you know what's going on?"

The woman dejectedly shook her head. Just then someone walked in wearing a dark grey suit, crisp white shirt, and a shiny blue tie. Walking along the length of the place, he looked at each of the chained people, inspecting them as one would look at the residents of an animal shelter. Returning to the front of the room, he turned and looked back at the menagerie.

"Hello, everyone. Thank you for joining us today," The man in the grey suit said amidst the gagged groans of the surrounding people. Watching him closely, she concentrated on what he had to say, searching for the remotest chance to escape and return home.

Almost as if he read her mind, he said. "Now, now. There's no need for any of that. Forget about the lives you used to have. They are over. You will never return to them. It would be best if you concentrate on what I have to say from now on. Your life depends upon you paying attention."

Among the muffled sounds of rising heartache, he continued.

"As of today, you belong to me. I own you. I went to a lot of trouble to secure you, and I mean to make up for my expenses. After you clean yourselves up, you will join others like you. Over the next two weeks, we will instruct you on how we expect you to behave. Good behavior will allow you to live. Bad behavior, well let's just say, you will learn just how unpleasant your lives will become. Training will be minimal; as your new owners will take on that responsibility."

"That's right; you heard me correctly. I own you. At the end of your training, I will sell you to the highest bidder."

The grey suit paused, letting the significance of his last sentence sink in.

"Moving on. I invested a significant amount of money in bringing you here. At your sale, I expect to make a notable profit. Pray that someone offers a high bid for you. Minimum bids barely earn me a profit. The higher the selling price, the more likely you will find a decent life down the road. Those that do not garner top money will repay me in other ways. Ways that I guarantee you will neither appreciate nor enjoy."

"Now, all I expect of you is to shower and clean yourself up. Take care of any business you need right here. The water will wash away any dirt and fluids you deposit. Use the soap and shampoo provided. No exceptions. Anyone who does not properly clean himself or herself up will remain here while my associates properly wash you. I assure you, they will take great pleasure, using rough scrub brushes, to clean you inside and out. If you want to avoid that, wash well."

"After that, get some rest. Tomorrow, you begin your training."

"Turn on the water boys," he commanded as he turned and walked out of sight.

Ice-cold water fell from the showerhead. Following the instructions, Katie took the soap and began washing. The glaring gaze from the guards and the stink of her body made it an easy decision. Some squatted and released their bowels and bladders.

"Gross!" Katie thought but realizing that she also felt the need. Hoping for something more suitable later, she held it.

Another woman wasn't so decisive in washing herself. Two guards walked up to her and grabbed her by the hair. Accusing the woman of not following directions, they roughly slammed her against the wall. Unceremoniously, they scrubbed the woman with rough bristle brushes used to wash floors. In no time, her skin was red and scratched, as she screamed in pain and embarrassment.

After they finished with her, they threw her up against the wall, spread her legs, and forcibly violated her. Yelling, the woman bounced up and down against the wall as they raped and sodomized her.

Katie got the message. She quickly and thoroughly cleaned up and shampooed her hair. Katie had just finished rinsing when the showerhead slowed to a trickle and stopped. Katie looked around. Most of her fellow captives had finished their bathing, though some hadn't thoroughly rinsed themselves.

"I'd hate to be them right now." Katie thought, shaking her head in dread. "I wonder what will happen next?"

She found out in no time when another guard walked along the length of them, pulling an enormous firehose behind. Finding an unfortunate poorly rinsed souls, he opened the valve. A large, steady and robust stream of water hit them full force, knocking them down. The chain shackling them to the wall was too short to lie flat, so they dangled by their neck as the tumult pummeled them back and forth.

Watching with fascination and fear, she watched as the firehose dug deep crevices into their soft flesh. The guards did little to rinse the soap away. Instead, they took pleasure focusing their attack on all the sensitive parts of their bodies. Particularly brutal was when they aimed the firehose at their heads, watching craniums bounce against the smooth slick walls.

Katie turned away. She couldn't watch anymore though she couldn't stop from hearing their screams and pleas for mercy. Their ordeal was horrifying.

"What the hell have I gotten myself into?" she silently asked herself.

When the guards finished with the slackers, one by one, they led them captives from the room. Without concern for her comfort, they pierced and welded a pair of steel rings through her nipples. The piercing wasn't so bad. It was when they welded the rings closed. The red-hot burn seared her tender flesh. For someone who wouldn't hurt a fly, it bewildered her to find out others behaved precisely opposite to her way of thinking.

Afterward, they led her to a small cell, just big enough to hold a small cot and a combination sink and toilet.

"Ah, gross," she thought to herself. "Do they expect me to pee and wash up in that thing?"

Knowing the answer before asking, she sat and used it. It was still gross. Turning towards the cot, she noticed a piece of paper on the mattress. She reached over and read it.

"Dry off and place the wet towel outside the cell. Put on the shoes and stand up straight in the center of the room. Clasp your hands behind your back and wait. You have ten minutes to comply. Failure to adhere to the time limit will incur severe punishment."

Katie realized she wasted valuable time relieving herself. Reaching down, she put on the high-heels. Unaccustomed to wearing heels of any height, she wobbled on her feet, trying to stay upright. Following the instructions on the note, she stood against the steel bars of her cell and stared outward.

She had just gotten situated when a guard came by to check on her process. Across the way, another person, a male, had decided he would not wear heels. That decision turned out to be a big mistake.

Four guards bounced on him, beating him within an inch of his life. It was astonishing, Katie thought. Using a towel wrapped metal bar, they beat him. Then, for good measure, they sodomized him over the cot. By the time they withdrew and locked the cell door, he lay moaning naked on the floor, barely able to move. By the end, he was wearing his heels, steel hoops threaded through his nipples, and sporting a brand new steel collar around his neck.

"Get up and stand against the bars." A guard commanded the beaten man. "Do it, or we'll beat you again."

Slowly and cautiously, the man crawled over to the cell bars and pulled himself up.

"Whew!" Katie whispered to herself.

Her petite tits poking between the bars, a guard approached and locked a strong chain to each of her new nipple rings. Concerned, she noted that the chain rested on the other side of the cell bars. She was or rather, her breasts were, intimately chained to the unyielding cell bars.

She couldn't contain the searing pain when the guard sadistically dropped the chain, yanking her painfully inflamed nipples. She loudly yelped. The guards laughed and went onto the next victim.

On and on it went, until they chained everyone to the cell bars.

Looking down at her chain, she wondered how long they would keep her like this. With her ankles wobbling, she might fall to the ground at any moment. She kept a firm grip on the bars to keep from slipping down. Should she fall, the chain would snag on the cell crossbar and tear her aching nipples.

As Katie pondered her precarious predicament, the man in the dark grey suit returned and began speaking.

"What? I now belong to him, bought and paid for? What the fuck?" Katie thought. "Am I now a slave, sold into human bondage? Is this what human trafficking means?"

These and a torrent of other questions filled her thoughts, unceasingly keeping her distracted as the man droned on. She didn't hear much more after the realization that she was an instrument to use, abuse, and dispose of when they finished with her.

Over the following days and weeks, they taught her how to walk on her heels, pirouette, and stand still on display. The whole exercise felt like what Victoria Secrets Supermodels do when showing off those fabulous costumes that no one would ever buy. The only difference was that they didn't wear specular outfits, only their high stilettos, and their nakedness. That seemed to be all they wanted her to do, walk the runway.

When she did not do it right, she paid for her failure with pain. When she did well, they didn't applaud her, but only minimally reduced her suffering. Having only worn flats her entire life, she dealt with far more suffering over the next two weeks. It took endless practice walking in those high-heels to make the bastards happy. They were never happy.

Midway through the second week, they chained her nipples to the cell bars and placed a ball gag in her mouth. Surprising her, they locked the ball gag to the bars, smushing her face against the cold steel.

After they chained everyone as she was, the man in the grey suit appeared once again and started talking. She didn't want to listen to him but to no avail. His commanding voice cut through her desire to shut him out.

"Good morning, ladies and gentlemen," he began. "I admit, I am rather pleased with most of you. The progress in your training is going very well. All but for one, that is." He said, glancing around the cells. "I am about to rectify that situation."

"What you are about to witness, could happen to any of you, without warning. If you do not follow the rules, this will happen to you. I require you to look forward at all times. Do not avert or close your eyes. We will watch each of you closely. If you do not follow my instructions, we will punish you, with extreme prejudice, and likely in the manner of what you are about to witness. There will be no warnings, no second chances. Do I make myself clear?"

As he talked, they rolled in a platform upon which sat a tall, upright post and placed it right in the center of the gathering. A pair of shackles and a rope tied into a noose hung from the top. Gagged from speaking, Katie watched and listened, fearing someone would notice she wasn't paying attention.

"I presume you know what this is. The rest of you need to know, that unless you do everything required of you, without pause or delay, what you are about to witness will happen to you."

"Mind you, I didn't say you may, but you will. Falter, don't follow instructions, give the guards problems, or don't do as instructed, and you will suffer my severe punishment. I guarantee it." Allowing a moment to let his words sink in, he spoke up once again. "Bring him."

As the man in the suit continued, guards approached the cell with the man who initially refused to wear the heels. Dragging him from the cell, they forced him onto the platform and shackled him to the post. The man glared in defiance as they draped the noose around his neck and pulled it taut.

Still sporting a ball gag, the man yelled garbled obscenities as the guards jeered. The man in the grey suit motioned the guards to step aside and approached the unfortunate man. In his hand, he held a whip, about four feet long.

Turning to the onlookers, he said. "This will happen to you if you do not follow instructions and not do well in your training."

With that, he turned to the shackled man and started whipping him. Katie pitied the man as he whipped him time and time again. She lost count on how many times the whip flayed him alive. As the whipping continued, the man yelled unspeakable things to the man in the grey suit. The suit only smiled and continued. After a long time, he covered the condemned man in nasty red welts and deep cuts. Blood oozed from his wounds, pooling at his feet on the platform.

Then the most horrific thing happened. As the whipping continued, the rope started retracting, eventually lifting the helpless man off his feet by his neck. Struggling and unable to breathe or yell out profanities at his killers, he strangled, dying even as they whipped him.

His victim hanging lifelessly, the man in the suit dropped the whip and turned to the audience. Bound as Katie was, she could only look forward, unable to look away even if she wanted.

"This is what will happen to you if you don't follow the rules. I trust this will provide the proper incentive to do well. Every one of you is failing at something. Improve, or you will suffer the same fate."

At that point, he turned and left the cell block. The guards meanwhile took up station nearby and kept a watch on them. No one dared to look away. For hours, they stood there, looking at the dead man hanging from the post. Katie, for one, did not want to suffer the same fate. She worked on strengthening her ankles while standing on her monstrous high-heels.

No doubt about it. She was in deep trouble.

Chapter Seventeen

"No,"

"No,"

"Yes,"

"No,"

"Maybe, I'll come back to this one later."

"Yes,"

The Chairman reviewed the new list of candidates, rejecting several while tagging others for pickup and training, to prepare for their auction to the membership.

In this batch, he noted the staff seemed to get lax in their selection criteria. Several were not a good fit for the Consortium. Too many had issues that might later come about and burn them. Rejecting them was easy.

He knew that he had to satisfy the membership with new, fresh stock regularly. Since he was early in processing this list, he tagged several for later follow-up. This batch seemed to lack sufficient candidates to meet the quota. Mentally crossing his fingers, he plowed on, knowing that it was better to select the right candidates than to choose ones that would bring trouble down on the Consortium.

"No,"

"Possibly,"

"Yes,"

"Yes,"

"Yes,"

"Maybe,"

"Yes,"

"Oh! Now, here's an interesting candidate," the Chairman mumbled to himself. His eyes opening wide, saliva flooding his mouth, he reviewed the file with hungry anticipation.

"There is something there with this one," he pondered as he continued reviewing her file. Here, the record included several videos of the woman in action. She was an aspiring mixed-martial arts fighter, good in the octagon. She was pretty, just his type. She wasn't very approachable, and in fact, she was often nasty to those around her. As a result, she had few, if any friends, and no current prospects for a contract. That alone should not have stopped her advancement into the MMA fighting scene. With her impressive record and her looks, she should have landed a deal by now. According to the file, she hadn't.

"Why?" the Chairman asked himself before stumbling upon the answer, "Oh, that's why."

His executive assistant had notated the file to let him know that it might interest the Chairman on this one, so they had surreptitiously suppressed any offers that might have come her way until he decided on her candidacy.

With renewed interest, he read deeper into her file. According to their agent's reports, she was stubborn, fighting dirty and wouldn't take shit from anyone. She liked rough sex, indulging frequently but never with partners lasting more than a week or two. She broke the arm of one of his agents amid passion.

"Interesting…" he mused. "I like this one" tagging his approval for pickup and flagging her file for himself.

Leaning back in his chair, he stared at the ceiling, closing his eyes after a moment. He envisioned his scenes with this bitch forcing her into submission, enjoying her rage along the way.

"Yeah, I'm getting bored with the usual fare. I think this one is just the one to energize me."

After several minutes of fantasizing about his newest conquest, he got up and poured himself a scotch. He had been coffee'd out some time ago, and water was always near at hand, he fancied something stronger at the moment. Something to match his excitement and growing need in his cock.

"Yes, she'll do just fine." he murmured as he took his first sip of the single malt over ice.

He was still pondering the girl when he heard a knock on the door.

"Come," he responded.

"Sir, I'm about to get dinner. Would you like anything before I leave? I'll be back in a few hours."

"No, go ahead. I'll be fine." The Chairman answered. "Oh, wait. I'm getting restless and in need of some exercise."

"Should I have the warehouse prepare one from stock for you?" the assistant asked.

"No, that won't be necessary. I'm thinking about something more strenuous. I need a sparring partner."

"Yes, Sir. What did you have in mind?"

"I think two would suffice — one this evening and then again, another tomorrow. I'm thinking two of the guards, one slightly bigger and heavier than I am and the other, a scrapper, smaller and faster."

"Sir, I know your capabilities. You realize that you could get seriously hurt."

"Yes, I am aware and thank you for your concern. I presume you will take care of them should they maim or kill me."

"Most definitely, Sir."

"Fair enough, but only if they do it on purpose. If it is accidental, then it's on me."

"Yes, Sir. If I may, why?"

"Good question. First, I'm getting lax in my exercise. I don't feel as toned as I normally am."

"Sir, you could easily take care of it in the gym. But this?"

"To be honest, I'm interested in a new acquisition who will challenge me physically. I need to be in tip-top form to subdue her. She can fight back, and I need to defend myself. I need to make sure I can control her and force her submission. I'm already salivating at the thought of taking the screams from this bitch."

"Do you have anyone in mind who can meet my needs?"

"I do Sir. The first is Willie, a black brute of a man. While he is careful not to damage the stock, he has no reservation about abusing and fucking his targets, male or female. I'd estimate he has twenty pounds and two inches on you. If you're not careful, he'll crush and snap you like a twig in no time."

"Sounds ideal. I've fought that kind before. He'll do. What about the second?"

"Well, I'm not so sure about this one. He's an Irishman, growing up in Belfast. He was an enforcer in a gang before coming to us. He's short and bulky. You easily have thirty pounds on him, but he's fast. I mean really fast. If he hits you good, you'll not see it coming."

"How is he with the stock?"

"He has no problem with the females. He'll rough them up and fuck them as necessary to get them ready for the auction. He likes all the free pussy we make available to him."

"And the males?"

"Well with them, that's another story. He has an aversion to doing anything even remotely sexual. All he does is beat them down and destroy them. He's afraid of being tagged as a fag, and will react violently should someone even suggest it."

"I could use that against him."

"Indeed, you could and now that I think of it, you should. He gets sloppy when enraged from something like that."

"Good. Let's do it. Set it up, please?"

"I'll get right on it. I may even skip eating tonight, just so that I don't miss the action."

"Whatever makes you happy." The Chairman laughed, slapping his assistant on the back playfully. "How's ten tonight for the first bout?"

"Consider it done, Sir."

"Set it up in the Bowl. Were the rocks removed?"

"Yes, Sir, last week."

"Good, let's do both bouts there. It'll give us plenty of room to fight without killing each other."

"Sir, I know that either of them may die, but if I may, Willie is a valuable asset as a guard. I would hate to lose him."

"Noted, my friend. What about the Irishman?"

"Him, well, whatever happens, is all right with me. I can get a replacement easily enough."

"One other thing. Keep them isolated from each other. I don't want them comparing notes or anything until much later."

"In case one of them dies in the Bowl?"

"That too."

"I'll take care of it, Sir."

"Excellent. This will be so much fun."

"Now Willy, out here, I'm your boss. I pay you very well, and you get all the pussy you like."

"That's right Sir, and I appreciate it. I enjoy working with you."

"This is not a deathmatch, but make no mistake, in the Bowl, I am not your boss. I am your adversary. I mean to do as much damage as I can on you. I expect the same from you."

"So, if I take your meaning correctly, this is a no-holds fight in the pretense of a sparring match."

"You take me correctly. Can you do that? Hurt me, I mean?"

"Yes, Sir, I can do that."

Slapping the black man on the back, the Chairman said with a smile. "Good enough."

"Now Willie, rest assured, after the match we'll take care of you. We will treat your injuries, and if you need a hospital, we take you to our private facility with a hospital wing where you'll get the best treatment, no expense spared."

"I appreciate that, Sir. I do."

"But you also realize that while I do not intend this to be a deathmatch, accidents happen. You could die."

"As so can you, Sir."

"Yes, I can. While I expect you won't kill me on purpose, I could die accidentally. I understand that. I doubt that will happen, but I am prepared and will spar with you knowing that."

"Sir, if I may?"

"Go ahead."

"Well, you see Sir. I'm bigger and heavier than you. I don't see this as much of a fair fight."

"Willie, you let me worry about that. You do your best to give me a good workout, and I'll do the same for you. I don't care who wins or who loses. I need to loosen up and tone up my reflexives."

"Yes, Sir. I understand."

"Good, then let's get started, shall we?" The Chairman said as he began stripping off his clothes.

"Okay–ah, Sir. No workout shorts?"

"No, Willie. No protective gear, for either your head or your balls. It'll be just you and me the way our mothers delivered us into the world."

"You mean naked Sir, completely naked."

"Yes, Willie, I mean naked, as in nude, bare ass."

"Ah, okay, Sir. I, um, don't enjoy being naked in public and all, but I guess it's all right, I suppose. Whatever you want. If I may, you said no holds barred. Does that mean I can kick you in the nuts?"

"Yes, Willie. If you can connect, you can kick me there. Just prepare for my response. I can do the same to you."

"Ah, I don't know Sir. I like my junk. I'd hate to see it smashed like a pair of grapes."

"Then you must take me out all the faster. A good offense usually beats a good defense, don't you think?"

"Usually, Sir."

"Well, there you go. Come on now, strip down. I'm ready to go. Once we start, there will not be a bell to pause the action. We keep fighting until one of us submits. Understood?"

"Or one of us renders the other unconscious or dies."

"Or that too. Yes, that's right, Willie."

"I'm in."

"Then let's get started."

***

Twenty minutes later, Willie was out cold on the sands of the Bowl, blood leaking from his mouth and an arm lying at an awkward angle. The Chairman was rubbing his side, where Willie landed a massive blow. The Chairman wasn't sure, but he thought he had a broken rib or two, bruised at least.

"Sir, I figured you had it in you. Admit it though, he was tough."

"Yeah, he was tough. I thought I had it when he got me into that bear hug from behind."

"That was a tense moment for sure, but you got out of it. Simultaneously smacking both his ears gave you an opening."

"Which I capitalized, bringing him down with a whirlwind kick to the gut."

"Followed up with a knee to the chin as he bent over. Yes, Sir, that was quite the moment. Remind me never to spar with you. You're outright dangerous."

Laughing, the Chairman slapped his assistant on the back. "Damn straight I am and don't you forget it."

"I won't, Sir. Are you going to be up for tomorrow's bout?"

"I wouldn't miss it for the world. Is he isolated as I asked?"

"Yes, Sir. No one but me will talk to him. I'm even bringing him his food so that I can be sure that no one else talks to him."

"Good. That's good."

"Come on, Sir. Let's get those ribs looked after."

Unconsciously rubbing his bruising, the Chairman agreed. "Yes, that'll be an excellent idea."

***

Three days later, the Chairman sporting a black eye and a follow-up injury to his ribs, now broken for sure, his assistant joined him for breakfast.

"Coffee?"

"Thank you, Sir. How are you feeling today?"

"Oh, I'm good. Much better off than my two opponents, that's for sure." The Chairman responded, pouring two cups and handing one off to his assistant.

"Yes, Sir. I'll give you that."

"How's Willie?" the Chairman asked.

"He's doing better. After a night in the hospital, he's back on site in his quarters doing well. No broken bones, but he suffered a dislocated shoulder and jaw. Both are on the mend. The doctors tell me he'll make a full recovery."

"That's good, very good. Send him some pussy when he can handle it. He'll appreciate that."

"Already taken care of Sir."

"As I knew you would. I'll stop by and visit him later."

"Willie will appreciate that, more than the pussy. He's worried that you'll take the damage to your ribs out on him."

"Good, let him think that. It'll keep him on his toes. I'll stop by anyway and see how he is doing. How's the Irishman? He got the worse of the deal, didn't he?"

"Yes, Sir, he did. You broke his back in the fight. The doctor's say it'll be a miracle if he recovers and even then, it'll take years to walk again, if ever. They say his chances of walking again are slim to none."

"Hmmm, that's unfortunate. So, he's useless to us anymore."

"That's about the size of it."

"Well, then it's decided. Give him a shot to sedate him and then put him down."

"He's sedated now and will be for some time."

"Make sure it's painless and that he just slips away. He's done suffering for the Consortium. Dispose of his body in the usual way."

"Yes, Sir. I had thought that would be your decision. I'll take care of it personally today."

"Very good. The eggs look good, and the bacon smells wonderful. More coffee?"

Chapter Eighteen

"Ladies and gentlemen, that concludes the treasurer's report. I, for one, am glad to know that the accounts are flush so we can continue working on providing the best product to satisfy your basic desires. Thank you, Finance Minister."

A round of weak applause circulated the room. As long as sufficient funds existed to continue their predilections, no one cared how much money the Consortium had. Individually, the membership each had more than enough to sustain their desires. Being part of this organization isolated them from the day-to-day needs to secure new stock to necessary to indulge in their wants and desires. What they wanted to know about was the upcoming auction, and what to expect in the coming year.

"Now, for a report from the Acquisitions Minister?"

"I'll get right to the point. The past several months has been exciting. Of the candidates submitted from around the world, we selected and collected what we think is the best of the crop for the upcoming auction. In all, we trained seventy-three prey for your consideration. They are all up for tonight's sale. We trust you will find one or more piquing your interest."

A solid round of applause interrupted his report. The minister politely waited for the clapping to die down. He knew from experience. The auction was what everyone was waiting for. The building excitement even twitched his loins, as he salivated over the stock he was about to buy to refill his dwindling inventory back home.

"Thank you, thank you," he said in successfully quieting the crowd so he could continue. "Ladies and gentlemen, I think it will please you with tonight's offerings. We have amassed an appealing selection of quality male and female candidates from various parts of the world. Let me tell you. Several come from South America, Australia, New Zealand, Japan, and Korea. We selected two dozen from Russia, Ukraine, and the Baltic states. Several countries in Western Europe supplied another couple of a dozen, and the rest come from North America, including both Canada and the United States. I expect that each will meet with your approval and yield some very spirited bidding."

More applause rose, drowning out his final words.

"As customary, we will send a menu of the selections to your tablets to review before the auction."

Again, the elite membership smiled, clapping their approval, unable to contain their enthusiasm.

Taking back control of the meeting, the Chairman moved on to new business.

"Now, for the future. I must talk to you about a serious matter. Please pay close attention."

Pausing until the attendees turned their full attention to him, the Chairman went on.

"As you know, we take great care in culling from the herd those candidates that offer the lowest risk of discovery of our actions. Over the millennia, we remain out of the public eye by placing agents in every significant government, corporation, and various entities to further our goals. We maintain the utmost secrecy of our worldwide operations to supply you with prime stock to feed your needs. Are we all in agreement?"

The Chairman looked around the room and noted the nods of the membership.

"Good, because I have my doubts that everyone holds to the same standards. My office is getting word that there may be loose lips by members in this room or with your staff. Contain it. I mean it. I don't want to take care of it myself. Am I clear?"

A look of shock and disbelief arose around the room as various people looked around to see if they could spot the culprit.

"Now, let's not get ahead of ourselves just yet. I am letting you know that we picked up communications from non-Consortium people that seem suspicious. I don't believe someone exposed us. However, I must reiterate that each of us must do what they can to prevent further contamination within your own house. I will handle the current concern among the parties involved. We have agents already in place at the institutions concerned, and I believe that we can shut this down quite nicely. My staff and I will continue to monitor the situation closely and take suitable action, including ending any offender without prejudice found within the Consortium."

The Chairman let that sink in for a time.

"I trust I made myself clear."

Just before this meeting, the Chairman had considered informing the general membership of the rogue team-leader now on the run but decided against it. The warning just given was enough.

"Good," the Chairman said, closing the topic.

"You've heard the Executive Committee report. I want to bring up one last topic discussed and approved by the Executive Committee. According to our charter, the general membership votes on all membership applications to the Consortium. The Executive Committee voted to forward the application to you. I know it's been a while since someone put an application to you for consideration, so I'll review the qualifications and procedures of the candidate member."

The Chairman waited a moment before continuing to catch his breath.

"As many of you know, the Executive Committee recently received an application for elevated membership. Following our charter, the Ministry of Investigative Services investigated and vetted the applicant. They did a deep and thorough investigation into the finances, resources, and proprietary to fit into our agenda. The applicant showed all the qualifications necessary to pass a membership vote in the Executive Committee. The candidate supported the application with the required application fee and provided verified proof of their willingness to subscribe to the tenants of the Consortium."

"Who is this candidate, and what proof did they offer?" Someone in the audience interrupted.

"The who I'll get to in a minute. The proof? The Executive Committee set up a personal demonstration by the candidate, witnessed by five executives via CCTV, two of whom viewed the willingness by the candidate. The candidate performed two demonstrations, one set up by us, and the other an impromptu and I might add, decisive desire to join us. It was this last demonstration that swayed us to accept the candidacy to proceed to this point."

"What were they?"

"I'm glad you asked. I'll be happy to tell you. In the first demonstration, the candidate bound prey to a wooden post, where they beat and whipped the prey, eliciting satisfying screams and begs for mercy. This continued for several hours until the prey nearly passed out. During the whipping, the skin broke in several places, allowing the prey to suffer the wounds and feel the building pain. Concluding the session, the applicant used a fillet knife to cut the throat, thoroughly coating the candidate in arterial spray. But that didn't stop there. The candidate went above the requirements laid out and severed the head before the prey died of exsanguination. In summary, the candidate manually decapitated the prey while it was still alive. After cutting the head off, the candidate held it by the hair to their lips and kissed the bloody mess before dropping it to the floor and walking off. We were all impressed."

"And the second?"

"The second caught us by surprise. We might not have even noticed this second execution if it not had been for the surveillance cameras. I'll get to that shortly. Here, the candidate literally fucked the prey to death. Teasing the prey into a false sense of security through sex, the candidate strangled it to death in mid-orgasm with her bare hands. It was a spectacular end to the demonstration and, of course, the prey. It was an impressive sight to witness."

After waiting a moment, he continued.

"The Executive Committee reviewed both executions. Afterward, and with some heated discussion, the committee approved the candidate's application for submission to the general membership."

"So, who is it?"

"Let me say that this candidate is an unusual candidate. We did not reach out to this individual. Rather, they came to us. Her name is Avril Gillios."

"Never heard of her. Who is she?" One member asked out loud.

"Hmmm, yes. That's the rub."

"Huh?"

"I doubt most of you know her. But now, as I recall, several of you know her well, very well in fact, though I doubt you remember her name."

"Stop dancing around the question, Mr. Chairman. Who is she?"

"All right, then. Avril Gillios is a member of my household."

"You mean she is prey? She's stock? This is unheard of."

"Yes, I quite agree. It is unheard of but not unprecedented. Roughly one hundred years ago, a similar item of one's possessions ended up becoming a valued elite member of our Consortium. There are other similar approved applications for membership, and, yes, many who failed and died. Those records are available to you on your tablets. That said, Avril is a member of my stock to do with as I please."

"Then kill her now, right away." Someone yelled from the back of the room.

"Yes, I understand your point. I've considered that idea many times..."

"Not enough," someone else yelled out.

"... all right, please settle down. Please let me finish."

After pausing for a time to let the murmuring die, the Chairman continued. "I mentioned that some of you know Avril well." Pointing at the complaining member, "You've had her several times at my dinner parties held at my home."

"Do you mean the fiery redhead?"

"Yes, that's the one."

"Yea, I grant you, she's a fine lay. One of the best I've ever had. She can go all night satisfying five or more of us simultaneously, man or woman makes no difference," the member said

Chuckling, the Chairman continued. "Yes, I must agree. She's quite the greedy little bitch. Over the past couple of years, she has proven herself very resourceful. I know she can equal any of you in your wickedness and do it with grace and dignity."

"But you are asking us to take your word for this." One of the protesting members spoke out above the voluminous cross-talking between the members.

"Have I ever let you down? Haven't I always delivered what I promised? Have I ever done wrong by any of you?"

"Mr. Chairman, may I have the floor for a few minutes."

"Yes, Madam. Please speak your peace."

"Thank you, Mr. Chairman. Esteemed members of the Consortium. I realize that this may seem unprecedented to you and this application out of order. However, according to our charter, anyone who possesses the qualifications for membership and pays the exorbitant membership fees can be admitted as a member. I admit, at first, I was skeptical about her application. In my opinion, Avril put that skepticism to rest. I believe Avril is a kindred spirit, with desires and means to fit in with our organization."

"Humph!" came from the middle of the pack.

"At any rate, I believe in her, and I support the application. Mr. Chairman, thank you for allowing me to speak my mind. I yield the floor."

"Thank you, Madam. Members, you've just heard from Madam Susie Chardonnay, a longtime member of the Consortium and maybe our oldest member. I should be so lucky to live to her age, remain spright and in good health. Tell me Madam Chardonnay, how was that last batch you purchased for your stables?"

"All used up, I'm afraid. I need to buy more stock." She answered.

Amidst the soft laughter that her comment made, Sir wasted no time to continue.

"Ladies and gentlemen. I know that this application is unprecedented in recent history. However, according to the rules, policies, and procedures of this organization, it is valid. Since she is a member of my stable, I will recuse myself from the vote, and refer all queries to her membership to the executive board. Which means, ladies and gentlemen, I will not pontificate on her behalf or campaign for her acceptance as a member of this body. This decision is entirely up to you."

"Does that mean you'll step aside as Chairman for the duration?"

"No, I will not. I will conduct business as normal, excusing myself whenever the matter of this application comes up."

"Are you expecting us to vote on this application today?"

"No, I do not. The vote will happen one month from today by secret ballot, deposited in your secure communications channel. You may vote any time once received — the vote concludes at midnight Greenwich Mean-Time one month from today. Further, only one vote per member and once submitted, you may not change it, even if submitted before the close of voting. The Executive Committee will post the results on the following day for all to see. That is when I will find out, along with the rest of you."

"Well, I, for one, will vote right now with a Nay."

"That is your right. However, please wait until the ballots arrive in your tablets. You'll get them tomorrow."

"How do we know you won't play with the numbers?"

"Sir, you wound me. I hold my honor and integrity above all such shenanigans. I will have nothing to do with the vote, either in submitting my vote or tallying the results. The Executive Committee will oversee that function."

"Well, I don't like it," a member voiced.

"Again, that is your opinion. To the rest of you, I urge you to consider this applicant, talk among yourselves, ask questions of the Executive Committee members. Once this meeting is over, I will not be available to answer them so, now is the time to fire away."

"Mr. Chairman, you said she had the means to pay the membership fee. Did I understand you correctly?"

"You did, and yes she does, as verified by the Executive Committee."

"Isn't it highly unusual for prey to have those kinds of resources?"

"I could say no, but you're right. Prey rarely have the resources to pay for their membership application. Here, the applicant did not know she controlled these kinds of resources. Its old family money hidden from her until she came of age. Unfortunately, her parents died at an early age before revealing to her the source of this income. Since she came into my stables, I used her money to invest, increasing its portfolio many times over."

"And as a member of your stock, that income is now yours, is it not?"

"Yes, I agree with you. However, she has proven her worth, not only to me personally, but to the Consortium. Those assets helped build the Bowl and funded the acquisition, transportation, and support of the primary resident of this facility. I mean the python Henrietta, of which you watched her debut performance with relish."

"Speaking of the snake, when are we going to see a repeat performance?"

"Soon. It's in the works. We are prepping a viable candidate to occupy the 'Bowl' with Henrietta. We hope to have it all ready at the next auction."

"Why the delay? Can't we put one of the current stock up for auction today in with Henrietta?"

"While it is possible, the value in Henrietta is feeding her suitable prey who is deathly afraid of snakes. The prey must also measure certain physical dimensions, or Henrietta might choke swallowing it. Oh, she would try, but in doing so, she would constrict the victim, quickly killing the prey, dropping the entertainment value of the spectacle. None of the stock up for auction tonight meet the criteria. I assure you, every care in putting together another show featuring the awesome Henrietta is in the works. If there are no more questions, I suggest we adjourn to prepare for tonight's auction. Do I hear a second?"

"Second."

"I now adjourn this meeting. Thank you, everyone. I look forward to seeing you all later tonight. What we have in store for you is awesome. Enjoy the show."

Chapter Nineteen

The day of reckoning had come. Today, they would auction her off to the highest bidder, and Katie knew it was about to go from bad to worse. To use the common saying, 'to jump from the frying pan into the fire.' The thing was, she didn't know what to do about it.

When they came for her, her dread faded, replaced with unadulterated fear. When the two guards reached for her, she backed away, screaming 'No' in the most certain of terms.

"Come here, baby. We won't hurt you — much." One guard laughed.

"No, please!" Katie whimpered.

Ignoring her pleas, they each grabbed an arm and pulled her to her feet.

"Listen, sweetheart. We'll carry you there if you insist. We'd rather you walk. It took a lot of effort to get you to walk in those heels. Now come on, or would you like an incentive?"

"No, no. I'll walk. Please don't hurt me."

"Then get with it, baby. Hop to it."

Cautiously, Katie stood up and took a tentative step forward, followed by a second step. Before she even realized it, she walked out of her cage, fearing her sale to who knows whom. The best she could hope for was someone purchasing her as a sex slave, satisfying their dirty desires without regard to her own. She refused to consider the worst possibility she might die a painful death within hours.

Without a doubt, she believed she was no longer the instrument of her destiny. They were, whoever they were.

Amidst a crowd of mean-looking guards, she walked along the lonely hallway, her heels clicking on the floor.

After walking the catwalk, she found herself sold to the man in the grey suit. One thing she knew for sure, he could be cruel. There was one other thing she knew about him. He had no problem with killing.

She shuddered at the thought of what was to become of her.

***

"Ladies and gentlemen, that concludes our auction for tonight. As customary, we will deduct your winning bids from your accounts. Those who purchased items, you may take them with you as you leave tonight or plan to have them delivered, naturally for an additional fee."

Pausing for a moment to let the instructions sink in, the announcer continued.

"For tonight's entertainment, we have something new for you. Before I tell you what it is, please give a round of applause to Mr. Fox, who is donating three of his purchases to tonight's festivities. As we speak, the prey is on their way to 'The Bowl.' Unlike previous entertainment, where the audience were the spectators, each member in good standing may take part. As usual, the betting lines will be open for additional excitement."

After another pause, the announcer continued.

"We will break now and gather at 'The Bowl' in about twenty minutes. Make use of the facilities and grab a fresh drink. Hurry, though. You won't want to miss the excitement."

The audience broke out into heartfelt applause, eager to get on with the entertainment. The Chairman was standing off to the side, making sure they made all the arrangements to his satisfaction.

Leaning into his assistant, who joined him a few minutes later, he whispered. "Everything on schedule?"

"Yes, Sir. The guards are finishing up loading the prey in 'The Bowl.' The quivers and bows are at the ready."

"Crossbows as well?"

"Yes, Sir."

"Are the arrows and bolts color-coded for each member's house?"

"Yes, Sir. We'll know precisely which arrow tabulates the results."

"And mine?"

"You will shoot?"

"Might as well join in the fun."

"To win?"

"Absolutely. I'm a member as well and have every right. However, in the interest of goodwill, I'll probably miss a few targets. I have to score some points to make it look good."

"I thought as much. I have a bow and a quiver ready for you. I coded the fletching red, black, blue, and green, in that order."

"Excellent. My colors and a nod to Avril. I like it. Thank you."

"Anytime, Sir. Shall we?" the assistant said, showing they should make their way to 'The Bowl' and take up their positions.

"My friend, are you shooting tonight?"

"Sir, thank you for your permission to partake in the festivities. However, I am not a member, such as the rest of the guests are. They will see my participation as an affront to their standing in the Consortium, and I wouldn't want to put you in an awkward position."

"I understand. Still, if you want to, tell me."

"Yes, Sir. I want to, but I'll defer."

"Then, it's settled. Let's make sure all is in the ready."

With that, the two of them went over to their usual places by the railing surrounding the arena. 'The Bowl' as it became known among the membership, was a recent addition to the auction house, the Consortium maintained. Built for special events and entertainment, it was the brainchild of the Chairman after they came across a massive python known to be a man-eater.

Almost a year ago, the Consortium opened the arena with a first-ever spectacle of a snake against a woman. The Chairman specially selected the woman for her inborn terror of snakes. Released onto the sands of the arena, the snake toyed with its prey before swallowing the woman whole. The membership still raves about the ghastly sight of watching the struggling girl fight for her life.

Her ineffectual exertions did nothing to deter the resolute snake. She slid slowly down the snake's throat, hopelessly screaming and begging for deliverance. Days later, attendees returned to watch the bulge in the snake's belly gradually shrink. Many stayed on longer than usual to observe the complete digestion of the girl's body.

The exhibition was so successful, the Chairman and the executive board kept the snake and planned on a repeat performance in about six months. The Executive Board later found it difficult to come up with a spectacle even approaching the impact of the snake. They hoped that this event would do the trick. Plus, it was so much less expensive to put on. They were still paying off the cost of building this facility.

Hosting death matches had become a regular event, forcing prey against prey, winner take all, and the loser giving up their life. So far, these had gone reasonably well. Finding good fighters was the problem.

Among the male contests, only the selection of that Costa Rican, Tomás Rivera, survived past three bouts, eventually dying in last month's auction warm-up entertainment. He held promise. As for the rest, no one generated enough interest in the crowd. Death-matches before the auction, warmed up the attendees, inspiring spirited bidding.

"I hope they like this." The Chairman spoke under his breath, despite the attentive assistant hearing the comment.

"I'm sure they will, Sir. The shooting gallery is again, a first-time match, at least in recent history."

"Yes, it is. It should work. After that snake episode, the membership no longer seems satisfied with simple hangings. They want more outlandish spectacles. Ultimately, it will be impossible to satisfy their blood lust every time."

"Yes, Sir, that may be true. I believe the members will understand. Limiting the wild performances to an annual event should at least give them time to get over the last one and whet their appetite for repeat performances."

"That's the hope. Still, this bunch is selfish, which granted, allows our continued existence. We selfishly feed our passions at the expense of the lives of others. Not that I have a problem with that. It's just keeping up with the demands."

"Sir, if I understand you correctly, it's a matter of supply vs. demand. If that's the case, then perhaps the committee should let the members orchestrate the spectacles and leave the big ones to when and if the committee can put something together."

"You know, my friend, that is exactly what the executive committee did. How astute of you. I may have to submit on your behalf, a membership application myself. But then, I'd risk losing a valuable assistant."

"No danger in that, Sir. If they gave me such a gift; it would have no impact on my loyalty to you. Thank you for your support."

"We'll talk about it soon. Everything is ready. Shall we?"

"It seems so, Sir. The members are filing in, quivers in hand."

"How much are we charging for the quivers?"

"As we discussed, ten thousand euros per quiver. Bows and crossbows are free. Each quiver contains ten arrows and members can purchase a second quiver if they wish."

"Why so many arrows per quiver?"

"Sir, issuing more encourages the membership the opportunity to toy with the targets, rather than kill them quickly."

"So, that amounts to about million Euros to the till. After expenses, the Consortium should pocket another million on our cut. We expect to earn over two million Euros on entertainment alone."

"That's about what we figured, including what Mr. Fox is getting for donating three of his purchases."

"No matter, everyone knows that he is not losing even a single euro on this deal. He'll probably make out like a thief."

Chuckling, the assistant agreed.

"I think we are ready to begin, Sir."

"Then, by all means, let the show begin."

Nodding, the Chairman, stepped up to the podium and waited for the din of the assembled crowd to die down.

"Ladies and Gentlemen. I hope you all enjoyed yourselves so far."

Clapping arose, forcing the Chairman to wait. After about a half a minute, he put up his hands in a motion to settle down and continued.

"And I hope you're pleased with your purchases and enjoy them for as long as they last."

More applause arose, not unexpectedly.

"For tonight's entertainment, we have something extraordinary, and a first in over a century. Tonight, we are allowing each of you to take part in tonight's event. Each of you purchased a quiver of arrows and a bow. For those of you who are unversed in the art of archery, we've made crossbows available to you. While easier to use, they take longer to load, which pretty much evens out the advantage of a regular bow. While easier to load and shoot, it takes skill to use a bow accurately."

"Now, you may think, all right, I have a bow and a quiver of arrows. What are the targets? I know you have an idea."

Laughter arose from the attendees situated around the 'Bowl.'

"Mr. Fox donated three of the prey sold tonight at auction. In a moment, they will enter the arena and face your onslaught. Thank you, Mr. Fox, for your generous donation. May I have a round of applause for to the esteemed Mr. Fox?"

The Chairman waited for the arousing ovation to die down. It took several minutes, but eventually, it did. The membership was eager to make the first kill.

"Yes, I know, it's akin to shooting fish in a barrel. However, it's a big barrel, and your prey will not stand around as you take potshots at them. Free of bindings and shackles, they are free to move about the sands, ducking as they try to evade your attack. There will be no place to hide, no escape from their fate. It's up to you to see how long each last before they receive the killing shot."

With more applause, the Chairman waited.

"Now, some rules are in effect. Few, mind you, but there are some. Anyone found to violate these rules will lead to disqualification."

"The first and most important rule is this. We color-coded your arrows to match your house membership. In that way, we'll know who scored what. We will film the event with high-speed motion cameras, to resolve contested hits. All scores will get reviewed, and a ruling made within minutes."

"The first arrow fired from bow or crossbow must not be a kill-shot, but a shot meant to intimidate the prey, ensuring that they know the event is for real and they are the target. Your job is to reinforce the mortal danger the targets face. You may wound as much as you like. We restrict only the first one from being a kill shot."

The crowd pondered this for a moment before the Chairman felt they were ready to continue.

"We will award points for each hit. A head or neck shot resulting in immediate death will earn two hundred points. A shot to the heart, killing the prey will earn one hundred points. A nonlethal shot to the chest or torso will earn fifty points. Arm or leg shots will earn twenty-five points while a minor wound to any other body part, will earn ten points apiece. Arrows that cut the flesh but do not impale the target will earn five points apiece. You may not target dead prey. Doing so will lead to disqualification."

"Does everyone understand the rules?"

Nods of murmur ringed the room.

"As always, we are accepting bets on the competitions. You will find betting lines in your tablets. Among the bets the house is offering include, who will die first, second or third; the number of headshot kills, heart shot kills, etc., time to first and last kill; time to first arrow wound, time to the first impalement of an arrow, whose arrow will strike first;

and so on. Place your wagers or offer a personal bet. I am sure someone will take it."

With that, they heard a fury of tapping on dozens of tablets around the room. As the membership placed their bets, the targets, a man and two women appeared, unceremoniously dumped into 'The Bowl.'

As customary, except for their collars and nipple piercings, all three were naked. For the first time since their arrival at the facility, they were barefoot, their footwear removed. With bewildered looks on their faces, they looked up at the crowd hidden in the shadows of the bright lights above them.

"Ladies and gentlemen, one more thing. I want to ask you a serious question. My executive assistant was key to putting this event together. Under our normal rules, we do not allow him to take part in an event. I've offered him an opportunity to do so, but he politely declined, assuming you, the membership, would take offense to him joining in on the fun. I ask you. Will you grant him an opportunity to take part? Say 'aye' if you agree, or nay if not. Do I have any 'ayes'?"

The room erupted with a chorus of loud 'ayes.'

"And nay's?"

Two nays sounded out, quickly silenced by the surrounding membership.

"The 'Ayes' have it. My friend, please take a bow."

"Thank you, Sir, for this opportunity, and thank you, members. It means a lot to allow me a chance to take part."

"You're welcome, my friend. Now, are everyone's wagers in?"

"Wait! I'm not done yet," a voice came from across the 'Bowl.'

"Step it up, my man. Why is it? I ask you. Why are we always waiting for your wagers?"

"That's because I am placing a lot of wagers." A minute went by before he spoke out, "Okay, I'm good."

"Good, okay then, archers load your bows."

The sound of the pulling arrows from quivers and nocking them into their bows surrounded the arena as the three people standing on the sands stood wondering what was happening.

"Pull" came the next command, and the sound of arrows rubbing against strings under strain reverberated.

"Loose" came the command when everyone quieted down.

Instantly, razor-tipped arrows pelted the two women and the man in the arena. The man seemed to be the favorite target, as dozens seemed to fly in his direction, and two of them slicing into his thighs and calves. Another embedded itself in his arm. One of the other women took an arrow to the leg while the last one, except for one small slice across her upper arm, seemed to escape unscathed.

The man went down to the sands almost immediately, feeling the pain of his injuries. It didn't take long before another arrow landed right beside him, narrowly missing his head. The prey scattered, running this way and that, as best as they could as arrows rained down upon them.

Dodging this way and that, the three people tried in vain to avoid the onslaught of flying arrows. The first to go down was a woman, an arrow penetrating the top of her skull and sticking out the underside of her chin. Falling to the ground, they counted six wounds and five arrows sticking out of her before the killing headshot.

The man was the second to go down. An arrow to the heart entered his chest just above his left nipple, and he fell to the ground. He died instantly, a second arrow hitting him in the gut almost at the same second as the heart arrow.

The third woman, realizing that all eyes focused on her, screamed. Trying to run and dodge as fast as she could, inevitably, an arrow landed on the top of her thigh, just below her groin. She stumbled and almost fell. However, in stumbling, she exposed herself to enough time that no less than six arrows connected, piercing her torso and arms before the final killing one struck her neck, opening up her carotid artery, spewing blood in all directions. By the time she fell face down onto the sands, three more arrows had pierced her body.

Cheers erupted as she fell.

As blood-soaked the sands beneath the kills, members and guests alike slapped each other on the back, gleeful in their role in putting to death three more of their prey. With more than a billion more available to them and their blood-thirst satisfied, they felt absolutely no remorse.

Chapter Twenty

The pool water had been warm, a pleasant eighty-four degrees, heated year-round. Avril was lying on a chaise lounge, relaxing. She was recovering from a workout in the fitness center and swimming a mile doing laps in the pool.

Over the years living with Sir, she had gotten used to the hour running on the treadmill in her heels. That is if you could call it running. The spikes on her heels prevented her from doing much more than a brisk walk. Still, it kept her in shape, her calves, thighs, and ankles stronger than ever. Overall, she had come to grips with her training schedule.

Now she was taking some earnest 'me' time, soaking in the sun gleaming through the glass walls and ceiling of the natatorium. That's what he called this room, a Natatorium. It meant an indoor room housing a swimming pool. Whatever! It was there, and she used it nearly every day.

It was easy to fall asleep while lying naked on the thickly cushioned chaise. Sometimes she did. Other times, her mind so occupied that there wasn't any way to relax enough to sleep. Staring at the heels on her feet, she considered her state of mind. It was in turmoil, and she was uncertain what to do.

Before Sir left on his business trip, he told her to figure it out, straighten out her mindset, and get back to business. That was easier said than done, but then again, Sir didn't care. He only wanted her to do as he said without argument or kickback.

Closing her eyes, she tried to block out the images plaguing her thoughts. Of late, arguing with Sir was all she seemed to want to do. She was tired of his silly rules. She was tired of trying to be the image of someone he desired. Couldn't he just want her, as she was?

No, instead, not only did he keep her as his slave, owned property and such, he wanted her to be like him. He wanted her to torment, torture, and kill people for pleasure. So far, he had forced her to kill. The first burned brightly in the front of her mind. Misty, the poor girl, died suffering for hours under her whip, slicing her skin with deep bleeding gashes, only to cut her throat, and not stop there. No, while he watched, she cut deeper and deeper until she finally severed the poor girl's head from her body.

She still couldn't get the image of holding her head by the hair, as the life in her died. Saturated in the poor girl's blood, she almost lost it. It took weeks before she felt like she had washed the blood from her body. To this day, over a year later, her soul remained stained with the blood of more victims killed by her hand. Hopefully, God understood and would grant her clemency on judgment day.

This latest session in the dungeon with that poor girl, she never got her name, left her drained in a way she never felt before. Sir thought she had it in her to enjoy his games, to enjoy making them scream in agony, to relish the resulting kill when she got bored with them. With this latest prey, she couldn't kill her. Instead, she tortured her in much the same way as what Sir did to her.

"What the hell is wrong with me?" she breathed.

"Nothing is wrong with you."

Startled, "Sir, I'm so…. I mean, I didn't know you were home."

When Avril started to get up, he stopped her.

"No, stay there. I enjoy looking at you all stretched out like that. You make my blood boil seeing you."

Avril stretched back out.

"May I join you?" he asked politely.

"It's your house, Sir. Do as you please."

Sitting down and taking his clothes off, he retorted. "Still passive-aggressive, I see. Did you not do as I asked before I left?"

Thinking about it for a moment, Avril realized he was right. She should have said, 'Please' and left it at that. But no. Instead, she let her turmoil get the best of her, and lashed out.

"Sir, I was wrong. Please, join me."

"That's better," he said, as he finished undressing, folding his clothes on a nearby chair and laid down beside her.

Avril turned to look at him. Try as she might, she could not keep from admiring his well built and toned body. No doubt about it, he was an impressive man. If only he weren't the cruel and sadistic bastard.

"How was your trip, Sir? Did you buy anything interesting for your stock?"

"Oh, several and one special one to boot. I will keep that one around for a time, isolated from the rest."

"Sir, that's so unlike you."

"Hmmm, yes, it is, isn't it?"

"Sir, what's so special about this one?"

"Oh, she's the bait to catch a bigger fish."

"I don't understand Sir. What do you mean? If I may ask."

"Avril, let's just say that this girl is important, and will attract someone I desperately want in my stables."

"Who is she?"

"No one special, if that's what you mean. She's just a single, unattached girl from Portland, Oregon. She's my type, though, and I'll enjoy training her. I've never had a girl who never wore heels in her life."

"She's in for a rude awakening Sir."

"That she is. Two weeks in the training facility only got her started. She's still wobbly on her feet. Her true value is that my real target loves this girl and knows what happened to her."

"Sir? That seems unlikely. As I understand it, you were on to me for over six months, tracking me, having people sleep with me, and dig into my background. Never in all that time had I any idea that anyone was targeting me for abduction. Even after being taken, I didn't know who you were or anything about the Consortium. You're telling me that this prey knows all about you and the Consortium and you're targeting her."

"Yes, Avril as strange as it seems."

"Sir, may I ask how?"

"Let's leave that for now. Also, I don't want you to play with her. I need to keep her pristine for now."

"Yes, Sir. I understand. Who is she? I ask as I don't want to make a mistake and accidentally take her to the dungeon."

"Fair enough. I'm placing her in your old cell. For now, she is to be well-cared. She'll arrive tomorrow along with the rest of the stock. What I want you to do before she arrives is to make sure the room is ready. Set it up just as you found it on your first day. Make sure you set her toiletries up in the on-suite. I need not remind you that the closet will be empty of clothing."

"No, Sir, I understand. I'll get to it right after we finish here."

"No rush. We have time. I'll give you a copy of the rule book and a note to go with it. I also want you to see to her needs. Make sure she's fed. I'll tell you when. Also, make sure she has clean linens, and she understands and abides by the rules."

"Yes, Sir. I can do that. May I ask you one further question?"

"You may."

"On my first day, you beat me with your belt and then fucked me to reinforce your dominance over me. Are you going to do that to this girl?"

"Yes, I will. Do you have a problem with that?"

"No Sir, it's just that you said you wanted to keep her pristine. It seems to me she won't be if you do that."

"Let's say then, that I won't harm her, but I will hurt her. She has to know who is her owner and master."

"I get that, Sir. Are we done?" Avril asked while starting to get up.

"Oh, no, my Avril. We're not. We're just getting started. Please, lie back down."

"Um... yes, Sir." Avril lay back, stifling a 'sorry.'

"Tell me about your week. I understand you made use of the inventory."

"Yes, Sir, I did. I was going over the session in my mind when you came in."

"Were you now? I'm intrigued. Tell me about it."

"Yes, Sir. After your last visit, I woke up finding you missing. At that moment, I wished you were still here. I felt a need to be near you. I surprised myself, in that I missed you."

"You did? That's wonderful. Tell me more."

"Well, Sir, I did, though I don't understand why. Perhaps it was the mind-blowing fucking you gave me. I don't rightly know. All I know is that I thoroughly enjoyed myself and wanted more. I guess that was what I was feeling at the moment. I'm not sure. All I know is that my pussy ached for more and you weren't there to fulfill the need."

"Nice to know. What happened next?"

"Sir, I found your note and worried that somehow I upset you. That's why you left."

"I left on business, as the note stated. However, you have upset me of late, and I hope you had the time to work out whatever is bothering you."

"I don't know Sir. To say otherwise would not be telling the truth. I'm working on it."

"Good. You do that. What else? Did you figure anything out?"

"I did one thing. You used to use me as the center of entertainment in your dinner parties. I came to like that. I realized that I like group sex, having multiple partners fuck and abuse me all at the same time. I don't understand all that much, but I accept the desire and need. That desire, in part, accounts for my foul mood."

"Well, that is something I can do something about. However, not just now. I have bigger plans for you, and that would not fit in with them. Soon. You must be patient."

"Patient Sir? I think I am being patient."

"You are. Just continue to do so."

"Yes, Sir."

"What else?" he asked.

"The rest is still a jumble. I am dealing with my situation, that much I know."

"Do you mean your place in my household? Or that you are my property to do with as I please?"

"The later I think Sir. Oh, I don't know. It's all a mess up there."

"Anything else?"

"Yes, Sir. Per your instructions, I took some stock to the dungeon to work on my dominance. It didn't go so well. I couldn't seem to make sure they knew who was in control, even as I elicited screams from them."

"Is that why you asked yourself earlier, what's wrong with you?"

"You heard that, Sir?" Avril said, worried that he might have determined the truth behind the question.

"Yes, I did."

"Go on," he said after she paused.

"Well Sir, I did something I swore I'd never do. I hooked them up to that damned electrocution machine of yours and let them have it. Oh, they survived, so you need not worry. I know how much you relish watching me kill them. I left that until you returned."

She lied but hoped he wouldn't detect it.

"Don't worry about that. There are plenty more. Why did you electrify them?"

"Sir, I suppose it so I could understand what you got out of electrocuting me."

"And did you?"

"No, Sir. I figured out I lashed out in anger, and that's why I did what I did to them."

"It didn't help, did it?"

"No, Sir. It didn't."

"What did you learn from the experience?"

"Sir, that being angry with someone is no excuse to take it out on someone else."

"Yet sometimes it is useful, though I will admit, that's rare."

"I'll take your word for that, Sir. I was using my domination and torturing them for all the wrong reasons. I got no pleasure out of the experience. All I got was more pain. It's all a blur, all mixed up and jumbled together."

"So, where do you go from here?"

"I don't rightly know Sir. Continue working on my feelings, I suppose."

"That's a start. I encourage you to push your limits. Until now, I've pushed your physical and mental boundaries. I think it's time to work on your feelings. Avril, my dear, there is so much more to you than you or I can even imagine. I see the potential in you. I encourage you to reach out and stretch your emotional limits. You'll find a whole new world when you do."

"I can try Sir though I don't know how to do that."

"Oh, I can help you there. I can easily put you in situations that will challenge you to the core. You'll experience emotional pain, pleasure, anger, frustration, desire, want, fear, joy, and satisfaction, among others. I expect great things of you Avril, and I know you will live up to those expectations."

"Sir, you're making me afraid."

"Good. A little fear always keeps us on our toes. It'll do you good."

"Sir, for the first year I was here, I was always afraid. I didn't like it then. Are you saying I'll like it less now?"

"Avril, it's all in your mental outlook. If you go into it expecting to fail, you will. If you go into it with a positive attitude, you will overcome the challenges I place in front of you. Think about it."

"I can do that, Sir."

"Good. Is there anything else?"

"Yes, Sir. I and my pussy still crave you. Do you have anything left after the flight you can share with me?"

"Come here, you greedy little bitch. Have I got something for you?"

With that, Avril got up from her chaise and threw a leg over his. Lowering herself, her pussy slick with natural lubricant, she settled down on his now raging cock.

"Oh, Sir, I need this."

"Don't let me hold you back. Do you want control? Now's your chance."

"Oh, thank you, Sir," she whispered as she leaned in and kissed him.

As the kiss lingered, she rocked him back and forth inside her, feeling him, feeling his pubic hair brush against her clit, his cock filling again and again. Probing his mouth with her tongue, she opened herself wide, both down below and above with her jaw. She felt like she could eat him alive, as her pleasure built.

"Sir, what is it about you? How can you bring this need out of me and fulfill me?"

"Shh! You're talking too much. Just enjoy yourself."

"Yes... Sir," she replied breathlessly, clamping her mouth on his while taking his face between the palms of her hands.

As she did, she slammed her pelvis down and clamped down on him, strangling his cock with her vaginal muscles. Over the past year, she had learned that when she did that, she inadvertently forced him out, as if to spit a watermelon seed. They both learned how to prevent that, as Sir pushed all the harder to remain inside her. She loved it. Together they laid there motionless, letting the pleasure and lust flow through each other, exchanging energies as they passed from one body to the other.

Soon enough, they rocked in unison. On each thrust of his glorious manhood split her apart, she felt her climb another small step towards a climax. The intense pleasure radiating from his cock seemed to force her consciousness from her body.

She lost all sense of anything but him, his cock, and his thrusting. She had forgotten that she was sitting on top of him, seemingly in control of their fucking. She left the physical world, and that was all right with her.

He was with her, and that was all she needed.

Swimming waves of ecstasy, she felt him grab a fist full of her hair and snap her head back. Simultaneously, he dove inside her. He penetrated her even more than ever, his cock piercing her torso as if to touch her heart. Her mouth wide open as he pulled her hair, she felt a guttural moan rise from her gut.

Feeling his hands entwined in her hair, the heat of his cock suddenly grew sweltering hot. Amid her climax, she sensed him plow past her cervix and shoot his ejaculate deep inside. She'd forgotten how heated his cock became when he climaxed. His cum filled her, and she squeezed him tighter, milking him with her vagina and draining his balls of his seed. This was truly heaven.

Not caring how long this climax lasted, she held onto it for as long as possible. She held her breath for the longest time. Her lungs burned, demanding air. She ignored it, letting the orgasm live a minute longer.

Eventually, instinct took over, and she could not stop the breath from happening. Sucking in a short breath, she pushed herself to feel the joy originating from her loins. Still, the magical spell broke, and the climax slipped away and died. Collapsing on her Sir, she sobbed in joy and pleasure, her breathing slowly returning to normal.

"Oh, thank you, Sir," she said before succumbing to her spent passions. It was sometime later she recovered enough to kiss him her thanks, pleased that he returned them with equal relish.

Chapter Twenty-One

"You know I can't offer an opinion. My brother will do what he wants, and usually, he gets what he wants."

"I know that Raven, but this is highly unusual."

"Are you suggesting that we don't give him what he wants?"

"I'm not saying that at least not yet. What I am saying is this application from one of his prey is highly unusual."

"Granted, but not without precedent."

"Precedence? You talk about precedence from something that happened a hundred years ago? That's not even relevant anymore."

Rolling her eyes, she stared at the phone. She knew everyone was asking the same thing.

She wanted to support her brother, the Chairman. She had her doubts on this scheme. She was happy to buy stock at the auction and dispose of them when their usefulness ended, but this was an insult. To welcome one of the fodder into their ranks irked her. She knew that the bulk of the membership felt the same way, but this was her brother.

For the first time in her life, she felt stuck between a rock and a hard place. More likely, a boulder and she was the flattened marshmallow.

He had supported her from the start, arguing for her acceptance into the Consortium. In the years that followed, he helped her refine her skills to find better ways to produce tasty live-roasted meat.

Sure, she had shared some good times with his property, and this Avril was exceptionally talented. She remembered the first dinner party he hosted that featured his new acquisition as the fuck slut after-dinner entertainment. Other such fuck sessions happened many times before but not with the likes of her. This one never whimpered, only begged for more until she was a quivering mass of flesh.

This bitch had staying power. She took what they gave her with relish, enjoying herself, eager for more. Fucking her ass as she whipped the girl's back was without a doubt a highlight of the evening. Since then, that fiery red mane only got her aroused and her pussy twitching. Even now, thinking about it, she looked forward to the next time he would invite her to play with his property.

Raven couldn't help wonder what hold she had on her brother. She had known no one, let alone captured prey, to lead and control him.

Here, this is precisely how it appeared to her.

And now, he wanted this bitch to join their ranks, and become a member in good standing. If that happened, she'd never fuck or play with that girl ever again. That would be a shame. She was fun.

"Was that the hold she had on her brother?" She wondered to herself.

"Raven, are you still there?" the member on the other end of the phone asked.

"Uh, oh, sorry. I was considering the situation. Where were we?"

"We were talking about precedence. I don't see the precedence or relevancy of something that happened a hundred years ago. Times have changed. The world is much smaller with the onset of global travel and communications in mere minutes or hours. What if she became a member and then alerted the authorities?"

"Look, in some ways, I agree with you. This is a bizarre application for membership, to be sure. But does that matter? So long as she has the means and desire to become one of us, why not?"

"Speaking of which, where did she come up with the money to pay her application fee? The Chairman would have drained all of her accounts and distributed the proceeds shortly after he seized the bitch."

"That I don't know. It is an interesting question. I'll ask him and let you know."

"You do that. I hope he tells you. I don't believe he adequately answered the question during the general membership meeting two weeks ago."

"I know. I meant to ask him about that, but I haven't had the chance."

"Well, I suggest you do. He wants a decision on the application soon."

"I know. I'll get to it."

"You're close to him. What else do you know about this application?"

"I expect not much more than you do. I know she's a good fuck bunny and plaything. I've had the privilege to play with her myself. She's a bundle of fire of entertainment. I know he enjoys tormenting and extracting his screams from her. Still, it's obvious he found something intriguing to keep her around for a while."

"There's got to be more to the story than that."

"I agree. I don't know what."

"Well, find out."

"Is that a threat?"

"A threat? Don't be absurd."

"Okay, then. Give me a chance."

"Raven, I don't mean to be rude, but this is too important to take lightly."

"Well, you are rude. Of all people, don't you think this turn of events would concern me? I am just as interested in this application as any of you, perhaps even more so."

"You're right. I apologize. Please let me know what you find out."

"Certainly. Now, if you don't mind, I've got some work to do."

"Thank you. I look forward to hearing from you soon."

Raven hung up the line before hearing the last words on the other end. If anyone understood her brother, it was her. As Chairman, he had done great things for the Consortium. Why shouldn't he get something for himself? Still though, elevating prey to equal standing in the membership was suspicious. Not that she felt her brother was trying to pull a fast one on them. She rather suspected that an emotional need blinded him. The trouble was, was it real or imagined? And if they gave him what he wants, would it come to hurt them or enhance their collectiveness? That was the question.

At that moment, her phone rang again. Looking at the caller ID, she ignored it. Everyone wanted to know what was going on. If she answered every call, repeating the essence of the last conversation for the umpteenth time, she'd never get to look into the question at all.

Grabbing a glass of wine, she pondered what to do next. Staring at the body roasting slowly on the rotisserie spit in front of her, a smile crossed her face. Thrusting the spit through the girl as she struggled, she almost climaxed.

"Brother, what are you thinking? What are you up too?" she asked herself.

She resolved to see him and put the question to him. First, though, dinner was almost ready.

***

"I am honored that you are here." Sir said as he greeted his sister with a kiss.

"I must admit, I am curious why you came. When you called earlier, you were most evasive." He continued. "I saw right through you."

"Yes, Brother, I know I was." Raven started, after kissing her brother back. Before she could continue, he interrupted her.

"I'm sure it's business, but that can wait. Let's have a drink, shall we?"

"I think that is a grand idea. Lead the way." Raven said.

Leading her to the common lounge, he spoke out. "Avril, attend us."

Avril, curious who would show up at such a late hour, was lurking in the shadows trying to keep out of sight. Not realizing Sir knew she was there, she jumped.

"Yes, Sir, right away," she stammered.

"What'll you have, Sis?"

"Hmmm," she hesitated. "I think I'll have a glass of that delightful Reserve Cabernet. It'll go perfectly with my mellow mood."

"Oh, I sense you had a good dinner tonight. I trust, no one I know."

Laughing, Raven added. "No, no one you know. Just one from my latest trip to the meat market."

Sir smiled, knowing what she meant. "Avril, a glass of wine for my sister, and I'll have a glass of my usual, on the rocks."

Keeping her opinions to herself, she answered, "Yes, Sir. Coming right up."

Not finding the wine in question in the bar, Avril went to retrieve the bottle from the cellars after getting clearance from her Master.

Avril, well-schooled in keeping her opinions to herself, shuttered inside as she too knew what her Master's sister meant. Years before, shortly after they took her, she learned that the woman vying to buy her out from underneath Sir at the auction enjoyed roasting people alive and then serving them as dinner entrees. If his sister had gotten her way, Avril knew she'd be dead, slowly roasted over hot coals on a spit inserted the length of her body. She narrowly escaped that fate. It was only much later that she learned that the woman was in fact, Sir's sister.

Retrieving the requested bottle, Avril returned to the lounge. Along the way, Avril stopped to check herself in the mirror, making sure she kept her disdain for his sister well hidden.

Fixing the drinks, Avril served them before taking her position near the bar to await a new command.

For the first thirty minutes, their conversation meandered along with many nonspecific topics. They stayed away from the purpose of the meeting. None of it interested Avril. If they had spoken about world current affairs, then she'd be leaning on every word. Instead, they seemed to relish outdoing themselves in stories of their sordid activities in their respective houses. As painful as her time with Sir had been so far, Avril decided that she had gotten the better of the two. Or, were they embellishing their stories for her benefit? Were they each trying to get a rise out of her?

Over the half-hour, Avril refreshed each of their drinks twice. One thing she learned about him and his sister some time ago, they could drink, holding their alcohol exceptionally well.

"So Raven, what do I owe the pleasure of your visit?" Sir finally asked.

Avril's attention perked up. She too wanted to know why his sister came by at such a late hour.

"It's about that one," Raven replied, nodding in Avril's direction.

"Ah, I see. Would you like to speak in private?"

"No, I don't care whether 'It' hears us. 'It' means nothing to me. It's just pretty prey, used, and consumed."

"It, huh? I see. You're here to talk about her membership application."

"Yes."

"You don't understand my motivations."

"I don't. Enlighten me."

"You ask an excellent question. I've been pondering the question for a very long time. I'm not sure I can answer you to your satisfaction. I'm not even sure I can answer it to my satisfaction."

"I don't understand."

"No, you wouldn't."

Raven then did something that surprised Avril. She waited, not speaking, just staring at Sir, patient for his answer. It was a mannerism that Avril observed in her Master time and time again. When Sir did it to her, she'd get uncomfortable, edgy and nervous under the scrutiny of his stare. His sister was now doing that to her brother, just staring, waiting for him to go on.

"Intriguing," Avril thought to herself. "Was he uncomfortable under her scrutiny?"

"Raven," Sir eventually started. "I'm not sure I can find the words to express what my feelings are in this application accurately."

Raven remained silent.

"So that's how it will be. All right then. I'll give it a stab."

Raven sipped her wine and waited.

"You've known all along how much I enjoy my life, my hobbies, my proclivities, and my position. Growing up, neither of us knew about the Consortium, nor our parent's role in it. Each of us dallied in our pleasures, getting into trouble, and our parents kept us safe from the scrutiny of the authorities. I always wondered why I enjoyed the things that everyone else abhorred. On the day they sat us down and told us about our membership in the Consortium, I discovered a freedom I never felt before."

"I remember," Raven affirmed, nodding her head.

"Yes, and then they set us up to indulge in our passions, even as they withdrew from theirs. Initially, I went overboard in enjoying my passions, extracting my screams with enthusiasm. They nurtured me in ways to keep us and the Consortium safe. I took those lessons to heart and learned. As I was enjoying my newfound freedom, I discovered that it came with a price and a hard lesson."

"It meant isolation from the rest of the world."

"Yes, that is exactly it. I used to think globally. Now, my world exists within the constraints of the membership. I read the papers from all over the world to stay in touch. It's not enough. Out of nine billion people on this planet, I have only a hundred I can share myself with, and of those, only one whom I can bare my deepest, darkest thoughts too."

"It?" Raven asked nodding in Avril's direction.

"Avril? No, sorry. But she may one day may become my second. No, I mean you, Raven. You're the only one I can trust with my real self."

"Why Brother, that is so nice of you to say. I understand what you mean, but tell me why. You have so much more than I do, more than I care to have. You are the Chairman of the Consortium. You have all the power. What you say–goes. Take the 'Bowl' for example. When you first broached the idea, you knew there would be resistance to such an extravagant expense. Since then, we've recovered the cost, several times over. I would also guess. The favor you curried with the membership set yourself up for the rest of everyone's lives."

"That's nice of you, Sis. I mean it. Thank you. However, being all-powerful and exalted for my accomplishments is not enough, at least not anymore. It hasn't been for some time now, several years at least. I used to enjoy being on top, directing the activities of the Consortium to get my needs fulfilled."

"But not anymore?"

"No, not anymore. I'm tired of the politics of being the Chairman. I make all the decisions and get what I want. As an authoritarian, I expect to have my orders obeyed, my wishes manifest. Over the past several years, I feel a yearning to fulfill a different set of needs. Needs that go beyond the purchase and playing with the prey I take down."

"I don't understand."

"No, why should you? Maybe it's our differences in sex. You're a woman. I'm a man. Throughout our evolution as a species, males are hunters and gatherers. We enjoy the hunt, sometimes even more so than the kill."

"Surely, you're not tired of that."

"No Raven, I'm not. Through my position as Chairman, the hunt for new prey takes precedence over the acquisition of stock for my stables. I enjoy seeking new candidates, tracking them, investigating them, hunting them, and taking them. The chase is still very much a part of me. Extracting their screams before killing them is getting passe for me. I'm tired of it."

Raven nodded, not wanting to interrupt her brother. The two of them fascinated Avril in discovering this new aspect of her Master. Her mind raced about, processing the implications of his revelations. "Was there hope for redemption in him after all?" She wondered to herself.

"For the first time in my life, I know I need something, something I am not so much as desire as need. I'm trying to figure out what that is."

"You think 'It' may be the fulfillment of that need?"

Looking over at Avril, Sir nodded ever so slightly.

"What can 'It' do that the rest of us cannot do for you? What can 'It' do that I can't do for you?"

"That's what I am working on. For one, we are siblings. I love and care for you dearly. I can't love you the same way as our parents loved each other. I saw something in what they shared, that is impossible between us."

After a pregnant pause, he continued. "I would like to have someone close to me with whom I can share myself with, as they did."

"Forgive me, brother. I don't understand. From what I can tell, we do that now. We share ourselves, our passions, our play, and even our bodies with each other. What more can there be?"

"The exact question I ask myself. Is there more? I believe there is, and it's more than the love you and I share. One thing I know, the rest of humanity enjoys bonding to another, often for life, to complete themselves. Not just to have sex, raise children, and maintain a household, I already have all of that. I don't have children, at least none I know of. But maybe that is part of the answer. You and I can not create a child together. That would be disastrous."

"I agree, on my many levels. But your need is more than that."

"Yes, it is. A child would not be outside the realm of possibilities, but I know enough about myself that I need more, much more."

"I think what you're edging towards is a companion."

"What do you mean?"

"Brother, you've said it already. You're looking for someone to share your life. Someone you can be truly honest with, and share your darkest secrets without judgment or recrimination. Then perhaps after that, someone to pass on your genes and your lifestyle. It sounds to me like you are looking for a mate. I dare not say a wife but a mate."

"Raven, that is what I am feeling. I want someone who will fulfill me in ways that prey cannot do."

"And you've selected It." Tilting her head towards Avril.

"Possibly. I want to see where this goes."

"Why not do it like the other members, find someone who is not prey, and establish a relationship?"

"I've thought of that. I've even occasionally tried. There is a problem. If you look closely at the mated members, their mates, wives, or concubines don't know about their alternate lifestyles. Still, they hide the most important part of themselves from their mate. I'm tired of doing that. Besides, the stuff in my head about the Consortium would bring us all down if it should get out. We operate in cells, isolating one another to protect the whole. There is only one element in the entire Consortium structure that knows it all. That's me. I can't even share some of that with you."

"You would with It?"

"No, not even then. I accept there are parts of me that would forever remain separated from everyone else. But I can share how I feel with another if she is the right woman."

"You think 'It' is the one?"

"In my search, she's been the closest fit to those needs. I suspect she recognized that even before I did. We've never spoken about it, but now I suppose we should. She's been listening to this conversation with the sharp eye of a circling hawk."

"Brother, I see your pain and recognize that you need something that I can't give you. But can you honestly tell me 'It' is the right course of action?"

"It has a name. Should this be the right course of action, I expect you to accept my choice and give Avril the benefit of any doubts you might harbor. If there are any consequences to this course of action, I will pay for them."

"Brother, that is where you are wrong. We will all pay for them. As you said before, you are the Chairman, the central figure in our community. What you are proposing is risky, and could be disastrous."

"I agree, which is why I am proceeding carefully and very slowly. I need to be sure."

"You had better be, or we will all pay for your dalliance."

"Sis, why did you come here? What prompted you to see me. You had months to ask these questions. Why now, tonight?"

"All right, I'll tell you. You may have swayed the executive committee on this application, but the general membership is not on board with this turn of events. You've recused yourself, as you rightly needed to do so. Therefore, the membership cannot reach out to you to help in deciding to go along with this crazy scheme. Instead, they are calling me. My phone is ringing off the hook with members trying to get answers or insights into why this is important to you. I'm tired of it. I want to stay out of it but I can't. You're my brother, and I will support you, even if I don't agree with you."

"You're saying that you would otherwise vote no on this application, but you believe it is me pushing the issue."

"Yes."

"You'll vote aye on the measure?"

"Yes, but I don't have to support you to the others. They need to make up their minds on the application."

"No, you don't, nor do I expect you too. Let me ask you, from what I've told you, has your position on the application changed?"

"I can say this. It's changed in favor of your position. I don't know whether it is enough to change my vote if it weren't for you asking."

"Is it enough for you to say to the membership that you understand my reasoning and can support me? After that, let them make up their minds?"

"Yes, I can do that."

"Thank you. That means a lot to me. Is there anything else on your mind?"

"One more thing. A member has to have the means to support our lifestyle. That includes the hefty application fee, annual dues, and the resources to purchase stock. 'It' is prey and nothing else. By rights, 'It' doesn't have any money. Where does 'It' have the means to be a member?"

"Raven, I thought I answered that in the general meeting."

"Not to everyone's satisfaction, you didn't."

"Can you trust me when I say that the money is not a problem and that Avril can pay her way?"

"I can, but I doubt the membership will accept that."

"Do I ask about your finances, or of the members? As Chairman, I can look into them, but I don't have the right. So, I don't. Why should you or any of the members know about my finances or that of Avril's?"

"Brother, you bring up an interesting point. You're right. We don't ask each other how we maintain our coffers. Still, I think the community would say that 'It' doesn't have the means to pay these expenses. Instead, you do. I tend to agree. However, you're telling everyone that

'It' can pay her way. Why is that?"

"That's where I refer you to what I said at the general meeting. I'd rather not discuss it further right now. Can I ask you to accept my statement and move on?"

"I've already told you I would. But how do I explain it to the others?"

"Oh, I'm sure you can manage that well enough. You have your talents."

"I do? That's very nice of you to say so."

"It's the truth. So, can I count on you to tell the membership that we've discussed this question, and I answered it to your satisfaction?"

"I suppose so. I think it will be a hard sell, but yes, I will do that for you."

"Thank you, Raven. I appreciate it. Is there anything else bothering you?"

"No, there's not. I'm tired. Let's go to bed."

"Sounds great. Would you care to have one from the cells join us and make a night of it?"

"You know what? Let's keep this between the two of us. I love your dinner parties and all, but now, I want to stay close to you. You may not realize it, Brother, but I need you too."

Arm in arm, the two of them left, headed for his bedroom. Avril too wound up, waited a while before making for her room. Overwhelmed with what she learned tonight, she remained awake for hours considering the implications of their conversation.

Chapter Twenty-Two

"Sir, about the other day. Can we talk?"

"You mean the night my sister came by?"

"Yes, Sir."

"You're bothered by what she and I talked about."

"Yes, Sir, well, maybe. I don't know. Surprised maybe, a little shocked for sure."

"So, talk to me."

"Well, Sir. I don't know. I don't understand something."

"What is it?"

"Sir, why does she refer to me as It?"

Laughing, he replied. "I wouldn't worry about that. It's just her way."

"But it's so–impersonal, derogatory even. It's like I mean nothing to her."

"You don't. You mean nothing to her. She sees you as game; hunted, captured, and in her case, spit-roasted for her dinner."

"Yes, Sir. That I understand, still, until the other day, I've never heard her refer to me as 'It.'"

"I suppose that's because she has a change of attitude towards you. Your application is being discussed among the general membership. There is a big divide on whether to vote for or against the application. To her, you're a big pain in the ass. She's being called onto the carpet, and she doesn't like it. Everyone thinks she can unravel your application and tell them why they should agree to it. Even now, knowing how much you mean to me, she does not support me on this matter. But she will never publicly voice that opinion. Either, she'll plead ignorance, which is near to the truth, or she will stay silent and vote her conscious when the time comes."

"Sir, I expected that. I knew it wouldn't be easy to get it approved. Still, I don't understand her attitude."

"No, I suppose you don't. Sometimes, I don't understand her either. What I can tell you in this case, is that because the members cannot reach out to me for information on your application, they are all over my sister. They are pestering her for answers she does not have. She's had it. As such, she's done with you."

"I see Sir."

"She'll get over it."

"When I'm dead, I'm sure."

"Oh, yes, but I expect sooner than that."

"Why, Sir?"

"Ah, that's the thing. You are less interested in how she refers to you and more interested in our conversation. Isn't that it?"

"I guess so, Sir."

"Let's talk about it then. By now, I expect you to understand my motivations for keeping you alive."

"Sir, it is true. I suspected you were in love with me long before we entered our agreement."

"Let's be clear, my Avril. You did not force me into anything. I chose this path. I will admit that when I proposed you choose between life and death; I did not consider you would have a counter to my proposal. I intended you to choose immediately. Your counter of applying for membership caught me off guard, and I needed time to think about whether to go along with it."

"And if you hadn't, Sir?"

"I would have killed you right then, extracting my screams along the way."

Avril nodded, having already known the answer.

"But I accepted your terms, despite my reservations." He finished.

"Even though you, Sir, are tiring of extracting the screams and anguish of the prey you torture and kill?"

"To answer you yes, without a doubt."

"Sir, back then I suspected that you were in love with me. But are you? I am still not sure."

"My Avril, I don't know the answer to that question. I may if I knew what the love of a woman was and that I could reciprocate it in kind."

"You mean Sir. You don't know how to love, is that it?"

"You might be right. I always thought I could love a woman. But with each passing year, that kind of love escapes me. I don't know what to do about it or recognize it if it should come to pass."

"I could help you with that, Sir. If not towards me, I could mentor you on the meaning of the love between a man and a woman."

"You might indeed. The thought has crossed my mind."

"Sir, is that why you let me live? You want me as your wife?"

"Wife? No, my Avril. I'll never marry. I'm not the marrying kind."

"What then, Sir, your consort, a companion, an ally?"

"Avril, you're already all of those and more. As you heard me tell my sister, I don't rightly know what I want. I know that something is missing in my life and that something is a woman."

"Sir, you already have all the women you want, and you get more all the time. I don't understand."

"The women in my life come and go, as you so well know. Beyond indulging in fulfilling my vicious needs, they do not fill the vacancy in my soul. If I have a soul that is, I don't know. All I know is that something is missing and with each passing year, the hole in my soul grows larger. I yearn for more. I desire someone special in my life. Someone who only wishes is to make me happy. Someone to share my life with, not as prey but by my side."

"But not as an equal? Isn't that the crux of it all, Sir?"

"I've thought about that. As much as I think she needs to be my equal, that can never be. I have too much invested in the Consortium."

"Sir, do you consider yourself depressed?"

"Depressed, no. Anxious and frustrated might be better descriptions."

"What about discouraged or despondent?"

"No, I don't think so."

"Sir, Are you unhappy?"

"Many times, Avril. I didn't think my life would turn out the way it did."

"Sir, are you no longer finding happiness in extracting your screams?"

"Often not. Sometimes I feel like it's a chore. The sensations I got years ago, the excitement, the driving force to get better at extracting them for longer periods is waning."

"Oh, surely not." She said, rubbing her ass involuntarily.

"That should make you happy, wouldn't it?"

"For me, yes, Sir. I don't enjoy giving you my screams, even though you pleasure me in the most delightful ways. I can certainly do without them, though that doesn't mean I'm willing to give up on my pleasures."

"Oh, setting terms, are we?"

"Oh, no, Sir. You own me, even if I should become a member of the Consortium. I know that, and I accept your ownership."

"Even though it comes at such a high cost?"

"One might think so, I suppose. I've not thought about my old life for a very long time. In some ways, I have found a better life."

"Oh?" the surprised Sir remarked. "Elaborate."

"Sir, I don't know. I want for nothing is one thing. You supply all of my material needs, such as food, shelter, warmth, companionship, and sex."

"Avril, I know you well enough to know that isn't all of it."

"Ah, no, Sir. I don't have to work for a living or pay for the upkeep on my apartment. I used to arrive home after work, exhausted after taking care of my bosses screwed over clients. It's tiring saving someone else from their shortcomings and never being noticed or thanked for looking out for them."

"You're referring to your old boss, Mr. Curlebba. You remember, the company fired him for his careless handling of his clients after you left his service. He later died."

"Yes, Sir. I remember."

"Do you also remember me telling you the executives of the company noticed your work? If you hadn't left their service, they intended for you to replace him."

"I remember Sir. I also remember that even if I got the job, they would have paid me half of what he made. It's unfair, and I don't miss it for the world."

"You remember correctly, and yes, I agree with you. Those old farts would have paid you less and given you more work on top of it because they knew you could handle it. They'd line their pockets with money coated in your sweat and blood."

"Sir, isn't that what I do for you, line your pockets with my sweat and blood?"

"Avril, you are a bright one, I have to admit. Unlike them, you give me your sweat and blood, plus screams. You also give me something they could never do."

"Sir?"

"Avril, this may come as a surprise to you. I enjoy having you around, regardless of my proclivities."

"Sometimes I wonder Sir."

"Wonder what?"

"What exactly do you get from having me around? Everyone needs something in a relationship. We're in a relationship. Granted, most people would consider it absurd and not normal. In a way, so do I. I know deep inside, they are wrong. For whatever reason, I like you."

After pausing for a moment, Avril continued. "Wow, I didn't intend to say that. I didn't even know it until just now."

"Yet, you did. You like me, even when I punish you mercilessly, hurting you until the brink of death?"

"I suppose I do, Sir. I suppose I do."

"Well, we're making progress. That's good."

"Sir, if you are looking for life companionship from me, I agree. However, if I may, your definition of a long, satisfying life differs from mine."

Chuckling, Sir agreed. "Yes, I see what you mean. I expect to be around for decades still, while you wonder whether I'll kill you today, tomorrow or next week. You find it hard to think about living beyond that."

"Yes, Sir."

"Even though in our agreement, I promised not to kill you. Have I ever broken a promise to you?"

"No, Sir but knowing your track record and having nothing to compare to it, how can I possibly trust you never to kill me."

"I guess then, only time will tell."

"Yes, Sir."

"Avril, I can assure you, that should we partner up and mate, you will die of a ripe old age."

Laughing, Avril added. "Mating, we've done that many times over. I admit it is a favorite pastime of mine. I never knew I could enjoy my sexuality as much as I do with you."

"My dear, it was always within you. I am only a path to let it out. You are one of the most sexual people on this planet today. You not only enjoy our copulations, but you also relish your time in groups, servicing several cocks and pussies at the same time. It's a big reason I enjoy having you around. You constantly surprise me with your hunger for it."

Tilting her eyes downward in a thought, Avril considered his worlds. With a slight devilish smirk, she added, "yes, Sir."

"But I'm not talking about copulation. I'm talking about something deeper, more intimate. Do you recall from the days before you came to me what you wanted in a man?"

"That was so long ago, Sir. I don't think I remember."

"You frequently said, you wished to find a man who could control you in bed, and take you sexually to places of extreme ecstasy or something to that effect."

"Sir, I remember now. Yes, I felt that way."

"And now?"

A teasing smirk in the corner of her lips, she said. "I found him."

"Thank you, Avril. That's what I wanted to know. Do you yearn for anything else?"

"Sir, I don't know if this is the time and place to say that."

"Go ahead. I won't hold it against you. But before you respond, let me speculate. You wish your freedom."

A look of surprise flashed across Avril's face. "Sir?"

"Ah, come now, my dear. Of course, you do."

"Well Sir, if I am to follow the rules laid out in the book, I am never to lie to you, just as you will never lie to me."

"Yes."

"Sir, yes, I wish my freedom, to step beyond these walls, smell the fresh air, scented with the flowers of the fields. I miss running on the streets of New York as well in the park. I miss lying out on a coastal beach, soaking in the sun as saltwater slaps the sand in wave after wave. I miss—well, I miss my parents and their guidance, even though I know they are dead and gone. I miss, well let's say I miss wearing clothing and walking around all day in sweats and bare feet."

"You know I love seeing you in skin and heels. I can tell you this. I honestly don't relish seeing you wearing anything else. You're a beautiful woman. You stand proud and confident in your beauty, just as mother nature gave you."

"I know Sir. Still, I miss them."

"What about when I permit you to wear an elegant outfit when I entertain guests?"

"That's all fine and good Sir, but I am constantly on guard to not spill anything on them, to spoil them. Besides, they're not everyday clothes, like sweats and a tee-shirt. They're for display, before being ripped from my body as your guests have their way with me."

"You seem to enjoy that."

"Yes, Sir, I do. I love being thrown up against the wall, groping me as they undress me. My knees weaken, and the only way to keep from falling is to give myself over to your support. If I fall to the ground, it's because that's where you want me. There's a kind of freedom in giving you or someone else total power and control over me."

"Which is why I do that. I accept your gift, offering great pleasure in compensation."

"Even when that includes a good flogging, whipping or electrocution?"

"Avril my dear, even then. The more excited and aroused you are, the more likely you enjoy and feel pleasure from the sting of the whip or the thud of the flogger. Sometimes I wonder whether you have an upper limit to pain when you get sexually aroused. When you're like that, the screams I extract from you are those of joy and not pain. In those moments, I can't swing the flogger or throw the lash of the whip against your body hard enough to cause you to cry out in pain. No, my dear. You have no boundaries while you relish the depth of your sexuality."

"If I understand you correctly, Sir, if you warm me up sexually, you can hurt me more, and I won't feel it much at all. But if you come at me cold without arousing me first, I crumble under the pain sooner, faster and hurt more."

"That's about it, Avril. When I need your screams of pain, there is no warm-up involved. You suffer at my will, and there is no mercy. When it's over, you are a quivering mass of flesh whimpering on the floor, unable to process the agonizing hurt you're feeling."

"Which can't last that long as I fall apart too easily."

"True."

"If you want to extend the session for as long as you like, having me a willing participant, you arouse me sexually. That's why I feel pleasure from the torment."

"That's about it."

"Tell me, Sir, have I ever exhausted you to where you could not go on yet, I could?"

"What an insightful question. Yes, you have. Frequently over the past year, I left you whimpering, not in pain but a need for more, as I could not continue. You're the best workout a man like me could have. I burn thousands of calories doing those play scenes with you. I'm sure you do too, even though you are not exercising in the normal sense of the word."

"Is that why I continue to maintain my toned body even though my gym workouts don't seem to do much for me? Is that why I can swim more laps than I ever could before I came to your service?"

"Yes, Avril, I suppose so. Even in your arousal, your muscles contract and relax constantly. In our marathon sessions between fucking and gleefully suffering my torments, I venture you burn more calories than you would in running a marathon. I bet you could win the New York City Marathon just in the condition you are right at this moment."

"Sir, I have to admit, sometimes I feel that way. If I understand you correctly, between the sex and dungeon sessions, I keep my body toned for anything in the outside world."

"Avril, there is no medical evidence to support such a conclusion. However, between you and me, I believe that to be the case. I used to think I had the stamina to take on any woman, either in bed or in the dungeon. With you, I may have met my match."

"The match for a lifetime partner and mate, Sir?"

"Maybe."

Avril slid up to her owner and whispered in his ear.

"Sir, take me to bed. I think it is time to test whether or not you have met your match. Besides, I need a good long, strenuous fucking right now."

"Now, that is something I can get into Avril. You're on."

With that, Sir picked up her and threw her over his shoulder and headed for the bedroom. Avril plastered his back with kisses as she swung in time with his footsteps cupping his ass along the way.

Chapter Twenty-Three

"So, how's the new heart?" The Chairman asked the member on the other end of the call.

He wasn't too worried about phone taps. The Consortium uses a highly advanced encryption that bounces across several global locations through an endless number of firewalls. Calls sometimes didn't work, which was okay. Better to protect the security of the Consortium than risk exposure.

"Fantastic. I can't thank you enough. I feel like a new man. I have energy again, ready to take on the world."

"That's good to hear. Don't abuse it, though. It's the last one you'll ever get from us."

"Yea, yea. I get it. It was a rush black market job. Because of that, I'm off the regular donation lists forever. As I understand it, if anyone ever did a tissue match between me and my new heart, they would get the surprise of their life."

"That's right. So, from now on, you only see our doctors, and most especially the cardiologist who did the transplant. I mean it. No one."

"All right, Mr. Chairman. I said I would, and I will."

"Good."

"Surely, that is not the only reason you called, just to make sure I take care of myself."

"No, it's not. I have two things to share with you."

"What is it, Mr. Chairman?"

"We've been monitoring you since receiving your heart. I don't appreciate that you've returned to your old, destructive ways. You'll destroy your new heart if you keep this up."

"Then you must get me a new one, Mr. Chairman. What do I care? It's the only life we have. I intend to enjoy it."

"At the expense of someone else's life."

"So? It doesn't bother me in the least."

"My point is, take care of your heart. I'm informing you, you must go through procedures to even get a chance at another, assuming I'll allow it. Candidate research usually takes at least six months, often resulting in a rejection."

"And I tell you this. Expect to get me another one. Start the search and background checks now. That way, when I need it, you will have a suitable candidate vetted and ready for the transplant."

"Don't count on it. I mean it. Something so specific as a match for a new heart is difficult to come by. The one we found for you fell into our laps by accident. In your case, we would have rejected the candidate after a cursory investigation. The risks on that one were too high."

"Whatever! Find the next one. You said two things. What's the second?"

"You recall that this was a rush job. You gave us too little time to find, investigate, and get you your new heart."

"Yes, I remember. One day I was doing all right and steadily moving up the transplant candidate list and the next, they gave me less than a week. That scared the crap out of me."

"Just as you like to do with your acquisitions." The Chairman jumped in.

Chuckling, "Yes, I suppose you're right. I like to scare them before I kill them."

"Well, let's just say that this is not over yet."

Interrupting, the member asked. "Whatever to do you mean? I have my heart. The donor is dead and gone, what more is there?"

"Just this, the family of your donor is hunting for their missing loved one."

"Yeah, so?"

"So, because of the rush job, we weren't able to do the full investigation we normally do with candidates. Our initial assessment of the identified candidate looked good for the taking. It was only after we completed the transplant, we learned that under normal circumstances, I would not approve this candidate. The family has connections and is making waves in their search for their missing family member."

"What has that got to do with me? Handle it as you normally do."

"I am, but don't put this on the Consortium or me. The issue I'm dealing with started long before you needed the heart. I checked. Your extravagant lifestyle destroyed your old one. You had no defects or genetic abnormalities. No, you did this to yourself, and because of that, you put the Consortium at risk. I am holding you personally responsible if this goes south."

"Oh, no, you can't put this on me. I had nothing to do with the crappy investigation job on my donor. No. This business is all on you. If you so much as try to put this on me, I will make your life a living hell. Got it."

"Don't play games with me. I'm doing you a courtesy in letting you know that anything involving your new heart is not over yet. It's your issue, not ours. We hope to resolve it in due time."

"And if you can't?"

"We'll deal with that if it comes to that."

"Is there anything else?"

"Yes, I'm glad you're feeling better and that our efforts on your behalf are paying off. On a personal note, I look forward to seeing you in person at our next auction. You've missed out on several excellent products going through us, not to mention the entertainment."

"Thank you. I appreciate it. I heard about the snake thing. I understand that it was spectacular."

"It was. I'm sorry you missed it."

"Well, I was under the weather. Will there be a repeat performance?"

"Yes, we're working on that even now. Though I can't give you a date yet, when we have all the players in place, we'll put it on the schedule."

"Fantastic. Though I expect that we only need a single player for this event, that shouldn't be too hard to get."

"You'd be surprised. Whoever we place in the 'Bowl' must be adequately motivated when they meet Henrietta."

"Henrietta? Is that its name?"

"Yes, it is."

"Who chose that? It's an odd name."

"That's a story in of itself. During her capture, the handlers were calling it Henry. We learned it was female after it arrived at the facility. So we changed its name to Henrietta. It turns out that female pythons are bigger and often more aggressive with their prey. It worked out better for everyone all around."

"Except for the prey in the 'Bowl' with Henrietta."

"Just so."

"Well, I, for one, am looking forward to the repeat performance."

"So am I to tell you the truth. It was a fun time all around."

"I'll bet."

"Again, I'm happy you're feeling better. Take care of your new heart."

"I will. I'll see everyone soon." The member said before ringing off.

"Goodbye," the Chairman said into the dead handset.

"Idiot." He added under his breath before dialing another number.

"Sir?" he heard through the speaker when his Adjunct answered.

"How's everything on the Senator investigating his daughter's disappearance?"

"From the last reports, so far, so good. There is something else of interest. A few weeks ago, the Senator suddenly canceled all of his appointments on the Hill and left for home and hasn't been back to work since. We're tracking him."

"Is that odd?"

"For him, yes. He's a workaholic and rarely spends time at home while Congress is in session. When he's away, he's campaigning for the next election or doing the speaking tour with his constituents."

"And he's not doing that this time around?"

"Well, he is, but he isn't."

"Explain."

"Sir, he's spoken at a few events but not enough to justify his time in Chicago. He's also traveling a lot around the country, outside the population his office serves."

"Has he gone back to the city we picked up his daughter from?"

"Several times, Sir. Not only that, he's traveling with his other daughter."

"But not his wife?"

"Well, she occasionally travels with him, but it's his other daughter he stays close too."

"I see. Anything else?"

"Yes, Sir. We suspect he doesn't trust the FBI or other investigators searching for his missing daughter."

"Why is that? Did we inadvertently drop the ball?"

"Not to my knowledge, Sir. The only reason we suspect his true intentions is that we discovered he purchased a burner phone for cash before leaving Washington. Fortunately, it was from a dealer we have on our payroll. From that, we have the SIM Card code so we can track him and monitor his calls that way. However, to date, he's never used it or even activated it. He may have already discarded it by now."

"I see. Buying a burner phone is a positive signal he doesn't want his whereabouts known."

"Our thinking exactly."

"We suspect that after he purchased it, that he may have dumped it in favor of buying new burners from smaller dealers outside Washington, Chicago perhaps. That's his hometown. He has connections from before the time he entered politics and came under our umbrella."

"If he purchased a burner phone, what's to say he didn't buy one for his other daughter, or several?"

"It's a possibility. We are watching both closely. You know as well as I do, they will take precautions to guard against anyone from monitoring their movements and conversations."

"I assume the team watching them knows of this development?"

"Absolutely, Sir."

"Good. How many teams do we have assigned to them?"

"Two direct teams and two indirect teams. The two principal teams are closely monitoring both the Senator and his daughter. The indirect teams float between Chicago and the cities they visit, doing the background checks and follow-ups from their movements. We have enough personnel that it would be tough for either subject to see one of our team members more than once in a month."

"Very good. Keep up the surveillance. These burners bother me."

"If he bought one, he bought others. We're trying to figure out how many and what their SIM card numbers are. We need to know what they are doing or saying."

"Agreed. Anything else?"

"No, Sir."

"From here on out, let me know of anything interesting, suspicious or not. These two individuals are not our usual prey. If they are onto us, it is our job to snuff out their curiosity."

"Yes, Sir. I'll keep you informed."

"See that you do." the Chairman closed and disconnected.

Leaning back in his chair, he stared out into space, not seeing anything really at all. His thoughts whirling, he considered the ramifications of what might happen if they could not squelch this suspicious behavior of the Senator and his remaining daughter. They were undoubtedly behaving out of the norm.

Thinking about it more, he tried to put himself into the Senator's place. What would he do if a loved daughter suddenly went missing? He had power. He had connections. He had the means to investigate on his own and outside the law. What would he do? What would I do?

"I would do what the Senator is doing," he decided.

Pondering the question for over an hour, he picked up the phone and called his Adjunct again.

"Sir," he heard through the handset.

"Do a deep dive on the Senator. Look into his associates from decades ago. A man like him doesn't rise to the powerful position he has today without connections and money. If I were him, I would tap those resources, leaving no stone unturned. He's covering his tracks as I would do. He is on a mission and searching for his missing daughter. He won't stop until he gets his answer."

"Right away, Sir. If I may, might it be safer to remove him from the playing field?"

"I'm considering it."

"Yes, Sir. I'm glad to hear that."

"Keep me informed."

"Will do, Sir."

In a plush downtown never visited Chicago library, the Senator and his daughter Heather sat next to each other reviewing local newspapers. They were researching recent events with the slim hope that some odd tidbit of news would direct them in a positive direction in the search for the missing girl.

"Nothing." She said frustrated, leaning back and rubbing her eyes in fatigue.

"Heather, how are you doing?" Her father asked.

"Okay, Dad. Tired, that's all." Tossing the papers down, she added, "This is getting us nowhere."

"It seems like it. Also, I'm tired, and that doesn't help. Don't worry, though. We'll sort this out."

"I know. I feel it too. It's what we find at the bottom that concerns me."

"She'll be all right, Heather. We must have faith."

"Dad, I know you don't understand this. Rachel and I, well... we can feel each other when we are apart. It doesn't matter how far away she is, I can feel her; I can't anymore. I am worried that she is more than missing. I am afraid she's dead."

"Don't talk that way, honey. We don't know that. Until we find out what happened, there is every chance we'll find her alive and well."

"I know Dad."

"Though I refuse to accept she's gone forever, we'll find out what happened to her and destroy them."

"That's what keeps me going. To find her and discover what happened to her."

"We will, honey. We will."

"So, what next? We've already retraced her steps, and we're no closer to finding her than before we started."

"The bugs we found in each of our homes and where I work would show that someone is watching and keeping us from finding out the truth. Heather, we must remain vigilant. Whenever we investigate, wherever we go, we must leave a false trail for those watching us. Make no mistake. Someone is monitoring our every movement."

"Dad, shouldn't the FBI or Capitol Police be dealing with that?"

"Heather, under normal circumstances, yes. However, both of us don't trust them at the moment. For all we know, they planted the bugs themselves, or know about them and won't do anything about them."

"It seems that way, doesn't it?"

"Something is bound to break. I can feel it. Something is just not right, and I'm determined that we find out just what went on."

"Or going on?" Heather added.

"Yes, that too."

"So again, Dad. What next? I'm sure Rachel did not return to Chicago at all, despite the evidence she did."

"That I agree with you, dear. It all has to do with the conference trip."

"Do you think she attended it at all?" Heather asked.

"Yes, I do. Otherwise, if someone else attended in Rachel's place, there would have been too many opportunities for something to go wrong. There might have been someone else there attending the conference who knew her. I think whatever happened to Rachel, happened after the conference. I suspect something happened before she arrived in Houston."

"Where she had her layover?"

"Yes. Though I doubt anything happened in Houston. She would have remained within the security zone during her layover. Getting her out and replacing her with a double would have attracted too much attention. Not to mention all the security cameras all over the airport watching everything.

No, I think whatever happened, occurred at her hotel on the night before she was to return home."

"Yeah, that's what I think too. So why can't we find out anything? Doesn't the hotel also have security cameras?"

"They do, but I'm told they didn't reveal much."

"Can't we go watch them ourselves? We know Rachel and her behaviors. Maybe we'll see something that no one else did."

"You might be right. No one knows her better than we do. The video might pick up something minor, insignificant to anyone else. However, if we do, it would be a clear sign to whoever is watching us, that we are investigating on our own."

"So what? Dad," Heather said emphatically, "even if we didn't know about our stalkers, we would have every right to view them ourselves. You have pull. Couldn't you make it happen?"

"I suppose you're right. All right then, we'll do that. I'll book the plane tickets. I don't see why we can't get a flight tomorrow. Take your regular phone and the burner with you. Leave the burner turned off while we travel. There's no sense in trying to prevent anyone from knowing where we are when we announce it. Just don't use your regular phone for sensitive communication. Keep conversations mundane and within the expected for two people dealing with grief."

"We are Dad."

"We are, aren't we?"

Chapter Twenty-Four

"Oh, my aching head," she complained.

Katie reached up in the darkness and rubbed her forehead. The sleep she got locked in this wooden box did little to ease her killer headache. From the moment two guards roughly dropped her here, and screwed down a wood panel over her, she lost all track of time. One minute she hung over the shoulders of a burly man and the next, he threw down, and the blackest of darkness enveloped her. So dark was it, she couldn't see her hand in front of her face.

Thinking back, she remembered she laid there for some time trying to sense what was going on. She accomplished little. Oh, they bounced her around a lot, as they jostled her box. At one point, she realized they put her on a truck, but she couldn't be sure. What she was sure of was that they placed her on an airplane which took off for parts unknown. The air travel was unmistakable with all the changes in air pressure and turbulence.

At some point, she closed her eyes and drifted off to sleep.

The next thing she knew, they were removing the cover of her padded coffin. A blinding light assaulted her optic nerves, elevating her headache further. Two pairs of arms grabbed her by the underarms and dragged her down a long hallway. Recovering from the assault on her eyes, she barely understood what was happening. She found out soon enough when they pushed her into a room and the door behind her locked.

Lying on the floor, between moans, she slowly opened her eyes. She found herself in a sparsely decorated room. Though there was room for furniture, she only found a bed on the wall to the right, and a plush, upholstered wingback chair opposite the bed. Other than the two closed doors to the left, there was nothing else.

Alone for a time, Katie rolled over on her back and stared at the ceiling. A single recessed light illuminated the room.

"Decent but uninteresting," she said to herself. A moment later, she corrected herself.

"What am I thinking? This is a cell, and I am a prisoner."

Struggling to stand, she took a closer inventory of her surroundings. Sure enough, she still had the metal band around her neck, her tender and aching nipples sporting the welded rings, and those ridiculously high spiked heels on her feet. On her hands and knees, she crawled over to the bed and used it to stand up.

Achy and her pressing in from all sides, she went over to the doors. Opening the first, she found an empty closet. Nothing hung from the rod, and there was no other furniture. Going over to the next door, she found a fully outfitted en-suite, complete with toilet, sink, shower, and jacuzzi tub. On the vanity, she found an assortment of her favorite products to care for her hair, face, and body.

"Well, finally, something decent," she thought. "First things first."

After using the inviting toilet, she finished checking out the drawers in the vanity. She found little of interest. She found what appeared to be a laundry chute and a wide, deep cabinet that seemed to have little purpose. There was also a linen closet, empty.

"Well, nothing here to hang myself," she jested to herself as she closed the door.

After washing her hands and face, she returned to the main room of her cell. Just to be sure, she tested the door. She found it locked, as she expected. Turning inward, she noticed a thick book on the bed. On top sat a piece of paper with writing on it.

Picking it up, she started to read:

> 'Welcome to your new home. I hope you will find your stay here comfortable and relaxing.'

Katie snorted, "Yeah, right."

> 'Unless otherwise directed, you will remain naked and wear only the high-heel shoes given to you at the training center, including when you sleep at night.'

"Wear the heels to bed? Do they really mean I must wear them as I did at that other place?" she squawked.

> 'On the bed, you will find a book outlining the rules I expect you to obey at all times. Failure to follow the rules will earn you severe disciplinary action. I sincerely hope you will avoid punishment. I assure you; punishments are excruciating. I will undoubtedly enjoy disciplining you should you violate a rule. Study it closely. Your life depends upon it.'

"No doubt," she conceded.

> 'There is an upholstered chair in the room. I reserve it for your new owner to use, namely myself. You may not sit on it. Should I give you clothing, you will wear them only as instructed. Your everyday dress is skin and heels — nothing

else. You will remain nude unless told differently. The same goes for your heels, you will wear your heels at all times, even to bed. You may only remove them to bathe, putting back on as soon as you exit the shower stall. Ignoring this rule will incur my wrath as you've never seen before.'

Taking a brief look at the closet door, she continued reading.

'I will have meals and drinks delivered to your room through an access panel in the en-suite. Assuming you follow the rules, you will be well-nourished. Failure to follow the rules will cause missed meals. You will keep the room clean and straightened up at all times. You will make the bed immediately after you wake and unless otherwise directed, it will remain made throughout the day.'

The note finished with one further command.

'You have one hour to shower and clean yourself up. Do not use the tub. I only permit you to shower. Shave your legs, underarms, and pubis. I expect you hairless from the neck down at all times during your stay. In time, you will receive laser hair removal treatments, making shaving obsolete. Put your heels back on immediately after you step out of the shower and then finish cleaning up.'

'As soon as you finish, kneel in the designated spot in your room and await me. See rule number fifty in the rulebook for my exact expectations. In the meantime, study the rulebook while you wait. How long or short your stay here is up to you. It should not surprise you. This is the last home you will ever have.'

Dropping the letter on the bed, Katie leaned back, supporting herself on her hands and stared at the note, not really seeing it. Disbelief slowly being replaced with a realization that her situation had not improved at all.

With a sigh, she removed her heels and walked to the shower.

***

After spending the bulk of what she thought was an hour, Katie went back into the main room, stopping short when she noticed the man in the grey suit sitting in his chair.

"So, you're finally done cleaning up. It's about time. You've kept me waiting. Not only that, you were not kneeling as instructed in my note."

"Ah—I'm sorry."

"You've also not read the rule book yet, have you?"

"No," Katie replied, frightened by the powerful and posture of the man sitting in his chair.

"What do you have to say for yourself?"

"Ah, I don't know. What should I say? I'm a prisoner held against my will."

"Let's settle this right now. You're not a prisoner. You're my property. I own you. You will behave and do as I command."

"I'm to be your slave then?"

"You're not a slave, just my property. Like this chair, I'm sitting in is my property. You have no rights, no say in what happens to you. I don't care what your opinions or beliefs are. You are my property, bought and paid for, to do with as I wish."

"That's illegal. You know that, don't you?"

"Illegal? You hope that some authority or police officer will come and save you?"

"You could say that."

"I just did. Don't snipe. It's unbecoming. As to your belief that someone will come and save you, put that out of your mind. No one's coming. There is no law here except for what I tell you. What do you think about that?"

Katie started to answer when he shushed her.

"Don't answer that. I don't care what you think. All I can about is that you obey. Just submit and obey."

"If I understand you correctly, requests for mercy and being let go will fall on deaf ears."

"We understand each other. One more thing, feel free to beg for mercy and relief. I will relish your pleas as I ignore them and continue extracting my screams from you. How does that sound?"

"Not too good."

"No, I don't suppose it does, at least from your perspective. In the meantime, you've still not answered my original question."

"Ah, I don't remember what that was. Could you repeat it?"

"SIR." He commanded, stopping Katie before she could utter another word.

Frozen in place for a minute, she finally offered in a questioning tone.

"I don't remember Sir."

"Is that a question or a statement?"

"Ah, a statement, I guess."

"Don't guess. Be clear, be specific. It will go easier on you."

"A statement."

"SIR!"

"Sir," Katie added.

"I said, you kept me waiting. What do you have to say for yourself?"

"Sorry. I didn't know you were waiting for me," quickly adding, "Sir."

"That's no excuse. The note said to shower and be back, kneeling while studying the rule book within an hour. You took nearly an hour and a half, not the hour as I instructed. This is the last time I will ask, what do you have to say for yourself to keep me waiting so long?"

"I...," she stammered.

"Don't stammer. It's unbecoming of even the lowest class of life on this planet, of which you're not too far above I might add."

"I have nothing to say."

"Why is that? Also, you didn't say Sir in your reply. You're digging yourself a deep grave."

"I... thought I took an hour. I was just about to come out, grab the book and kneel."

"Were you now? How can I believe you when you didn't follow my simplest instructions? Such as using my title, which you missed yet again."

"Sir, I thought I took an hour. I'm sorry."

"See, yet again, you violate another of my rules. If you had read the rule book, you'd know why. I suggest that as soon and I leave, you pick it up, kneel and start studying it. Your life depends upon you knowing my rules inside and out. Do I make myself clear?"

"Yes, –Sir."

There was an uncomfortable silence between the two. Katie was seething. Sir was about to continue when she interrupted.

"On second thought, who the fuck are you to keep me here? What right do you have to kidnap me off the streets? What right do you have to tell me what to do and wear, how to walk and speak, and make me call you 'Sir?' There's no way in hell I will call you 'Sir.' You are a despicable individual and haven't earned the privilege to call you that honorific. I will not."

Katie was about to say more, but he interrupted her. In a flash, Sir jumped from his chair and backhanded her across the face. Katie fell to the ground, the side of her face turning a bright red. That didn't stop her rant, however, and she continued to yell at him from the floor.

Sir stood over her for several minutes, hearing but not listening to her complaints. Eventually, she slowed her verbal dump and eventually transitioned to silent tears running down her cheek.

"Are you done?" Sir sneered.

Katie was about to resume her tirade but decided against it.

"Good, now get up," he commanded her in the sternest of tones.

"Make me."

Smiling, Sir leaned over, wrapped a mighty hand around her upper arm and yanked Katie to her feet. So roughly and brutally he picked her up, for what felt like several seconds, he lifted her completely off her feet, holding her suspended by her arm.

Then, as if she were nothing more than a rag doll, he threw her across the room to land face down on the bed. Even as she sought to roll over, he leaped on top of her, pinning her to the bed. Struggling against his weight, she tried to find some advantage to push him off her. Not caring whether he sexually assaulted her, she tried kicking him in the balls, instep, and other vulnerable spots on the human male. He deflected her attacks easily.

Before she knew it or could do anything about it, Sir stripped his waist belt, folded it over, and began spanking her ass. Admittedly, it was more like beating her ass. Katie screamed, more in shock rather than in pain. Never in her entire life, had anyone spanked her so brutally, so viciously. She quickly lost the ability to keep up with the feel of the strap on her skin before the next one landed right next to the previous one.

Try as she could, she could not break away from his heavy hold on her, and the beating continued without pause. Her legs flailing, enduring the pelting of the belt, she began sensing he was talking to her. His stern voice was somehow soothing. She couldn't figure out why. She only knew that the fire in her ass was slowly lessening with each sentence. Utterly confused, she stopped struggling. Her mind stretching out, almost leaving her body in pain, she felt and heard him in a way she never expected.

He seemed to be with her, part of her misery, and part of her very being. It was a disconcerting feeling. In a way, it felt like her episodes in bed with her lover. Shelby would sometimes get rough with her when they had sex. Not at first, but later after they had gotten to know each other well, and slept with each other many times over. Each of them seemed to sense their needs, what the other wanted or needed in and out of bed. It was a warm, comfortable sensation, and Katie hated the idea that it might all be over.

Yet this time, the sensation was completely different. She trusted Shelby but this bastard, definitely not. The portion of her mind not tortured by the brutal assault knew who was in control and who had all the power. Taken, not given, his power over her overwhelmed and subdued her.

He must have sensed her mind. As she came to this understanding, he stopped beating her with his belt and climbed off her. She laid there for a minute. Her face rested in a spot dampened by her tears. As she rolled over, her bloodshot eyes shooting fire-bolts at him, she was about to retort.

Sir held his finger in a 'Stop' gesture. Katie understood the message and complied.

"If you continue to fight me, you can expect to receive more of the same, only more of it, and all over. Will you comply?"

Katie thought about it a moment before giving him a hesitant, affirmative nod.

"Use words. I want to know without a doubt, you understand and comply."

Nodding her head again, Katie whispered, "yes."

"Yes, what?"

"Yes, I understand."

"Insufficient answer. Try again."

After a moment thinking about his retort, Katie responded. "Yes, I understand Sir."

"Good, very good. Now, you must know you're off to a rough start. Not as bad as some of your predecessors, but worse than most."

"I'll bet," Katie replied surly.

"Sir. I'll bet Sir," he corrected her.

"Yes, Sir. I'll bet Sir," she repeated with an attitude.

"Good, now to continue. You're off to a bad start, especially since I put you into opulent quarters. Would you like to live in a four by six cell with bars like the rest of my purchases?"

"I still don't like it. I never will."

"SIR!" he snapped.

"I still don't like it. I never will, Sir."

"I don't care whether you like it. You are mine. You belong to me. I will do whatever whenever I wish with you. You have no say in the matter. Behave, and you will live to see tomorrow. Misbehave, and you may not see another day. Do I make myself clear?"

"Yes... Sir."

She paused before using his title, almost not caring if she used it. Katie figured that no matter what, this bastard would find any excuse to beat her, perhaps kill her.

"Ah, I still see resistance in your tone and body language. You're a smart woman. You must know, you will spend the rest of your days as my property. You will live here and die here. You will never see what you thought was your old life, ever again. Make the most of it."

"You have no right... Sir."

"I have every right, and you have none. Make the best of it."

"Whatever...," Katie said, her words trailed off, her tone evident to any casual observer that she was dismissing him.

At that moment, Sir reached out and casually grabbed a chunk of her hair and stood her up on her feet. Dragging her by her hair, he slammed her face-forward against the wall. Seconds later, his hard cock against her dry anus, he invaded her. Lifting her off the floor, his body pressing hard against her, she cried out.

Struggled to deal with his powerful assault up her rectum, he reached around to her breasts squashed against the wall and mashed them with a firm grip. So powerful was his attack on her body, her feet dangling off the floor, her hips bouncing against the wall, he repeatedly thrust deep into her.

Sometime later, he threw her to the floor, his cream leaking from her anus and walked out. Katie laid there for the longest time. She had almost passed out during his assault while her body dangled on his erection like some friggin rag doll.

"Fucking sadistic bastard. You may have beaten me this round, but you've not broken my spirit."

Alone and in pain, she closed her eyes and blacked out.

Chapter Twenty-Five

"Come in, Avril. Come see what I'm up to."

Sir stood, contemplating the specimen in front of him.

"Sir, who is that you have there?" observing a bundle of rope in his hands.

"Ah, oh, you mean her. Ah, I don't remember. What's your name, girl?"

"Lara, Sir." She replied, trembling in fear.

Lara was standing in the center of the dungeon, spotlights illuminating her from all directions. She was naked and in heels, as was typical for all his playthings. However, her stilettos were some of the highest Avril had ever seen. They were so high as to make it look as if she were standing on her toes. The pose reminded her of a ballerina standing on pointe. It had to be an uncomfortable position.

"Avril, please tie a chest harness on her, if you please," Sir ordered tossing the rope to Avril.

"Yes, Sir." deftly catching the bundle and unraveled it.

"Clasp your hands together on top of your head," Avril told Lara.

"Please, don't do this. I beg you. Please let me go." The trembling girl whispered to Avril. She didn't expect the slap across her face that immediately followed.

Shocked, tears welled up on Lara's eyes, her lips trembling in fear.

"Surprised? I'll just bet you are. I'm not one of you. I'm with him. Now shut up and take it. Oh, you can still scream and cry if you like. He loves hearing screams of pain and agony."

Lara dropped her head and closed her eyes. Meanwhile, Avril took the bite in the rope and wrapped it around her chest, just above the girl's breasts. After two more wraps, she added more underneath her tits. Knotting the bindings together behind her back between her shoulder blades, Avril tossed the ends over one shoulder and looped them between the girl's boobs, cinching the wraps together, pinching her breasts between the wrappings. Tossing the last of the ends over the other shoulder, she tied everything off behind her back.

"Excellent Avril. You did a fine job. Nice and tight, just as I like it. See how firm you made her tits? Wonderful. Hard as a rock. I like it."

"Thank you, Sir. I'm glad you like it."

"Now, tie a groin harness," he said, tossing her another bundle of rope. "Make sure it's tight around her waist."

Nodding, Avril got to work. By the time she used up the entire length, she had cinched Lara's waist with several wraps, and it looped between her legs, and up her butt crack and tied off behind the small of her back. Sir had to give her a bit of instruction while she tied the harness to ensure that the cording bisected the girl's pussy lips and pulled them apart.

"Perfect. What do you think?" Sir asked his protegé?

Grasping and pulling the segment reaching down from her waist and through Lara's legs, Avril said. "I like it, Sir. I don't know what you have in mind yet, but we're off to a good start."

"We are, aren't we? Well, I have something special in mind for this one. See how toned yet soft she is?"

"Sir, it's obvious that she's taken care of her body. It's almost a shame to disfigure it."

"Ah my dear, I don't plan on disfiguring it. I do, however, intend to do something risky. I don't know how it will turn out."

Lara, hearing the first half of his reply to Avril started to breathe a sigh of relief, only to have those reassurances dashed by the second half of what he said. She whimpered.

"See Avril. I gave her a gift. A glimmer of hope thwarted knowing that this would not go well for her."

"I saw that fleeting look of hope and a sigh of relief Sir. How quickly you turned it around."

Tossing another, a more substantial length of rope to Avril, he said. Thread that through the hoop above her head and let it dangle.

"Yes, Sir. A suspension scene in the works I take it."

"Hmmm, not quite my dear, but you're getting close. I'll keep you in suspense a little longer. In the meantime, you have more binding to do. Tie her arms behind her back, please; wrists and elbows if you would."

"Very good, Sir. May I assume you want them tight?"

"As usual, my dear. Don't forget to rotate her arms at her shoulder sockets, making it easier to bring those elbows together."

"Sir, I'm surprised you felt the need to remind me of your teachings.

I know full well what you want."

"My apologies, my dear Avril. I don't know what came over me." Sir replied, teasing her.

With that, Avril tied Lara's hands behind her back, cinching her wrists and elbows tight and elbows touching.

With Sir scrutinizing the tie, he remarked. "Avril, your technique is getting better. She has some fine lines to her body, which you embellished with flair. I love the geometry of her upper arms coming down in a triangular shape, and her lower arms trailing in a straight line following her spine to her tailbone. Beautiful. I especially like the protruding shoulder blades popping forth, trying hard to deal with the unnatural position."

"Thank you, Sir."

Meanwhile, Lara, as fit and toned as she was, was struggling to maintain an upright position. Arms bound and standing on her toes; she was teetering on the perch encasing her small feet. All the while, she was whimpering under the straining of her bindings.

"Sir?"

"Yes, Avril."

"Seeing she has a high waist as I do, I love the lines she offers you. Would you tie me like that one day?"

"I can arrange that. I suggest you wait until we finish this scene before you confirm that request. You may have second thoughts. In the meantime, let's finish this scene."

"That makes sense, Sir. Knowing the depth of your sadism, I can only imagine what comes next will not only be new to me but awful for the object of your sadism."

"Avril, you are smart. That's why I enjoy having you around. This scene is a test to see what I want to do is possible, and whether one can survive it without serious injury."

"Then Sir, I'm glad you're trying it out first before doing it to me."

"I thought you would appreciate it. Can we continue?"

"By all means, Sir. I'm eager to see where this goes."

"Loosely tie that rope above her head to her chest harness to keep her from falling. Just support her, not lift her."

A minute later, she tied Lara off from above, keeping her from falling over. Avril and Sir stood back and stared at the helpless Lara.

"Beautiful, isn't she?"

"Yes, Sir. You know, you could leave her there overnight in the dark and see how she fares."

"I could, but then I wouldn't get my answers from this scene."

"You have a point, Sir. I withdraw the suggestion."

"That doesn't mean we can't do that again, even have dinner over there while she struggles to stay awake and upright. We could replace the support from the chest harness with a noose around her neck, as an added incentive."

"That's an idea, Sir. Something to think about anyway."

"I agree. Okay, let's move on." Sir said, slapping Avril's ass as they disengaged.

"Thank you, Sir," Avril added as she smiled back at him, appreciating the touch of his hand on her backside.

In the meantime, Sir went over to a cabinet and opened the doors. He extracted from the darkness two stainless steel hooks. One was gently bent into a curve and contained a small stainless-steel ball on its end. The other looked like a stylish check mark, with the steel curved outward from the 'V' of the hook. With both hooks, one side was twice as long as the other and capped with a steel ring.

"Oh, Sir, I see where this is going. Will it work?"

"Time will tell, my dear. Let's find out. Slip the ball hook into her ass, making sure you seat it between the rope between her legs."

"Certainly, Sir. No problem. I presume then you want me to tie a line to it and slip it through the ring over her head?"

"That's the idea, Avril."

Squatting down behind the bound girl, Avril split the two lines through her groin and slipped the anal hook deep into Lara's rectum. Tying a cat's paw with the bite of another length of rope, she fed that line through the suspension hoop above the girl's head and pulled it taut, ensuring a deep, secure fit inside the girl's ass.

"The other one I presume is for her pussy?" Avril asked.

"Yes. Make sure they are both firmly seated, splitting the lines separating the labia. I want the groin ropes to pinch the lips against the cold steel."

"Yes, Sir, no problem."

With that, Avril took the stylized hook and squatted down in front of Lara. Looking at her pussy for a second, Avril leaned in and kissed it, licking the lips.

"Ah, very nice Avril. I hadn't expected that. Were you adding wetness to ease the insertion?"

"Just came over me, Sir. I couldn't resist, but now you mention it, I may have done exactly that. I don't know for sure. All I know is that I wanted to kiss her and enjoy the moment."

"Nor should you. You are very much a part of this scene. Enjoy yourself."

"Thank you, Sir."

With that, Avril fed the short side of the hook between Lara's pussy lips and pushed. It slipped in easily. Tying another line through the eye of the hook, she threw the free end through the hoop and pulled it taut.

"Put your weight into it. Make sure you seat both hooks deeply inside her."

"Yes, Sir." Doing as instructed, Lara groaned as Avril partially lifted her off the floor.

"Tie all three lines off above her head, making sure they are taut. Just make sure the chest harness isn't carrying any weight. I want all the weight carried by the hooks."

"Yes, Sir. I understand. The chest harness line is to keep her upright but not carrying a load."

"You understand correctly, my dear." He said as Avril went about tying off the free ends of the overhead lines.

"Anything else Sir before we lift her?"

Lara whimpered and begged for mercy. Sir and Avril ignored her, and slid together, arm in arm.

"No, I think that's about it. Let's pause and enjoy the moment."

Each stood there, gazing at the fearful girl, enjoying the moment, enjoying the dramatic scene, letting the knowledge of what was about to happen sink in. Each knew that the hooks would do the job. What they didn't know was whether the hooks would perforate the soft tissue inside, flooding her lower abdomen with blood and excrement. Since Sir would do nothing to treat the condition, either was fatal.

Each stepped back, and ate a snack from a side table set out with fruits, cheeses, and drink. Sir poured himself a single malt scotch as was his habit and an icy cold Russian vodka for Avril. Both sipped the drinks, occasionally consuming another bit of food.

"Come on. Let's take this to the table over there and sit, eat and watch the fun."

"Yes, Sir," Avril replied, picking up the small plate of food while Sir took their drinks over to a small round table with two chairs. After Sir sat down, Avril placed the food down on the center of the table and sat beside him.

Clicking their glasses together, Sir toasted. "Here's to the fun. Let the games begin."

After each of them sipped their drinks, Sir pulled out a remote control from his pocket and placed it on the table.

Avril stared at it, knowing precisely what it was for and what it did. It controlled the winch that raised and lowered the hoop in the center of the room.

"Go ahead. Activate it. But just enough to put her weight on them."

"Sir?"

"Go ahead, Avril. I give her to you. In a way, it's a present."

"Present Sir?"

"In due time, my dear. Now lift her, but only a little."

Picking up the remote, Avril put her thumb on the up button and pressed. The activated winch started up, making a soft sound as the slack in the lines disappeared, firmly seating the hooks into the girl's lower torso. Avril took her thumb off the button just as the girl began to lift off. Between her cries to stop and let her go, her toes struggled to remain planted on the ground, her heels no longer touching the floor.

"Watch Avril. See how gravity is slowly doing its work. In a minute, those heels of her's will soon touch the floor, at the expense of the hooks driving deeper into her belly."

"Sir, I see that. What I would like to know, can they support her suspended off the ground while not ripping her to shreds?"

"Ah, that is the question, now isn't it? First off, her pelvis will sit nicely on the hook in her pussy. As you know, the skeletal structure of the pelvis has a lateral section of bone crossing just above her pussy. The hook in her pussy will use that to support her frame."

"And the hook in her ass?"

"With all that soft tissue, not so much. It will, however, provide stability to keep her from falling backward as the hooks lift her off the ground. Anyway, that's the theory."

"And the lines from the hooks I threaded underneath the wrappings of the harnesses, will provide upper body support, assisting the hooks to keep her upright and vertical."

"Just so, yes. At least that is the plan."

"How long will you leave her up there, Sir?"

"Avril, I should ask you that question. She's yours to do with as you please."

"Again, Sir, I don't understand."

"In time Avril. In time. Now, do you see? Her heels are touching the floor once again."

In response, Avril tapped the remote, and the winch activated once again, but just for a moment. Lara harshly hoisted up off her heels once again, her toes still touching the floor.

"Nice touch, Avril. However, do you see anything wrong with how she is hanging?"

"Sir, now that you mention it, it seems that too much of what's holding her up is not from the hooks but the chest support. I know you want all of her weight on the hooks, but that's not what's happening."

"Very good. You see it. What are you going to do about it?"

"I'll adjust the center rope to transfer her weight to the hooks. The center line's only purpose is to keep her upright and rest on the hooks."

"Perfect. Please go ahead."

"Yes, Sir," Avril answered as she adjusted the tension on Lara's support rope.

"That's better. What do you think?" Sir stated.

Stepping back and reviewing the mechanics of the lift, Avril smiled.

"Thank you, Sir." She responded; her eyes glued to suffering Lara. "I think this will do, at least until she stops settling on the hooks."

"I like it."

"Thank you, Sir."

Over the next ten minutes, Lara and gravity did its work. Slowly, repeatedly, Avril tapped the button lifting Lara in small increments. Eventually, there came a time when her heels didn't drop. Avril stopped there, the two of them enjoying the moment.

"Avril, it's time, don't you think?"

"Yes, Sir. I'm just giving her time to think about what's about to happen. A little psychology."

"Yes, I get it. I've done that often. You're learning."

"From the best Sir."

"Thank you," he said, as he reached into a pocket and withdrew a set of clover clamps connected with a chain. He placed them on the table and took another drink.

"Ah Sir, I like your thinking. Three clamps? Will there be room on her pussy to clamp her clit?"

"We'll see, won't we?"

"That we will Sir."

A few minutes later, her nipples tightly clamped, she sandwiched the third clamp beneath the hook, crushing the girl's clit. It had to be painful.

"I wasn't sure I could get it in there, Sir. It took a lot of wiggling to get it under the hook."

"Yet, mission accomplished."

Smiling, Avril reached for the remote. "Ready Sir?"

"Ready."

In no time, Lara was hanging several feet off the ground. The girl was alternating between yelling, screaming and whimpering, begging for mercy, wanting down. Her cheeks were glistening under the lights from her drenching tears. Soon her tears coated her chest, dripping from her tits.

"Nice! Very nice Avril. How about some dinner? Besides, we have our dinner entertainment."

"Thank you, Sir. I am getting hungry."

"You'll find hot meals over there in the cabinet. Please serve them."

"Right away, Sir."

After serving, Avril sat down and waited for permission to eat. Getting it after Sir started on his meal, the two of them ate quietly, watching Lara dangle before them. Lara did nothing to contain her painful discomfort. They were halfway through their meal when Avril spoke up.

"Sir, what's this about giving her to me as a present. Why?"

"Out of patience, are we?"

"I suppose so, Sir."

"Fine. You've waited long enough. I brought you here to tell you something. It's taken a while, and it was touch and go."

"What was, Sir?"

"Patience, my dear. I'm getting to that."

"Sorry, Sir."

"Are you apologizing? You know that is against the rules."

"Sir, uh, no. A figure of speech is all."

"Fair enough. Remember, even as a member of the Consortium, you still belong to me, and subject to my rules. Understand?"

"I belong to you, and I follow the rules. I don't understand what? A member of the Consortium?"

"Ah, sunlight dawns. Yes, my dear. By the narrowest of margins, they approved your application."

Jumping up, Avril hurried over to Sir, wrapped her arms around him, and kissed him. "Thank you, Sir. I won't let you down."

"You're welcome, Avril. Welcome to the Consortium."

Epilogue

"Hello, may I help you?" Heather asked the woman standing at her front door.

"No, I'm here to help you."

"I don't understand."

"No, I'm sure you wouldn't. May I come in?"

"What's this all about."

"I have information about your sister Rachel."

Stunned, Heather quickly invited her in. Closing the door behind the woman, Heather started to open her mouth. Immediately taken aback, Heather looked shocked when the woman put a finger up to her mouth.

"May I?" the woman asked, showing she wished to whisper into Heather's ear.

After a moment, Heather nodded.

Leaning in, the woman spoke at such a low volume that Heather could barely make it out.

"My name is Shelby. I'm about to tell you something, but you must not speak up or act excited. It's for your own sake."

Biting her lip, Heather paused before nodding to let the woman continue.

"Good. Now, the first thing you need to know is that your home is bugged. People are watching and listening to you."

Surprised, Heather jumped back, stunned by the revelation. Again, Shelby put her finger to her mouth in the universal sign to stay quiet. After a moment, Heather nodded and leaned into the strange woman.

"I know what happened to your sister."

"What?" Heather whispered.

"Shh, they may hear you. What I am about to tell you may seem incredible, unbelievable even but it is true. Believe me."

"Okay," Heather nodded her agreement.

"Good. Both you and your parents are under surveillance. Your father, the Senator even more so."

"I don't understand," Heather muttered low under her breath.

"Just accept what I tell you is the truth. I can prove it. I can tell you where at least one of the listening devices is right here in your living room. After I leave, you can verify its existence for yourself and decide whether to believe me."

"Go on."

Directing Heather's attention to a nearby table lamp. "Do you see the intricate detailing on the lamp?"

Heather looked over and nodded.

"I hid the bug in the lamp. It's just below the socket holding the lightbulb. It's small, barely a quarter inch around. It's colored to match the metal of the socket and easily mistaken for the screw holding the socket to the lamp."

Heather nodded once again.

"There are more bugs hidden throughout your apartment. They are everywhere, and I don't know where they all are."

"How do you know someone bugged my apartment?" Heather whispered.

"I placed some of them myself."

Stunned again, Heather backed away from Shelby, anger and fear building in her body language.

"Please, I understand. However, time is short. I don't know how much longer I have to live."

Shaking her head in disbelief, Heather stood there for a minute before moving in closer to Shelby.

"Go on."

"Heather, it's important. Not only is your apartment bugged, but you have been under intense scrutiny and surveillance for months now, even before your sister went missing. Your father, too, though I don't know more about his surveillance. Someone else is taking care of him, and a third person is watching your mother. All three are under surveillance, their homes and offices bugged."

"What a minute. I don't understand something. My father? He tells me they sweep his offices at the Capitol for bugs regularly. How can they be bugged?"

"Trust me, they are. There are some well-placed people to oversee these things. There was once a time I headed up a team whose job it was to look into the backgrounds of individuals, watch them, and report back our findings."

"Report back? To whom?"

"Heather, this is where the story I am about to tell you is unbelievable. For a long time, I didn't believe it myself. I do now, and as a result, I am running for my life, afraid that they will kill me before I finish telling you my story."

Heather nodded.

"I work for, at least I used to, an organization that calls themselves the Consortium. It highly secretive and operates in the shadows where no one looks. I don't know everything about them. They operate in tight cells. Members in one cell do not know those in another cell. They keep it that way on purpose. If someone compromises a cell, they cannot take down any other cells. However, what I know is enough to get me killed."

Heather was about to interject again when Shelby silenced her.

"The Consortium's been around for a long time. For how long, I don't know. They may have existed for hundreds of years in one form or another. They have a singular purpose for their existence. That is to meet the personal needs of their membership."

"Which is?"

"Whatever they want, whatever they desire, that they cannot legally get."

"What has this got to do with my sister?"

"Heather, I'm sorry to tell you. They took her. By they, I mean the Consortium. By now, she is probably dead. I'm sorry."

Heather's face turned ashen, and her knees started to give out. Shelby reached out and helped steady the grief-stricken girl.

"Why?" Tears were pooling in her eyes.

"I don't know. All I know is that the Consortium wanted her and so they took her. She had something they wanted, something they could not get elsewhere."

"I don't understand."

"Yes, that is understandable. I don't get it myself, but they noticed something about your sister they liked and needed. Therefore, they arranged her kidnapping."

"But you don't know what it was about her they wanted?"

"No, sorry, I don't. What I know is that it was a rush job. Normally, they take their time investigating candidates before deciding to take them. Often this can take several months up to a year. Most times, we find the candidates unsuitable for their needs. They are the lucky ones, never knowing we targeted them for an abduction."

"But my sister wasn't so lucky."

"No, she wasn't. In Rachel's case, we had only a few days to investigate her. I don't know why everything was so quick. I only know that there was an urgent need."

"But you don't know why?"

"Like I said, no. I don't."

"You said candidates, as in plural. They take others?"

"Oh, dozens each year, maybe hundreds, maybe more. I don't know how many. All I know is that they have urges they cannot satisfy by other means."

"Hundreds? That's unbelievable."

"I know. I can scarcely believe it myself."

"So, they took her. What did they do with her?"

"Again, I don't know. All I know is that once they take their game, they disappear forever, never seen or heard from again."

"Game? Is this a game to them?"

"I wish I knew. What I know is that in this case, the term 'game' is referring to the prey they hunt, just as the lions of Africa are big-game to the hunters there."

"They hunted her?"

"Yes, that is what they did. They hunted, took, and likely slaughtered your sister."

"What happened after her abduction?" Heather whispered, her eyes full of tears, on the edge of a breakdown.

"They loaded her onto a plane like cargo and took her somewhere in the world. Where? I do not know. I never wanted to know."

"So, you think she's dead?"

"Yes, I do. Again, I'm sorry."

"I don't understand. How do you know about this Consortium?"

"I used to work for them."

"You used to be a member of this Consortium?"

"Oh, no. I don't think I could afford to be a member. Only the elite rich, the one-percenters, meet the requirements to apply for membership. No, I only worked for them."

"As what?"

Gulping, Shelby stopped a moment before admitting. "As a hunter."

"A hunter?" Heather exclaimed, her voice rising uncontrollably.

"Shh." Shelby tried to quiet her down. "Yes, a hunter I am ashamed to admit."

"A hunter," Heather voiced quietly, "—a hunter. Why?"

"The pay was excellent — more than I could ever get with a normal position. I was superb at my job. The Consortium recruited me when I was young, hungry, and without a family to support me. I had nowhere to go. They trained me, fed me, gave me a home. They became family to me, and I was loyal, so loyal. Over time, I became good at it. Eventually, they asked me to lead a team that included experts in surveillance, background investigation, computers, hunting, and other talents."

"Talents that included people stealing people off the streets."

Nodding, Shelby whispered repentantly, "Yes."

"How do you know about my missing sister?" Heather asked, almost dreading the answer she didn't want to hear.

"Because I'm the one who took Rachel and handed her over to the Consortium."

###

Connect with the Author

website – RichardVerry.com

Facebook – richardverrywriter

twitter – @richverry

blog – RichardVerry.com/blog

Author's Notes

Thank you for reading this chapter in Avril's story. If you enjoyed it, won't you please take a moment to leave me a review? Telling her story preoccupied me for months, demanding to be let out of my mind and written down. With the success and demand for more, I came up with an idea for the next few segments of Avril's story.

In this next edition of her captivity, 'UnderCurrents' continues Avril's story trying to balance her survival with her desire to take down the Consortium. She knows enough of her situation that escape is impossible. Even if she can get away, Sir would use the resources of the Consortium for hunting her down and returning her to his clutches. Her only hope is taking down the Consortium, granting her a chance to return to a normal life, even if it's not her old life.

Her strategy to keep herself alive seems to work. Unfortunately, she's no closer to taking down the organization that stole and sent her into a life of bondage. Forced to serve and submit, spending time in his dungeons extracting her screams was a necessary consequence to her plan.

Putting her plan into action requires decisions and behaviors she's uncomfortable with, knowing they may forever damn her soul. She murdered others, knowing full well she will never forgive herself. Her only hope for redemption is her hope that God will forgive her, saving innocent souls from suffering her fate.

I appreciate your sharing this book with your friends and acquaintances and posting a review.

Also by the Author

About the Author

Richard Verry is an Information Technologies Engineer who has coded and supported computer systems for decades.

He wrote many stories in his youth all lost to history. He wrote his first short story as an adult in 2007 and over the next few years, dabbled in writing stories, not expecting to publish any of them.

Along the way, he created a vast gallery of artwork of oil and watercolor paintings, sketches, and drawings. In 2012, he began writing full-length novels and novellas where he is finally able to capture some of the ideas and story concepts steadily invading his mind.

Richard grew up and lives on the North-East Coast of America where he lives with his life partner, Janet. He enjoys skinny, sugar-free vanilla lattes, Kamikaze cocktails, red wine, single malt scotch and a good steak.

Richard ponders, sometimes to the point of excess, the myriad of images and scenarios, mostly including the captivating nude female form, streaming through his consciousness. A rare few eventually come to life in his artwork and writings.

https://richardverry.com

Made in the USA
Coppell, TX
02 May 2022

77310689R00128